Odds and Sods

Lawrence Gray

Supported by

香港藝術發展局
Hong Kong Arts Development Council

The Hong Kong Arts Development Council fully supports freedom of
artistic expression. The views and opinions expressed in this project do not
represent the stand of the Council.

Lawrence Gray's short stories and texts were written as the antidote to his screenwriting. The story, 'The One Legged Rickshaw Boy' illustrates his view of the absurdities of the film and TV world. And so in **ODDS AND SODS** he allows himself to have fun with words alone. Characters in this world change their lives as if they are changing their clothes. They view reality as a shifting negotiation between moments of insanity. And when they want to fly, they take flight without reference to budgets. He buries the conventions of one form of writing within those of another. French farce clashes with Chinese opera. Science fiction translates into Chinese fairy tales. Sitcom meets Shakespeare. And the lyrics of Blues songs create narratives for the lives of those attempting to recreate them musically. Literary greats turn up as bit-part players. Samuel Taylor Coleridge mingles with Punjabi Rap artists. Tang Xianzu of the Ming Dynasty bumps into George Feydeau. Antonin Artaud has a walk-on part, and if one wants to look, one can find Julian of Norwich, medieval mystic, stealing pencils in the dark. In Gray's final piece, he gives a stimulating and unusual view of Hong Kong's chequered history.

LAWRENCE GRAY was born and educated in the UK and took BA honours in Economics and Politics from Leeds University. He has lived in Hong Kong since 1993. Gray founded the London Screenwriters' Workshop, which became Europe's largest screenwriters' organisation before evolving into the many UK screenwriting organisations and courses which are now part of the UK cultural environment. In Hong Kong he founded the Hong Kong Writers' Circle and chaired the group for twenty years, publishing many collections of stories from a wide variety of Hong Kong writers.

Gray has taught screenwriting in various cities around the world, and was one of the first to professionalize the industry. He has written, produced and directed a number of films in both English and Cantonese, and has worked on numerous screenplays for various film projects from India, to China to Hollywood. He has won the PAWS award for drama and the Hong Kong Film Finance Forum's award for best Hong Kong film project of the year. He is currently directing a feature film. He has worked as a television scriptwriter in each of the UK and Singapore, contributing episodes to popular TV series.

As a writer of prose he relishes the nuances of his own northern English culture and the subtle twists that many years in Hong Kong have produced; but fears that the very things that make his topics interesting to those who experience such cultural displacement make it less accessible to the wider world; hence his persistence in writing screenplays and now in directing feature films aiming to break down this resistance.

The world is more united than ever and whereas he has little faith in the concept of universal stories, he does have faith that all stories, presented well, can within the context of modern technology gain at least widespread, if not universal, recognition and appreciation.

Odds and Sods

Lawrence Gray

Proverse Hong Kong

Odds and Sods
by Lawrence Gray.
2nd paperback edition published in Hong Kong
by Proverse Hong Kong, January 2016.
ISBN: 978-988-8228-18-8
Copyright © Proverse Hong Kong, January 2016.
Printed by CreateSpace.

1st published in paperback in Hong Kong
by Proverse Hong Kong, 19 November 2013.
Copyright © Proverse Hong Kong, June 2012, November 2013.
ISBN 978-988-8227-16-7.

Print edition(s) distribution
Hong Kong and worldwide:
The Chinese University Press of Hong Kong,
The Chinese University of Hong Kong, Shatin, NT, Hong Kong SAR.
E-mail: cup-bus@cuhk.edu.hk Web site: www.chineseupress.com

United Kingdom:
Christine Penney, Stratford-upon-Avon, Warwickshire CV37 6DN, England.
Email: <chrisp@proversepublishing.com>

Enquiries: Proverse Hong Kong, P.O. Box 259, Tung Chung Post Office, Tung
Chung, Lantau, NT, Hong Kong SAR, China.
E-mail: proverse@netvigator.com Web site: www.proversepublishing.com

The right of Lawrence Gray to be identified as the author of this work has been
asserted by him in accordance with the Copyright, Designs and Patents Act 1988.

Cover image by and with kind permission of Helen Gray.

British Library Cataloguing in Publication Data.
A catalogue record for the first edition of this book is available from
the British Library.

PREVIOUS PUBLICATION ACKNOWLEDGEMENTS

'The One Legged Rickshaw Boy', in *CityVoices*, Ed. XuXi, Mike Ingham. Hong Kong, Hong Kong University Press, 1999, pp. 158-168.

'The Lubrication Zone', in *The Silverfish Collection of Asian Stories*, Ed. Professor Ronald D. Klein. Singapore, Silverfish Books, Sdn Bhd, 2003, pp. 68-75.

'The End', in *Dimsum: A Journal of Good Reading*, Ed. Nury Vitacchi. Hong Kong, 1999, pp. 95-105.

'Digital Deficiency Syndrome', Prize winning *South China Morning Post* (SCMP) Short Story competition, Hong Kong, nd.

'Replicas', in *The Wild East Magazine*, Ed. Lawrence Gray. Hong Kong, Hong Kong Writers' Circle, 2003, pp. 12-16.

'The Immortals', in *Haunting Tales of Hong Kong*, Ed. Lawrence Gray. Hong Kong, Hong Kong Writers' Circle, 2005, pp. 119-129.

'The Immortals', in *Silverfish 5*, Ed. Professor Ronals D. Klein. Singapore, Silverfish Books, Sdn Bhd., 2006, pp. 62-80.

'The Chinese Farce', in *Dimsum: A Journal of Good Reading*, Ed. Nury Vitacchi. Hong Kong, 2004, pp. 139-145.

'The Chinese Farce', in *Haunting Tales of Hong Kong*, Ed. Lawrence Gray. Hong Kong, Hong Kong Writers' Circle, 2005, pp. 69-79.

'The Devil's Work', in *Sweat and The City*, Ed. Diana McPartlin, Mio Debnam. Hong Kong, Hong Kong Writers' Circle, 2006, pp. 30-47.

'Soft Boiled Egg', in *Hong Kong ID*, Ed. Dania Shawwa. Hong Kong, 2005, Haven Books, pp. 83-95.

'Going Gweilo', in *Hong Kong Whodunnits*, Ed. Diana McPartlin. Hong Kong, Hong Kong Writers' Circle, 2007, pp. 31-53.

'The Pussy Man Blog' in *Love & Lust*, Ed. Tammy Ho, Jeff Zroback. Hong Kong, Hong Kong Writers' Circle, 2008, pp. 77-88.

'In Mid-Sentence', in *Fifty/Fifty – Essays on the political condition of Hong Kong*, Ed. XuXi. Hong Kong, Haven Books, 2010, pp. 64-80.

'Anchorite', in *Gupter Puncher Magazine*, Issue 2, Ed. Oli Johns. Lamma Island Hong Kong, Zizek Press, 2010, pp. 16-19.

'Entropy Meant To Be', in *Gupter Puncher Magazine*, Issue 3, Ed. Oli Johns. Lamma Island Hong Kong, Zizek Press, 2010. pp. 16-19.

'The Tattooed Man', in *Gupter Puncher Magazine*, Ed. Oli Johns. Lamma Island Hong Kong. Zizek Press, 2010. Online.

LARGER THAN LIFE CHARACTER
TAKES US ON A TOUR

ODDS AND SODS is a collection of short stories and essays from Lawrence Gray, a much-loved screenplay writer who has lived in Hong Kong for many years.

Like the man himself, the work is unpredictable and varied. The items range from straightforward tales in classic short story format, to pieces of writing which are more experimental in nature.

And, also like the man himself, the stories range from being funny to being thought-provoking to being clever to being downright annoying! And sometimes they mange to be all these things at once, but overlaid, of course, with more than a touch of English charm.

Gray, whatever you think of his opinions, is always worth listening to. He has a distinctive style, a strong sense of fun, and a high level of passionate energy. And in classic British style, he manages to avoid getting too angry, even when dealing with controversial subjects. There's always a genial, laid-back, consider-all-the-factors stance.

He has also had a fascination with cultures and identity. So although he is very English, he is also clearly intrigued by "foreign-ness" and by the ways cultures interact with each other. And one gets the view that the many years he has spent in Hong Kong have changed him, too, and detached him from his roots. So as well as the "Englishman Abroad" elements, you'll find many Hong Kong references in this collection, and other elements, such as references to Hindi rap music.

By being a literary activist, organizing writers' groups and movie-industry gatherings, and being founder of the Hong Kong Writers' Circle, he has become well-known in his adopted home town. And so this book provides a thoughtful smorgasbord of items, perfect for dipping into, giving us a refreshing journey around the mind of one of Hong Kong's larger-than-life characters.

Nury Vittachi
Hong Kong, 2013

Dedicated to Helen, who thankfully never bothered to find out
what she was letting herself in for
and has remained unperturbed ever since.

ODDS AND SODS

TABLE OF CONTENTS

AUTHOR'S INTRODUCTION

I have discovered over the years that the fun of the short story is that one does not have to conform to rules. Where one would flinch at reading two hundred pages of experimental prose, bizarre plot lines and eccentric characterisation, a reader can actually enjoy them in the shorter form. For me as a writer, the short story is less a place to practice the craft of writing, than a place to test one's limits.

Characters in my dream world change their lives as if they are changing their clothes. They view reality as a shifting negotiation between moments of insanity. And when they want to fly like a great crane across the face of the moon, they take flight. They are actors who pick up the script as given to them, and are often as not a compromise between the writer's intention and the limits of availability and the casting budget.

This is not the case in all the stories. Some of them are firmly grounded in reality and they are what they are. Perhaps significantly these are set in the UK, whereas when my work is set outside of that firm base, my imagination slips into all manner of fantasy, pretty much as my life shifted on leaving the UK to live in Hong Kong.

If there is a technique behind all of this, it is found in my combining the conventions of one form of writing, with those of another: French farce clashes with Chinese operas; science fiction translates into Chinese fairy tales; the poetry of Samuel Taylor Coleridge mingles with the dictates of Punjabi Rap artists, and the lyrics of Blues songs create narratives for the lives of those attempting to recreate them musically.

I have avoided topicality and been oblivious to trends in writing, whether they come from the University English departments, or the hardcore commercial publishers. Even so, I discover that despite myself, the fashionable subject of "Identity" has crept in and I find myself talking about "the text" when I discuss my stories with anyone. The characters, unlike their author, constantly seek some amalgam of what they are with how others perceive them and repeatedly challenge themselves with alien cultures. Their author though is an Englishman Abroad and for some reason that seems to rule out all doubts about his identity and no culture is alien to such a creature.

Consequently I cannot say I am writing about any particular place or society. I am merely writing within the context of the physical and cultural environment that I stumble across with no particular plan in mind. My subject is me, but then again, the me that is a subject, has a habit of disconnecting itself from any firm footing and fracturing into many parts, none of which bear any resemblance to me. In a similar "Beckettian" vein I should announce that there are no symbols where none are intended. The fictional I and me are neither.

Before you think I protest too much, I think this is the existential occupational hazard of having always been a writer of some sort. My main claim to success if that's what it was, has been writing episodes of British TV dramas, which for some reason had large non-British casts. Even my brief spell writing medical dramas had me writing about a rampaging Iranian doctor who probably was the first ever Iranian character on British TV to hold forth on the iniquities of Western culture. Recently I have delved into Singaporean TV dramas, with not a single Western character. And during the compilation of this collection I have been working on various multi-cultural film projects. Some of them have been Chinese historical dramas and others have been Bollywood movies. Not to mention the short Cantonese films I have produced and directed myself. All of which has taken me a long way from Flamborough Head, the village my family comes from. And to hammer home the point, in theory, this century – I can be no more specific – should finally see a Hollywood production of one of my scripts, a comedy entitled Fat Englishmen. This brilliant and some would say hilarious conceit concerns the drunken exploits of a bunch of Englishmen in Japan who mistakenly get involved in a Sumo wrestling competition and lose, despite cheating outrageously. Ironically the first thing asked of me when I arrived in Hollywood was "Do they have to be English?" Next was, "Do they have to be Fat?" And so I look forward to its Hollywoodised version, "Fit Americans" about a bunch of men with perfect teeth and healthy lifestyles who challenge Japan's finest Sumo wrestlers, kick ass and write sentimental e-mails to their loved ones back home. Perhaps some of the extravagance of my stories can be traced to the influence of Hollywood, though in a very British sort of way.

In short, I write mainly to entertain just about anyone who can read English, and hopefully also to enlighten, though because these are short stories and there are no great budget requirements and little demand upon the time of the reader, I allowed myself the freedom to go wherever my mind wandered. So if you are of the mind to say, why are they fat, why are they crippled, and what the hell has Antonin Artaud got to do with any of this, then I reply, pay me what Hollywood would pay and you can have everyone living in a nice big house, on a hill, overlooking a little stream and listening to the bluebirds singing. In the meantime, this is what I write when left alone in a room with a keyboard and decide to have a bit of fun – My kind of fun.

Lawrence Gray
Hong Kong 2012

DIGITAL DEFICIENCY SYNDROME

When he woke from the coma the first thing that he noticed was that he could not see his wife. He could hear the murmur of her voice in the hum of the hospital noise, but where the voice came from was a void around which dazzling light from a window fitted with slatted blinds flickered. Was it Jean? Jane? June?

When Dr Thism loomed into view his grinning face was clear and his words cut through the buzzing and clanking, words like "stroke", "lost mental functions", "speech impairment".

Apparently things were serious, but not hopeless. Was this then, the famous Dr Thism, whose therapy and scientific credentials were so impeccable that the rich and famous brain dead called upon him for second opinions?

A nurse helped the patient sit up and the rush of blood away from his head dizzied him. As he became used to the idea of sitting, he found a name that he thought must be his own. Silas, yes, he was Silas, in the silence and this was a hospital made of music.

Next thing he was aware of was being shaved and clothed and taken for a walk around the hospital. He felt that it should have been a run, but the connection between his head and his feet seemed precarious. He blew in the wind like a flower stalk and thought how good it would be to make mountains of rubber so that everyone could climb without injury.

In Dr Thism's office Silas enjoyed being the object of close scrutiny. Dr Thism in his white coat and rimless glasses, stood before a row of photographs of celebrity mental degeneration. He broadcast the message to the assembled crowd that Silas was a unique case. He had blown a gasket and worked himself into a syndrome worthy of a scientific paper. Silas the walking grant generator, he called him, to much amusement.

Silas was proud of this diagnosis. If one was to be ill, one should be uniquely ill. If one was to be excluded from work, one could achieve usefulness in being the cause of usefulness in others. If he had been poor, with a stroke, he would have been of no value, but as he was, he had Digital Deficiency Syndrome, and was thus a useful member of society.

Dr Thism patted Silas's head, and with a magnifying glass showed the depths of the void of Silas's pupils to his students. Injected with fluorescent dyes and poked with iron prods, the eyeballs of Silas were walking symbols of sedentary post-modern life.

"One does not merely ask, how you are feeling, but 'What do you mean?'"

Dr Thism handed a buzzer to Silas. He was to press it every time he saw a light flash on a screen. Silas did nothing though and tried to explain that although he knew he had a buzzer in his hand, he could not imagine what one was supposed to do with it. Nor did he see any flashing light on the screen. And he was not even sure what this screen was, other than something flat.

Never mind, he was beginning to feel less panicked by strange gaps in his world. Bit by bit he would fill them in with whatever took his fancy. A freeway became a roller coaster because he could not imagine what a freeway was if it was neither free nor a way of life. Time also meant nothing and he would have it as long as he liked, in whichever order he fancied. So life was very easy. He was comfortable, relaxed, bothered by nothing. He was the centre of inexplicable interest, and food appeared as if by some miracle.

Life was beginning to shape up. He learned that he had a job and a house and a car as well, though the car was a bit vague in his mind, but he sensed the truth of the statement that he had one. There was a family, a history, and he could recall it, though almost as if it was somebody else's. He remembered vividly that the often ignored prologue to Shakespeare's *Taming Of The Shrew* involved a drunken man coming round to find his friends pretending that he was a Duke with amnesia. Well, he was a dog with amnesia, or maybe a god, though, more likely, he was a bicycle.

Bells were ringing and focus returned to his eyes as he wanted to explain the revelation to Nurse... Was it June, Joan,

Jane, Jean, or maybe Jim? Was that his Nurse or his wife? And the name of his wife was... The name escaped him.

Instead of his nurse or wife he found Dr Thism, shaking his hand and saying, "welcome back" and almost as soon as Silas had worked out what welcome back meant, he was being driven away.

He patted the seat, the safety belt, the windscreen, and all were solid. This was the car. It never stopped at red lights and changed colour at green ones. It had a large bell on the roof, and a team of huskies pulled it. Then out of his right eye he thought he could see the steering wheel and maybe the driver.

He heard her voice and translated it somehow. He was going home. He would have time to relax. He would eat well. They would go on a holiday. To the moon. And although there were lots of messages from work, he was not allowed to turn on his computer and begin answering them. E-mail had killed him once before. No computer then. He knew the word but not the thing.

He was home, sitting in front of the TV, so he was told, though where it was he could not fathom. There was something out there but he could not understand what it was. It smelt of electricity though.

He forgot the warning and found his desk. He was apparently a dotcom entrepreneur, running a large dotcom business. He was a computer wizard, a boy genius who became too old and he had not been to the moon, but had once had a dog when he was a boy before he was a genius. He remembered it all so well, but at his desk he found nothing but a flat screen and a keyboard. The voice warned him not to switch it on but he could not tell whether it was on or not.

A bell rang and he was told that lunch was cooked. And in the kitchen he could see a steaming plate of food emerge from a haze of more steam. A door clicked shut and then he was sat at a table with knives and fork, eating and hearing birds twittering in the gardens outside. He remembered running through grass, chasing a dog, and riding a bicycle.

"I want a bicycle," he said and the voice laughed. If Dr Thism said it was OK then it would be OK.

Bicycle therapy was obviously scientifically reputable.

He began to cycle to the hospital on a regular basis and Dr Thism explained to the gathered students that illness is not only a matter of being unable to do things but a matter of not wishing to. All pills and potions are useless if the patient refuses to get well. If one can persuade sick people of the truth of this then only the truly sick remain sick, and only the truly sick are dead, for which he was also working on a cure. And Dr Thism bowed amidst the laughter.

His therapy for Silas was thus to hand him a video camera and have him film his life. But Silas could not see the video camera.

"Pretend you can see it," said Dr Thism, "And pretend to reacquaint yourself with the world! From pretence comes reality!"

"Yes yes!" said Silas, "Shakespeare. The forgotten scene."

Silas took his pretend camera to make a pretend film that Dr Thism could pretend to watch. As Silas understood it, the meaningless object in his hand which had mass, volume, and shape, was a device for transforming what he thought knowable into the unseeable so that Dr Thism could see whether he really saw what he thought he did not!

Although he had no idea whether he had pressed a button, the imaginary camera made a satisfying "ding ding". It was thus like a curious bicycle bell and he felt comfortable with that. Levers, he understood. Pedals were very solid. Gears and cogs were a source of fascination. So his first project was to make an imaginary video of the town museum where great chugging machines, built in England, worked up the grease on steel pistons. And he "videoed" them. At least he thought he did when he heard the imaginary camera go ding ding. On looking through the imaginary viewfinder, he could see nothing but the reflection of his own dark pupil but when watching the videos with Dr Thism they both would howl with laughter.

"All this thrusting, all these pistons, all this steam blowing off! It is a sign that you are thinking of resuming your sex life with your wife."

At the next video session Dr Thism was most pleased.

"Your wife is hot!" yelled Dr Thism as he excitedly called in all the members of the psychiatric unit to witness this breakthrough. "Now how can you say that you cannot see your wife? Tell me! How could you make this movie using a video camera and not know what the camera is?"

Silas thought this was a valid point. If only he had not thought that all he had shot on his imaginary camera was an imaginary bicycle ride through the imaginary local woods where the trees were columns of rock n' roll and the leaves semi-demi-quavers riffing with the wind section!

"What are you trying to tell me?" asked Dr Thism, when Silas brought him another imaginary video and described what was on it for him.

"This is Jane, and that's her dog. That's the big fire in her sitting room. And that's me on the telephone telling my wife I won't be home for dinner..."

"But you are home, with your wife!"

Saddened with his progress, Silas found that he was not bicycling home, but in another direction. He rode his bicycle all the away across town to his company where, as soon as he walked through the door, he found he was the centre of attention. Strangers who seemed familiar to him greeted him. He was sure he would discover their names. He was ushered through the cubicles full of young men and women sat at empty desks staring into empty space. Inexplicably he felt cold.

"How's it going partner!" said a concerned young man. "We're well placed for the next quarter. Do you want to be brought up to speed on developments? I'll get all the papers over to you. How's Janet by the way?"

Silas heard the words but could not see the point from which they came. Then he heard a strange gargling sound but it meant nothing. There was a momentary image of red face, poking tongue, bulging eyes, and flaying arms, and he heard himself utter the words, "Die you supercilious little bastard!" But the words faded into mist and he could no longer imagine what he was doing there, so he rode away on his bicycle. He flew into the air, flapping his wings. He was a bird. He ate pizza. He barked. And Janet loved him and cleaned out his cage every night. Or was it June this time?

Dr Thism was very disappointed.

"Never mind, because here we have no failures," said Dr Thism, "Only set-backs."

Silas growled. He felt much better. The old dog was back.

THE LUBRICATION ZONE

I was hurrying towards my only appointment for months when the trap shut. The Martians had got me again. There was nothing important in the offing, merely a film crew waiting for me to play sleazy *gweilo* number three, but this time the Martian Snafu Ray hit me in the very seat of my humanity: my car. They had timed it so that the car belched, hissed and expired just as I was turning the corner into a little place in The New Territories called Nowhere Convenient. Then to tighten their death grip on my sense of well being, Ali in his oily pajamas, smiling a yellow-toothed smile, emerged from the stacked rotting wrecks of "Ali's Asian Lubrication Zone", saying, "It is just a burst radiator. It will be ready tomorrow morning."

So I went home to stare at the telephone and wonder what the hell I was doing in this place! My agent was dying to call me with good news though. He was bound to be out pounding the streets of LA and London, simultaneously, trying to rescue me, trying to get me back into the swing of the Western world I had somehow slipped away from.

But tomorrow came without the call and I took my trip to the Lubrication Zone only to be greeted by Ali's, "Is it tomorrow already?"

Is it, I wondered?

Taking taxis to "Nowhere Convenient" is grueling at the best of times, especially if the driver is on the fifty sixth hour of a fifty five hour shift and thus mentally dive-bombing buses to keep awake, but, frankly, I think taking taxis back home again is even worse. Why? You can never go back home, but my impatience, my ennui, was of no importance to Ali.

"B-B-But ..." I stammered, on the next visit, this time in a taxi with a dashboard display of seven dwarves on springs, "The engine you are now putting in is twice the price of the engine you said you were putting in."

"Twice as good," explained Ali, on his haunches with his cousins, sifting through the smoking remnants of the first engine installation attempt.

"OK!" I said, "Just get on with it; otherwise it'll be another wasted day."

"Wasted?" Ali pondered this concept. "But if you wait, you will have a car. That is not a waste."

Maybe he could tell from my stereotypical western purple-faced look of exasperation that I needed placating in some way. And as steam rose off me, Ali looked at the Prophet's words inscribed in Urdu upon a plaque on the wall, and held out his two hands as if weighing up all possibilities. Then he made a number of irate phone calls featuring expletives in four different languages, none of which got me a new engine. Ali took it all in good part.

"We charge by the hour, by the way," he added, "but for you it is a specially long hour."

He grinned. Ali was making a sort of joke. I sort of laughed, but even so, my sixth sense told me that at home my agent was leaving frantic messages saying I had to be in business class that very evening to take the meetings and schmooze the money, or else the whole deal would be lost. Telling this to Ali would not help, nor would strangling him, though that might have made me feel better. More atavistic behaviour, I thought, not uncommonly displayed in the roles handed out to me by Asian film producers in such epics as "Cop Castrator", in which I played a victim of the eponymous hero.

"Patience," said Ali, sensing my agitation as I relived one of my more painful scenes, "is a virtue."

"Is that what that says?" I said, pointing to the Prophet's words.

"It is a plea for tolerance," he explained, "Blacks, Women, Slaves, they are all to be given due respect. Very advanced for its time."

"Hmm," I said, thinking it a pity The Prophet did not write a car-repair manual as well. There was no alternative but to try the serene approach. As I awaited the starter motor's grind, I began to flick through the thumb-stained calendar hanging behind Ali's desk. I flipped over the pages to find every month was September and each year contained thirteen of them.

"I bought that in Sheung Shui market," he explained, "There they are very cheap."

"I bet they are," I said.

"Every year for me," he said, making another sort of joke, "Is a big year."

"That's almost a joke, Ali."

"People do too much chasing about, if you ask me."

"You are a fountainhead of ancient wisdom, Ali. When are you going to have the car fixed?"

As I watched his cousin biting a spark plug and polishing the spark gap on his sleeve, the appeal of Ali's calendar began to make perfect sense. The scribbles and appointments and promises that annotated various dates were all pre-packaged with the excuse: "It is here in black and white, underlined in red. And what is all this inhuman rush for anyway?"

Ali had got me by the credit cards and gained my undivided attention. Trying to forget that frantic phone call my agent must have been making, I told myself not to be so hard on Ali, for maybe there *was* wisdom to be gained from this collision of worlds.

Why should not every year be a big year, and why should not every day be as long as it takes? What was fortune, achievement, fame, anyway, when it was merely to be noticed by strangers, or in Ali's case, customers, all of whom spoke *stupid* and knew no other dialect? So who needed that big deal? Who needed the bank balance, the profile, who needed to add to the accumulated ornaments, trappings, and trivia?

I mean, the novelty of transforming my perennial promising into world beating accomplishment was palling. So why not spend the rest of my life under the Martian yoke watching Ali's uncommonly yellow teeth? There was wisdom indeed! Bugger that, I thought, and went home to call my agent and beg him to make my day.

He was in a meeting, so the secretary told me. "It's nothing important," I said, thinking how another birthday was coming, and that I still did not have a car, nor a career, for that matter.

There was a time though when I, young, righteously impoverished, performed in small theatre venues until I gained a lucrative contract drinking a pint of Old Black for TV advertisements. I had to smile to the camera and wipe the froth off the lip: the F.O.L. moment, as it was annotated in all the scripts. It became a Brand Identifier, a B.I., as *we* called it in the business. When they discovered they could B.I. without my lip for the F.O.L, I was sucked under the door by a Martian with a vacuum cleaner who must have read my thoughts concerning fear of returning to abject poverty. He then blew me from the nozzle gasping upon the dried riverbeds of what I like to call international media work. A beer commercial in Dubai, that well known beer drinking capital of the world, led to a spate of work in Africa, India, Australia, and somehow it all gets misty. The drift, the haze, the one air ticket, the one airport, the one beam me up, beam me down too many that led to worse than Nowhere Convenient, but Nowhere in Particular.

Then many days later, the phone rang. My pulse raced. My sinews stiffened. I thought maybe it was him, the agent telling me good, or perhaps bad, news. I was too young, not young enough, too old, too English, too American, too ... not enough ... dark ... light ... However, it was merely Ali to say the car was ready and that he could not drive it over because it was Ramadan.

I decided to look at the positive side, even if it meant a trip in a taxi through the crazy container dumps and rust fields of an industrial society that disliked paying for sewage processing. But why rant about such things as these? When the time comes, all will be done. That, I was sure, was how Ali would see it. Ali's will be done.

On arrival, suitably dazed, the garage was locked. When I called at Ali's home, a bracing fifteen minute walk away, with the rain, as the Chinese say, hou daaih lohk yu, very big, there were wives and kids and skinny balding dogs all reeking of spices and howling before a TV set. Ali told me he had to call his brother who had the keys.

"I'm glad you've got that organised by now," I said.

"But not to worry, the car is in good condition," explained Ali.

His wife, red lipped and purple chiffoned, offered some *galub jamin* which I proceeded to drip down the front of my shirt.

"And what brings you here?" she asked with a flash of big brown eyes.

"Shush!" said Ali, giving her a flash of the big evil eye as he headed for the door. She killed him with a mere wag of her finger.

"And tell your fat oaf brother," she added, "that he is not to come round here ordering my maid to clean his car, or I will kick him in his ulcer!"

Then she asked me about my life story: when I married, how many sons, daughters, cousins, and so on, leaving Ali to his shame at having married a pagan. That is assuming he had not merely decided Ramadan a good excuse that I, in my ignorance, would not question. For that matter, that was assuming she was indeed his wife!

"Ah, so you are nearly someone," said Ali's maybe wife, impressed by my description of myself, but then less impressed on hearing my usual coda of betrayal, frustration, and bad luck that my agent's silence had brought me to blurting out in ever increasing bursts of self pity. I tried to explain my theory of the Martian Snafu Vacuum Cleaner Ray, but it only seemed to cause her eyes to glaze over.

"Well," she said, relieved, "He is back."

"We have fixed it brilliantly," said Ali proudly as one of his – or someone's – sweaty and wet brood breathlessly handed me the keys. Both he and his father – uncle? – had run through the rain to and from the brother's house – whose brother?

"It was a tight fit but we shaved a little off here, pushed a little there. A mechanical engineering feat of enormity."

I clutched the keys to my heart and stifled a tear and all interest in the geography of Ali's life.

"Your customer," said his – let us say – wife, "Is almost somebody important. But he is very humble."

"No doubt he has much to be humble about," said Ali, taking my money, and then handing me his business card.

"In case of trouble," he added tapping the side of his nose.

"What sort of trouble?"

"Oh," he said vaguely, "just trouble in general."

"I'll remember that," I said, "During the next missile test or radiation leak, you're my man!"

I shook his hand heartily, the keys reassuringly jangling.

My new engine roared into life, minus a few hoses that were, according to Ali, of no importance. Thus, I prayed, there would be another year of being a step above pedestrian. In fact, I prayed for a lot more but the phone still did not ring, E.T. was dissected, and I played sleazy gweilo number four in a car commercial and thought why am I here in Hong Kong and not in LA? I could think of no good answer other than that Martian Snafu Ray.

Then it was Ministry of Transportation Vehicle Registry Test (MOT) time. Big Hollywood stars would never know the joy and the sorrow of such a moment. Those that lie abed ignorant of such days would count themselves accursed if they knew. And those I despised whose lives consist of little else but MOTs rightfully point at me and say, there, you are not so special after all.

The garage I chose for the MOT was slick, clean, with Chinese mechanics wearing brown overalls and carrying clipboards. They peered under the bonnet, tut-tutted and muttered to each other about *gong daaih wa a ma*! – the "Big Talk" they might have to commit themselves to and then phoned back to the main office on their mobile. There was a problem and I had to speak to the one person with the authority to hand out bad news. The Engine, I was told by a much-embarrassed young lady, in impeccable English, had no serial number and that would mean the MOT form could not be properly filled in, at least not without big talk, which was big problem. Now I knew the trouble Ali hinted at.

"Everybody is stupid," explained Ali, as he rescued me. "I personally will get it the required certificate. I will vouch for it. My word will count. I take cash by the way, but a cheque will do. Make it out to Hassan."

"Not Ali?" I enquired.

"Oh no. That is the name of the garage. I am doing this as a personal favour to you."

"And you're not Ali?"

"He was the owner who painted the sign. But that was many owners ago and now we are all Ali. But today I am Hassan. It does not matter as long as the car gets its certificate."

His yellow teeth sparkled crookedly at me. They were, if anything, yellower. As well as the turmeric scrub, he was now slapping on life threatening doses of gloss after coat for a long lasting finish. His twisted teeth, I suspected, would one day be dug up by eight-tentacled, green skinned archaeologists picking over the remnants of our civilisation. They might even find them at Ali's garage and surmise that these must be the sabre toothed Ali's, but they would be wrong. But to Hassan, obscurity was of no concern. To me, though, the end of civilisation was still worth an ulcer or two but next year the car would be one of those rusting hulks heaped high amongst the bamboo and bananas in the backyards of the environmentally challenged. This sleazy gweilo was, yet again, on the road to be righteously kung fu'd.

"You know, What-ever-your-name-is," I said, "I think that's the way everything works. Wars, famines, plagues of pustules and even the decline and fall of the British Empire, are but the background. Whereas the MOT, the Ministry of Transportation Vehicle Test, that's foreground, that's life, that's where the real action is."

Hassan nodded and laughed.

"Yes," he said, "You are making some sort of a joke?"

He probably understood. We were both in the Martian Snafu Vacuum Froth On The Lip Lubrication Zone where everything was slipping and sliding away and the jungle was in danger of reclaiming it all. I laughed. What else could you do?

THE IMMORTALS

Ah Wong's head floated down a stream, buffeted by the torrents of water, breaking on the rocks, breaking to gales of laughter. The poets beneath their umbrellas, along the banks of the winding stream, served by the giggling girls with lotus feet, skilled at rhyming when drunk, boasted and bragged and demanded a contest: the person who found the head must sup a skull's worth of wine and compose a verse to conjure a world of poetry, a world that a suffering man might make to distract his thoughts.

There was applause. The men loved the sentiment and watched the skull bobbing in the water. It would either wash into the hands of a poet or pass through the picnic area down to the lake or maybe sink to be rubbed smooth in the whirl pools, turned to a pebble, ground to a powder, dissolved in the lake, sucked into the sky, and rained back down. Instead it washed onto the dangling fat feet of Mei Mei, the oldest and the ugliest of old women, who poured wine into the skull and began the story of her lover.

***

His day began, she said, when a blinding blue light poured into his eyes. He blinked. The light flickered and clouds assembled, subtly changing colours as they moved picking up the browns and greens reflected from the earth. Dawn was perfection awaiting the corruption of night.

I, Mei Mei, his love, in a flowing gown that flapped lightly in the breeze knelt as I served breakfast beneath the canopy of the Morning Pavilion, Ah Wong's favourite morning place. I handed a bowl of congee to him and he admired its perfection. The willow patterning on the side was a world in itself and he could watch the lovers meet upon the bridge, sigh, recite their poetry, and promise never to forget each other for eternity. I smiled and watched as he ate the contents of the bowl.

"Lacking impermanence," he said, "We have become ugly."

Ah Wong held out his hand and ran it over my cheek. I giggled as my gown slid to the ground and left me naked. I was perfect: my breasts, my thighs, my waist, my neck, were all composed in the most pleasing and perennial proportions. I was soft to touch, my skin smooth and brown. Ah Wong wallowed in the smell of my perfume. He filled his lungs and held the moment. But the moment, despite longing for its permanence, had to be fleeting as that is what gave it its perfection.

"Do you love me?" he asked, and I sighed and asked Ah Wong in return: "Do you love me?"

"Of course," said Ah Wong, "How can I not?"

"You have chosen me to be the perfect object of your love," I said, "but is that perfect love? Surely perfect love can only be for that which you have not chosen?"

"What does it matter whether I choose love or love chooses me?" said Ah Wong.

I acted the beauty. I could act otherwise but I chose beauty. I do not need to embody it. There is ugliness, otherwise there would be no beauty, and somewhere in the world there are those revelling in ugliness and think beauty ugly and ugly beauty.

He lay back naked as I caressed him. He reached out his left hand and it met Ling Ling, who was as different from me, as she was beautiful. Her breasts were long rather than round and firm. Her thighs were round rather than undulating. Her eyes were large and hypnotic where with me, it is the lips that one longs for. Ah Wong kissed me as Ling Ling stroked Ah Wong. Then the moment was over. As ever the disappointment flooded Ah Wong's mind. As ever he had found the perfect person and then wondered what it was to have two of us and then why not four, sixteen, two hundred and fifty six… Was not the love of all greater than the love of one?

"You must choose," I said. "But your choice will make no difference, because I too make my choices and I too wonder if that choice is the best possible. This is our situation."

"Oh," said Ling Ling, "It is more of a philosophy day than a passion day today. Perhaps I should return in the evening?"

"And that is why you should stay," said Ah Wong, "Defeat your own will and defy the limited conventions you habitually create for yourself."

Ling Ling hesitated, but then decided and disappeared.

"She defies defiance itself," pronounced Ah Wong, "The principle of No Rule, even this rule, is perhaps the most difficult to live by. To choose not to choose is a choice and then to choose not to choose it. This too is a choice. It is inescapable and yet we must escape."

We spoke of the inescapable as we walked among the blooming bougainvilleas, violet and humming with a myriad butterflies, each with silvery scaled wings.

"The minds of the insects have their own systems of beauty that are not ours but can be appreciated by us," I said. "This is proof of our common ancestor and its origin in light itself."

"Proof," said Ah Wong softly, "Is a difficult word."

We arrived at a forking path and I walked to the left as Ah Wong walked this day to the right. He sought his schedule. Today he decided was to be an organised day after all. He was to defy defiance. The morning was innocence, the evening was knowingness, and between these thoughts he scheduled things in four headings: What to do? Who are you? Who am I? What now?

The scholar's desk appeared, complete with ink-stone and brush rack. He sat at it and turned to his great cabinet of miniatures with each drawer full of its treasures. He opened randomly a door to discover a miniature elephant carved out of ivory, or was it a carving in ivory of an elephant, or even an ivory elephant? How intrinsic to its nature was the ivory, or the elephant, or the intention of the carver? Ah Wong left off the question; it was a meditation for another day. He opened the door where the day's news had been deposited. Amongst the items was an event that Ah Wong found immensely interesting: a baby had been born.

He would have liked to have been with the thousands who gawked and tried to catch the sound the baby made naked in the air. Better still he would have loved to have gone in close and caught a whiff of the child. Smell, being such a primitive sense, was always the most authentic, the most essential to the nature of man. It was, Ah Wong suspected, the first sense we are ever aware of, but in the crush he would have had to settle for the mere rumour of the smell. It was said to smell of unlimited potential but Ah Wong, as you no doubt recall, had declared at the debating forum that, "The limits we have are a disappointment but at the same time they are our assurance of authenticity."

The forum buzzed with responses. The pessimists and optimists divided themselves equally: the limits were sources of spiritual harmony; the limits were sources of frustration; the inability of humanity to finalise the debate was a sign of its evolutionary dead end; the inability was a source of endless wonderment for there were still things left to discover.

And remember, he posed one final question before leaving the chamber, just to see what ripples it would make in the great sea of minds: "Was it possible that we are merely bound in a nutshell within a nutshell and viewed pitifully by gods of greater powers, or are we truly destined to be the pinnacle of perfection?"

Ah Wong turned the pages of his correspondence. Answers ultimately were of no interest. What he liked was turning the page. He liked the rice paper. The sensation of his finger tips staining the delicate membranes with his sweat gave him a sensual thrill. Oh, he sighed, to have been there when the paper was hand-made and not merely an approximation to all paper, but the individual sheet with all its imperfections, incapable of reproduction! Time was uncapturable. You could imagine the past, but never return. You could move into the future, but never back. Was this a disappointment or a blessing? If he was to invade the past, he would destroy the quality he longed for.

"Mei Mei," shouted Ah Wong, "Have you prepared the family tree?"

The doors of my garden opened. I was playing shuttlecock with Ling Ling and Ah Wong watched as we skipped from side to side and into the net and back. In his mind he ran us naked and then ran us clad in nothing but wisps of silk and then perversely he ran us as nothing but skeletal frames. Was it the running or was it merely the way the upholstery rebounded as we ran that he found so attractive? A mind controlling muscles that stretched and contorted facial expressions was more attractive than one lacking the ability. Beauty was skin deep, though, without the mind, the skin would lack the beauty and without the skin the mind would be of no interest.

Could he make himself find other things attractive? He could view the world as if he was a dragon-fly elegantly swarming high above looking down upon Ling Ling and me. But he found himself forgetting his reason for being there. Smells and strange colours excited him, but not naked Mei Meis and Ling Lings. The dragon-fly world had its own interests.

Ah Wong entered the garden carrying a silver tray containing the most fragrant tea that could ever have been created.

"Interesting," said Ling Ling as she savoured the flavour of the tea. "There is a hint of honeysuckles, and something that blew in the air circa 1641 in the foothills of... the Himalayas. This is Indian tea, dried by a Nepali and packed into a hard slab and trans..."

"Yes! Yes!"

"It could have come through Tibet, but no... this went through the Karakorum to the West of China."

"And?"

"And," I added, in case he thought that I was less knowledgeable than Ling Ling, "Of course brewed in the presence of a Sandal Wood mosquito repellent?"

"Remarkable."

"Yes," I said, "There is a whole history in a cup of tea."

"No," said Ling Ling, "All history is in a cup of tea!"

"There are many," said Ah Wong, as he sipped his tea, "Who believe in the future tea, the tea that has not yet been perfected, but I believe that tea is about history. How can one have tea without history? Tea is intrinsically a retrospective experience."

Ling Ling and I bowed to the great connoisseur and then led him along the path toward the trestle tables that I had laid with the charts Ah Wong required. All the names of all predecessors were spread out before us, with all their relationships explained. Here was the great chain of being.

Ah Wong pondered the charts. They stretched out as far as the eye could see. The relationship between him and any one of the millions of people annotated before the great discovery of everlasting life, seemed far too distant. What could he have in common with them? How could their concepts still find homes in his psyche? What was beautiful to them was as alien as the beauty beheld by a cockroach. It all made little difference now. Like that ever-repaired sword, he was no longer quite the blade he was. And yet, he shared the history.

"What a tragedy," Ling Ling exclaimed, "To be in the last generation to die!"

"The last person to die demanded to be allowed to," Ah Wong told her.

"Why on earth did they demand to die?" asked Ling Ling.

To explore the situation, I became an old woman. Ah Wong found this disconcerting.

"If one was to remain old," Ah Wong said, "Then death was the only option."

"Not necessarily," I said, "People will look after you. And that can be pleasurable."

"Why anyone would look after you when you looked like that," said Ah Wong, "I do not know. The dead puffy skin, the watery eye, the grey thin hair and crooked back do not enhance your beauty."

"They test love though," I said. "If one truly loves the younger version, one will love the older."

"The generations that died often left their old women to live alone," said Ah Wong, "But if the old man lived longest he would attract a young woman to look after him."

"Few people ever have true love," sighed Ling Ling.

"Love is not a test," said Ah Wong.

"Then why do you love Mei Mei more than you love me?" asked Ling Ling. "I love you no matter what. But she constantly tests you. And you love her all the more."

"I certainly do not love her when she looks like that!"

"What a shallow person you are," I said, returning to my glorious youth. My hair shone, my skin glowed, and I moved with grace and flexibility. My face showed the passing of my thought, whereas my old skin had hung like a mask hiding me.

"And your thoughts were not authentically old," said Ah Wong, "They were those of our kind. The prospect of death did not haunt you, the uncertainty of memory did not plague you, and the knowledge of having completed the life cycle did not inform you."

"My youth is no less inauthentic," I said, "in being the box in which an immortal lives, so why should my age be inauthentic?"

Ah Wong turned his mind to recalling his childhood, but although he could run the memory, he felt that perhaps it had been implanted in him. A perfect childhood would make a happier person and so all the imperfections of his childhood had been erased and even the erasure had been erased.

"We should forget this obsession with authenticity," whispered Ah Wong, "it is indefinable and can drive us mad."

"Language," said Ling Ling, "Is over-rated. We should simply make love. Would you like to make love for a moment at least?"

Ah Wong sighed as he contemplated the vast task of reviewing the record and discerning the rule that controlled his heart. It would defeat him and in that there was an authentic human experience, but it was not perfect even in its imperfection. Language, he thought, was not the way to go and so he allowed the garden to fade into twilight and his last thought before love was made was of the many mothers embracing him, for the last time that he believed he was the centre of the universe.

We no longer embodied the characters of the Ming Gardens. We became empty vessels ringing in harmony with each other. Our music grew layer upon layer, from a simple rhythmic pulse, to a syncopated melody, to counter melodies and layers of tones and half tones, and incidentals. We played together. We were the music.

"The metaphor that is not a metaphor is the only metaphor to express the experience," uttered Ah Wong, as he recovered his composure.

"You have to be there," I said, smoothing my silk gown back into some semblance of tidiness.

Ling Ling wound her hair back up and pinned it in place with black lacquer hair pins.

"He loves me more," said Ling Ling, "Because he is kind to you."

"He loves me more," I said, "Because he beats you!"

"Which of us do you prefer?" asked Ling Ling.

"Which?" I asked. "You must let us know or we shall live forever in pain."

"We seek to express our situation," said Ah Wong, "And yet it constantly eludes us."

"Never mind," said Ling Ling, "What would it matter if you could solve every single riddle written on every single lantern in the universe?"

"But," I said, "This is not every single riddle. It is but one! Our one! Ours alone!"

"These are good questions," said Ah Wong suddenly realising that he was standing alone at another fork in the garden path.

He heard Ling Ling giggling and the sound of water splashing and so took the fork towards the lake and joined us by the jetty. We climbed into the rowing boat to row out into the lily laden lake where we would sit, fish, and grill whatever we caught.

"I have a riddle," said Ling Ling, "I am not welcome, and yet there can be no harm in me. I am not known, and yet once all feared me. Once, only I was eternal and now I no longer exist. I never existed, that is my nature."

"I have a riddle," I said, "I have lost my past and have no end. I have no needs and everything that I want. I have no goals and have no pain, my story has been told, but I cannot begin again."

"I too have a riddle," said Ah Wong, "I live but a fleeting moment, but believe that I live forever. I have never existed and there is no future. What now?"

The words of the riddles implanted themselves upon the sides of the rainbow coloured lanterns that now lit the shoreline. The cormorants, the great shaggy black birds that listened to all the riddles, sat upon the granite pedestals positioned like chess pieces upon the misty lake and never answered them. Answering the riddles was not the game, merely posing them. To answer would be to end the game and the answers would be too trivial to warrant a riddle in the first place.

Dusk upon the lake was Ah Wong's favourite time. The mist rolled across the rippling water in dreamy clouds illuminated by the lanterns. Other boats drifted in and out of the mist, their own lanterns reflecting upon their wake, and their fellow fishermen waved and bowed to anyone who could see them.

A fish attached itself to one of Ling Ling's hooks and she squealed with delight as she hauled it in and with a flash of a blade, in the light of the great round moon that now filled the sky, she gutted the fish, skewered it and held it over the charcoal burner.

"We end the fish's life," said Ah Wong, "but know it to dream."

"It is the nature of the fish to die," I said. "It is no longer our nature."

"But we are no longer part of the cycle of being. We need no food."

"Spiritually we do," said Ling Ling.

"Ah," said Ah Wong, "The usual excuse for perversity and selfishness!"

We ate the fish, dangled our feet into the lily pad lake, watched the moon, the light of the lanterns, the grey of the clouds. The great cranes flew, sweeping through the sky, so high they could barely be seen, barely be heard, their creaking squawk winding down through the wind. The mountains of the moon could be touched if anyone so wished, but not tonight.

"Tonight we go to the temple," I said.

The temple of ten thousand faces was on the island in the centre of the lake upon which many of the boats converged as if drawn to the flickering lantern lights like so many fire-flies.

"Tonight we should try breaking through to the final experience," said Ah Wong, making us laugh for he said it each time. "When I stop saying it, enlightenment will be mine."

"Whatever that is," whispered Ling Ling, giggling.

"Now that it's dark," I added, "We move into the darker thoughts, the strange and perverse, those of pain, in which there seems to be most life."

"To live in pain," said Ah Wong, "Is to be constantly aware."

"There is nothing to gain, if you're in pain," I said, "It was the pain that drove us to this solution."

"What solution is that?" asked Ah Wong.

"Our solution to our problem," I said. "You will see."

"There are no solutions," said Ah Wong, "Only more riddles."

But Ah Wong was intrigued and to the island we flew, taking the cue from the bugs that rose from the lake. Like a dream they rattled their wings, followed the tail lights that said 'ready for mating'. The simple joy was a moment without thought and Ah Wong exclaimed: "Oh, how the simple life, brief and with structure, is far the best! A beginning and end, with in-between, moments of elation, moments of pain, hope and suffering, hunger and satiety, too hot, too cold."

"We can have that now," I said. "We merely act it and it is so, over and over, until we get bored, and then we change our clothes, and disappear."

"Ling Ling, Mei Mei!" cried Ah Wong, but we raced ahead. "Ling Ling! Mei Mei!"

Ah Wong flew with the flock, across the face of the moon, seeking his lost loves. This was his nature. He could not die. But he could live the part of those who did. At every crossroad he believed that one path led to oblivion, but he would never know which. And so he flew, as a great dark bird, crying "Ling Ling, Mei Mei!" And he hunted us through the mountains of the moon and thought he would be alone until dawn when he is always ready to begin again, fearing in the blinding blue light, that there is no more to come. But then the great bell clanged. The monks on the island sat astride the dried tree trunk that they swung from a great tripod of pines to clang the bell, which resonated throughout the universe, shook foundations, destroyed great cities, awoke the great dead poets who gathered as ghosts shaken loose from the ground, murmuring their life's works.

And there, before the temple gates, Ling Ling and I, still panting from our game, waited for Ah Wong.

"What a performance," said Ah Wong with delight and excitement. "This is a new ritual, the calling of the dead to entertain the forever living! Did they know they lived once? Did they know they lived again? Were they living? But then, were Mei Mei, Ling Ling, or anyone else alive in my world?"

Ah Wong had long debated this and concluded that I and Ling Ling must be real because so much was beyond his experience and control and unless he was everyone then he was but one among many.

The great hall of ten thousand mirrors opened before us, candles lighting the way, flickering in the mirrors, and here and there dark faces, some our own, looked back at us: a million billion souls, some living, some dead, some yet to be, so the monks said.

"Look deep into the mirrors," said the monks, "And you will see traces of everything that ever was and ever will be: the murders and the rapes, the disembowelling and the slow lingering tortures inflicted by man upon man, spider upon fly, snake upon rat, the maddened dream of a suffering god!"

The great temple shook to the clash of the swords that shattered overhead, clattering before the feet of Ah Wong, who – terrified at the sight – cowered behind Ling Ling who cried. We were trapped, as the door swung closed and around in the dark nothing could be seen any more as the voices growled. This was the show tonight.

The ritual began.

"Mei Mei do you love me?" screamed Ah Wong, his head pulled down by his long black hair by the monks, a great sword swinging towards his neck. He looked for the last time into my eyes.

Ah Wong's head flew through the air, propelled by the blood, splattering over the mirrors, his eyes flickering in recognition of every reflection of himself. An end at last? Was that the case? He could still think, but that would fade as the blood coagulated. The system would collapse and consciousness would leave. He was supposed to have no feeling if dead, so how was it, that he was not? But of course that was the point, he was not, could not be. This was eternity and death an illusion.

The cruelty of the trick was not lost on him when a prick rammed in his mouth. He choked surrounded by boars that squealed and stank of bad breath and pus. Their curling elongated pricks quivering to take turns. Boars are not particular. They shit where they fornicate. They snorted and gnawed at his nose. It re-grew to be re-gnawed. He heard us laughing and giggling and looked into the boars' eyes: Ling Ling and Mei Mei, we two boars, our tusks gold, peeling off his skin with our rough tongues. We laughed as we skinned his skull. He screamed but not with pain, that had faded and he knew this could not go on, it must end and he would be the same, or would he? There was doubt. This was not new, he reasoned. He had been here before. It was a ritual and in the light of day would be no more.

"Are we not beautiful," asked Ling Ling.

"Are we not perfect," I asked.

What he silently mouthed, we could not tell.

***

Mei Mei drank one last gulp of wine from the skull and then cast it back into the stream where it swirled, and clattered against the rocks, on its journey towards the great lake.

"Thank you for providing our inspiration," said Mei Mei, "Thank you for helping us immortals, gathered about the rhyming stream, take the night and create the next day. From your skull life and death come, and all points in between. Puppets dancing to their own tunes, your skull set them free. They have stories, they have needs and conflicts and obstacles to overcome. This story, my story, is all your stories in one!"

"But yours has ended and mine has begun," cried Ling Ling, swooping down, net in hand, scooping the skull from the stream. "I drink to my friends! Listen to my story! My story has no end."

THE ONE-LEGGED RICKSHAW BOY

I was on a mission to find a one-legged Rickshaw Boy. I told Mr P about my story idea and he said it was a very good one. Mr P was my producer, which means, as you can guess, that I am in the TV business.

My agent arranged our initial meeting in a wine bar in London's Soho. To my astonishment, Mr P told me the cheque was in the post, that I was his man, and that he loved my shoes. "Policeman's boots," he called them, and then showed me his own moccasins. I didn't understand the significance, but I think it was his way of telling me to relax and buy some more comfortable shoes. We drank a bottle of Merlot each and I told him my story idea. He said the one-legged Rickshaw Boy element was a hoot. I said I thought it a very important statement. This made him laugh.

That was how I came to be in a cockroach-infested apartment eight thousand miles away from home without toilet paper. More important members of the film-crew were put up in a four star hotel, but there had been some deal over real estate and this apartment was available. Apparently I was very lucky to be put up there. Long term stays in hotels, so Mr P told me, were unnatural, as well as expensive. Apparently, someone once stole his shoes from his hotel room. He had a thing about shoes, did Mr P.

So I was met off the plane, dumped in the apartment by a driver called Larry Lau, and left without maps, food or phone numbers. Extremely annoying, but there was little I could do about it then.

I had succumbed to jet-lag and was dreaming, for reasons that escape me, of three legged turtles when the telephone rang.

"Where are you?" asked the phone.

"What?"

"Where are you?"

"I wish I knew," I said.

The voice at the other end said she was Mr P's secretary. It was ten o'clock in the morning and I was late for work.

"Then send a car for me," I said. "And have you found the one-legged Rickshaw Boy?"

I heard a giggle as the phone went dead. I could tell that my quest was a true crusade. We would have a disabled actor hired if it was the last thing I did. I would also have it credited that no tiger penises were used in this production. Like I said, it was a very important statement. There were disability and environmental issues at stake here, all of which were very important in my world of wine bars and UK creatives.

When I looked out of my un-curtained windows, I thought Hong Kong looked promising. The sky was smog laden. Dogs howled. Pile drivers drove. Horns hooted. And schoolgirls in white socks paraded below in the sloping mess of streets. I had imagined an anthill of snake eaters in pursuit of money. And here it was. Just the place where an artificially legged Rickshaw Boy with a penchant for blow-torching his victims crispy-skinned might operate. It was an entertaining prospect.

I dripped like a rusty tap as I waited on the sweltering unknown street for the Toyota. The driver, Larry Lau, wore a yellow T-shirt rolled up over his stomach. He also had a mobile phone and pager strapped to his belt. I think he suffered Bandwidth Anxiety problems. For a man obsessed with communication, it was surprising that he rarely spoke.

Larry pushed an LPG canister off the back seat onto the floor. I assumed this was to make me more comfortable. However, sitting with legs straddling the cylinder had an unnerving effect. It occurred to me that I was being taken off to have my blood drained and my body dumped piecemeal into the water tanks of tall buildings.

This was cop-show writer anxiety syndrome. There is no known cure.

I dreamt of falling off the roofs of financial institutions and plummeting with the Hang Seng Index. Then the car rumbled down ramps into a basement car park and woke me. Luckily, we were beneath the studio and not the lounge of a chainsaw-wielding, rolling-eyed madman. I do not know why, but somehow I associate such characters with this mission.

Mr P leaped about his office explaining that "heroes never sit down."

"Heroes never sit down," I repeated as I jotted the words into my notebook. "Because?" I asked.

"Because they don't," he replied. "Heroes do what heroes do. And one of the things they do is always stand."

"Except when they drive cars?"

"They'd do that standing up if they could," he explained. "But mentally, they are on their feet."

Then he regaled me with many stories about his buckskin moccasins. He took his shoes very seriously, and since it pays to ingratiate oneself with the man who gives the pay check, I smiled and nodded appreciatively at his insight into life and footwear. As he spoke, he fed ant-eggs to Martian goldfish swimming in a small tank on his desk. Every so often, he had a bug-eyed expression on his face not too far removed from that of his fish.

"I tell you, thingy," he said. "Jet lag is shit lag. I haven't been for two weeks. Heh heh heh!"

"Yes Boss," I said. "It sure seems that way."

There were limits to my sycophancy and I suspected that he could see them approaching. So tiring of my company, he pushed me through a door into a darkened room and introduced me to one of the film editors. "Hi Ed," he said, "Here's thingy, you know, the writer, come to do some work. Heh heh heh!"

"Hi thingy," said Ed. "Sit down."

"I'm being heroic."

"Ah, you know, he's right. Look at this lot. They don't sit down."

Ed had a grizzly look about him. He sweated before images of scrawny, sinuous men in greasy vests bouncing, kicking, and dodging bullets while never sitting down. I recognised Larry the Driver on the screen in mid-death throe, screaming like a young Jamie Lee Curtis. Driving was obviously his forté.

Ed frantically cut and slashed at the rushes. He grabbed the strips of film from big wheeled tubs, slapped them onto the Steenbeck editing suite, and seemed able to run the film upside down and backwards and still know where to make the cut. Even so, he groaned, "Oh God! Call that acting? Don't they understand anything?"

"Well at least they don't sit down," I said.

On the screen a hairy-chested, muscle-bound monster wielded a flame-thrower and growled, "Eat death scumbag!"

"Oh Jesus!" groaned Ed. "Can't we kill that bastard?"

I was not sure whether Ed referred to the character, in which case it would have been my fault, or the actor. I plumped for the actor.

"He was cheap," I said.

"Well he's costing them plenty now." Ed replayed the line over and over again and I realised that the hero was actually saying "Eat beth thcumbag!"

"To think," muttered Ed. "I could have been in Hawaii working on an Eastwood movie."

Ed had not seen daylight for fifteen years. In the darkness, I think he was secretly crying. He was definitely sitting though.

I escaped from the editing suite to look for the one-legged Rickshaw Boy. There had to be such a character or the whole episode would make no sense. The Korean casting lady said I was insane. She was an ex-porn star whose last acting role was a naked hog wrestler. She snarled when she spoke and exhaled cigarette smoke from her nostrils.

"But," I pointed out. "In movies the serial killer always has a physical disability."

"Never wear panties, darling," she snarled. "That's the only rule that means anything in this business."

She called herself a dragon lady. It was a well rehearsed little speech for the likes of me. She was show business. I was an upstart. She was the old China hand. I was an ignorant fool. We got on like a house burning down.

"One-legged Rickshaw Boy!" she snarled, exhaling more smoke. "You gweilos haven' got a clue, have you?"

I felt ignorant, but there was a moral imperative to hire a disabled actor. It was my contribution to human rights. Something that I felt more people should know something about.

The golden reflections of Hong Kong's unblinking lights swam across the wet windscreen of my black Toyota. I scoured the streets seeking limblessness. My driver Larry, if I read his sign language correctly, knew a one-legged beggar who would fit the role. However, when we found the man, he was sprawled on the concrete floor of an overhead walkway with two legs: granted crippled, but bi-pedal nonetheless.

"He has to be able to pull a rickshaw," I mimed to Larry, hopping and tugging at the air. Larry nodded as if he understood. "And of course, avoid sitting."

We bent over the beggar again. He was not sitting, but he was lying facedown on the floor, banging his begging tin like a Saturday afternoon TV wrestler submitting.

I dropped him a hundred Hong Kong in memory of my grandmother howling down the ancient English wrestling personality called Billy Two Rivers, doing his stint of tag and grudge matches at Bridlington Spa. It was one of those moments when one wonders how one got here from there. Indeed the beggar was probably thinking much the same thing. One moment his mum was wiping his nose and drying his eyes, and then suddenly he wakes up a stain on the pavement.

"Even if we chop a leg off it won't work," I said. "And I don't think we can budget the recovery time for trauma."

Larry looked at me and grinned. I grinned back. We liked each other because although we could not speak the other's language, we could see in our eyes that we knew the truth.

I returned to my apartment saddened that I could not reach the day's goal. Inside the room, it was dark. I switched on the lights and noticed that even though I switched, nothing went on. On closer, groping, examination, I saw in the shadows that all the light bulbs had been removed. I wondered if somewhere there was a god who knew the reason. Maybe they had never been there in the first place? Maybe I had a rare form of stroke that disabled light bulb perceiving brain cells? Maybe there was a market for stolen light bulbs in Hong Kong run by one-legged Rickshaw Boys? It was a mystery like the source of our dreams and the course of our lives.

Since there was no light I went to bed and dreamt that I was in a sampan. An old woman in a black frilled straw hat sat at the tiller. She gnawed on a live snake that was featured in episode three, and saw that I had fifty thousand Hong Kong in my wallet. She called her husband, who had a chopper.

It was the sort of dream that conjured up one-legged Rickshaw Boys who would spit on my dismembered parts, call me a devil, and tell me I had no right to appear in their dreams.

Then I remembered how part of my research for this project was viewing a documentary on Cambodia. It became clear whose dream was being dreamt, and the fragments of my reality were but bits of shrapnel randomly blown in my direction.

I woke up, more or less, and telephoned Mr P.

"Landmines," I muttered to his recording machine. "Cambodia! Princess Di just before the mystery assassins caught up with her, or not. Good publicity for everyone, that is the cause, not the assassination, or not, but the "Good Cause." Anti-anti-personnel mines. Authenticity found in using a real victim. And a mere..."

I almost said, "hop away."

I did say "hop away."

I made a note to castigate myself for bad taste, but also breathed a sigh of relief. I had discovered I wasn't completely crazy, merely geographically off-centre. The mission could thus be accomplished. I hoped, before I drifted off into exhausted slumber, my crazed memo would not be taken as a sign of mental breakdown, more of inspiration.

Either way it was, as we say in showbiz, a done deal.

I spent the next day writing the script for episode six. It featured a story about doping horses for the Happy Valley Races. I thought it would be amusing to have a bunch of hapless criminals try to get a doped horse into a high rise lift. When I told Mr P this, I thought he would tell me what a hoot that was and I was his man. Unfortunately, he told me what a pain getting a horse into a lift would be. He said I should do the same story with cockroaches instead. He had heard of triad run beetle races, how in Mexico City people painted beetles, sprinkled diamonds on them and tethered them to their shoes as decoration.

It did not seem quite as challenging for a gangster to get a doped cockroach into a lift, diamond studded or otherwise, but Mr P told me to use my imagination. He said maybe there was one special cockroach and it got loose in the building with a small nuclear detonator attached to it. I said I was not quite sure that the animal rights angle would be fully exploited in this situation. I think he noticed that I was almost angry. He looked me firmly in the eye and told me God had an inordinate fondness for beetles. "But," I said as I stared into his wild bug eyes, "what has he done with my light bulbs?"

Mr P decided that he had to go to the toilet at that point. I was passing into a typical scriptwriter faze of unreasonable insistence on common sense. So I took my notes and decided not to write any more that day until I had digested all these ideas, or gotten drunk enough. I settled on getting drunk. Then I'd get back in the correct state of mind for working like this.

Larry took me to a bar in Lan Kwai Fong. It was a ghetto for Westerners, and thus a place held in much contempt by Westerners who liked to think themselves above the sort of Westerner who hung about with no one other than Westerners. However, nearly all the customers in the bar were Chinese. Larry left me alone as he went off with friends. I did find one Westerner though, drinking pints in a corner. He was an English soundman from the film crew: a miserable pot-bellied man with podgy fingers. I told him all about the impossibility of trying to think up a story about cockroaches. He told me he hoped that I would fail.

Like Ed, he too could have been on a shoot with Clint Eastwood in Hawaii. Instead, he told me, he was sitting in cesspools trying to catch the essence of the East, or rather, avoid catching it. His main sources of complaint so far were lizards that could not act, trained monkeys that ran up sides of buildings to plummet to their doom before startled tourists, and the hog-wrestling scene...

The Hog Wrestling Scene?

I was thankful he did not mention one-legged Rickshaw Boys, but my left eye began to twitch. I could feel sensations creep through my mind like rats through the sinking corridors of the Titanic.

"The hog wrestling scene?" I said.

"Whoever thought that one up," he said, "must need his head examined."

"Don't look at me!" I protested, increasingly concerned. It was always possible I had thought that one up in the same way as I had thought up the cockroach racing.

"Have you ever seen a frightened pig?" gurgled the soundman into his lager. This sound was supposed to represent the intestinal activity of a frightened pig.

I immediately went and dragged Larry away from a Filipina dressed in what looked suspiciously like a Minnie Mouse costume. Every time my eye twitched, she said "Screw the British!" I did not know whether she was making an offer or an insult.

"Diu!" snapped Larry. I guessed by the look of his face that the word was Cantonese and not an offer.

"Take me back to the studios," I demanded as I discovered my voice had raised an octave.

He glared at me as I mimed him driving and said "studios" three times in varying degrees of hysteria. He put a cocktail stick into his mouth and chewed on it a moment. Finally Larry said "Che!" and walked out. I followed, and he drove me to the studios in silence, apart from the noise of a jiggling plastic cat on the dashboard.

"Hello Kitty!" I said as I pointed to the curious writing on its side. "The Trend of Life Style" said a sticker on the dashboard. I couldn't help reading it out loud to try see if its meaning could be shaken loose.

"Chisin!" said Larry, spitting bits of the cocktail stick down the front of his T-shirt.

"I am doing this for us all," I explained to him. "Everything must have a meaning."

"Wah!"

"It is what makes us human," I added, stating the essentially humanistic and benevolent goal that motivated my urge to make money through my writing and bring a little joy into the otherwise humdrum lives of the masses.

At the studios I went to see Ed, who sat in one of the film tubs smoking a large cigarette and giggling. I told him that I wanted to see the Rickshaw Boy episode.

"Yeah," he said. "But I strongly recommend you smoke one of these before sitting through the whole thing."

"The whole thing?" I said as I threaded the film into the editing machine. "They finished it without my politically correct anti-anti-personnel devices Cambodian?"

Ed burnt what I hoped were useless out-takes of film. They melted and dripped to the floor as they emitted startling whizzing noises. Finally I sat back and watched a mad moustache of a Vietnam war veteran in hot pursuit of a one-legged Rickshaw boy. As the stuntman hopped down Queen Street, it was obvious that his spare leg was strapped behind.

Mr P stepped through the door, perhaps alerted by Ed. I think there was an emergency red button that could be pressed when the writer demanded to see the rough-cut.

"Hey thingy, don't worry," whispered Mr P. "If we get hold of a stump for some close ups, then people will be too frightened to look closely! Heh heh heh!"

"But he's got two legs!" I choked. "Didn't you get my memo about Cambodia? That country is full of limbless people."

"But can they act?" asked Mr P.

"They can act limbless."

"No," he said. "The Americans would not like it. And we're pinning our hopes on cable syndication."

I felt a sting of defeat. There was no arguing with American taste.

"Ah," said Mr P, spying a consolatory opportunity. "The Hog Wrestling Scene!"

I sank down into my seat and saw my hairy-chested hero grab a squealing pig, slip on something disgusting and fall flat on his back like a clown.

"I thought you said heroes never sat down," I whined.

"The pig's good though," said Mr P. "He'll be a star. Or is it *she'll* be a star?"

"But it makes no sense," I cried. "It's a piece of shit!"

Mr P placed his hand on my shoulder and pointed at the screen.   "With a bit of work, you can make it make sense. You can polish it till it shines. I believe in you, thingy! You're my man."

I looked up and studied the film from a professional perspective. The soundtrack was not yet finished, so I could add a few pieces of dialogue over the back of people's heads.

"Hey there, you guy," I tentatively ventured as Ed sat down beside me. "You not point that thing at me!"

"I don't think he'd say that," said Ed with a smoke-fuelled giggle.

"Well what would he say?" I snapped, trying to make sense of my pig-wrestling movie.

"Well," suggested Ed, "He's supposed to eat the guy so he'd say something like, "You might be stirred but you ain't fried yet!"

I looked at Ed, who burped and giggled, then I looked at Mr P, who nodded sagely. I heard a rumbling from deep inside myself. It was hysterical laughter. I suppressed it and calmly said, "The guy does not have any teeth. He cannot *eat anyone!*"

Ed examined the situation, running the film backwards, forwards and then backwards again. "Why the hell did you want a one-legged Rickshaw Boy?" he asked.

"God knows," I said as I buried my head in my hands.

Then something came over me. I turned to Mr P and said, "You know, some people say travel broadens the mind and art is a means of increasing ones understanding, empathy, and spiritual health. But I'm not quite seeing it somehow."

"Whatever," said Mr P with a shrug.

"Excuse me," I said, "I'm going to scream."

I slipped out of the door into the warmth of the night and took the lift to the roof. I found a washing line hanging with dried fish. I studied it for a moment and decided that once they must have been wet: therefore to dry them, one hangs them on the line. It made perfect sense. Then I looked down upon the hazy streets and imagined sending parcel bombs to prominent cultural figures. That too made perfect sense.

"It's a jungle out there, Mr Wong," I muttered as I looked down upon the people scurrying from shopping malls to housing blocks. They were crying as well. Which also made perfect sense.

I quickly returned to the editing suite, slapped Ed on the back, and gave him the "jungle" line that would lead into the end credits where it said: "No tiger penises in this production."

"And you know what?" said Mr P. "There ain't!"

After that, work proceeded relatively smoothly, though there was a revolt by the camera crew over the cockroach story. It then became a grasshopper story, which they thought more acceptable.

"Right," said Mr P. "There's this singing grasshopper with the same frequency that sets off bomb alerts in the cross-harbour tunnel."

"And the guy who steals the light bulbs in my apartment, lets off a swarm of these things to disguise the fact that he really does have a bomb!"

"But why?" asked Mr P.

"One of the mysteries of the East?"

"Exactly," he said.

"And my toilet paper keeps going missing as well," I told him, which made him smile.

I decided Mr P was the result of a UFO abduction and artificial insemination. I suppressed the thought though. I suspected it was crazy. And also, I might have to work for him again.

At the wrap party a pig's skin was roasted and served. I was certain we were eating the famous pig. The evening ended with Mr P going to every table, yelling "gon bui", and shooting down several shots of XO brandy. He made a speech about synchronicity and then with a wink at me, told us how a Red Indian pro-wrestler called Billy Two Rivers warned him that his pig skin moccasins were slippery when wet.

"But," said Mr P, his eyes focused upon each other, "I never really heard him until one stormy night – Heh heh heh!"

Even those that understood him failed to laugh, which must have meant the job was over so we no longer had to. Mr P sank into the shadows in an alcoholic stupor that apparently he never left until the next series was underway. Mr P considered himself a people person, and if he was not entertaining or bullying them, he didn't exist at all. It was a sign of his calling.

Larry drove me to the airport. We shook hands and I presented him with a new T-shirt that he immediately put on over his old one. He handed me a box with a dried tiger's penis in it.

"We'll work together again," I said.

"Che!" he said, "Could a-been in Hawaii!"

My mind immediately started to work on the next project. I was already late in delivering a script on "Country Nurse." I needed an outline and the flight back to London would give me plenty of time to think and write one. I was on a mission to find a set of Siamese twins for Nurse Kilkenny to deliver. I was on a mission to encourage compassion. I was on a mission to stop the world crying, especially in Nicam digital stereo between the hours of eight and nine p.m.

THE END

I woke up and decided that he would have to change his life. He wanted to leave it behind and take up with somebody else's. One option was to offer it in part exchange, but he might want it back and doubted that he would get much for it. Another option was to leave it at home cleaning up the place, but he knew from his experience that it would probably sit in front of the television awaiting food until the electricity failed whereupon it would expire in the dark. He had struggled with this tendency night and day and it was one of the reasons he wanted to take a holiday from it. In the end he decided that he would turn it loose in the wild where the cycle of habit might be broken.

He had first come across the idea when he noticed a newspaper advertisement about new role-modeling technology making it possible to choose from a list of popular fictional characters and turn them into ones own life. Don Juan, of course, was already taken, but there were still a few interesting ones unclaimed. He considered Mr Pickwick for his baroque charm but although he had the benefit of not ending tragically, he was merely a comic figure. "I" wanted to be taken seriously. However, since few people read the classics, except under duress at school, the majority of characters on offer were modern fictions, and these seemed designed for people who would rather watch the movie. He had lived that life already! In the end he had ditched the idea until further technological advances produced the Whole Life Catalogue offering organic real lives much more to his taste.

After ditching his life in a forest far from the city, he sat in his car flipping through the catalogue. He flirted with Martin Luther King and Florence Nightingale, but decided he did not want an exemplary life; he wanted one lived on fast forward. There were a few dead rock stars that he admired, but he suspected that they had hangovers most of the time. Political supremos seemed to offer the best mix of romance and self-love, so he considered Napoleon. However, Frenchmen and lunatics opted for Napoleon and "I" did not want to appear gratuitously French or insane. This brought him to Stalin, then Hitler, both of whom, although clean living, had their drawbacks. Hitler liked children. Stalin liked folk dancing. And besides, given their ever-popular genocidal proclivities, they were probably already taken.

He finally opted for "M", who seemed a racy sort of choice with his reputed penchant for young girls, writing poetry, and smashing things. "M" was rock'n'roll without hangovers and being Chinese he had the benefit of being part of the largest population on the planet, thus about as supreme a supremo as one could get. He also died very old surrounded by sycophants, rather like Buddha – another option that "I" considered, but decided against because he sat around too much. He wanted change, not justification. Picking up "M"'s life was easy. He phoned up the take-away service and it was delivered to the door by a cheery little Willow Pattern girl, all in blue with lotus flowers in her hair. She told him to be very careful with it because it was liable to career out of control if not handled well. She recommended that he take training lessons where he could learn a few simple commands like, sit, stay, and mobilize the masses. But as soon as he had taken delivery he felt an overwhelming urge to get busy smashing the bourgeoisie.

He took "M" for a test run by writing furious letters to the local newspaper about capitalistic exploitation of the proletariat but none of them were published. Maybe writing them in bright red Chinese caused the problem. He had not anticipated this problem despite the label at the back of his life with the government warning announcing that living other people's lives had contextual problems. He should have understood what this meant when he heard how Jesus had been arrested when drunk in charge of a bus. Apparently it had contained five thousand dried kippers and baskets of very stale sliced loaves. He never explained why because he never understood the context in which he had to.

"M", as "I" liked to think of himself now, decided that he should go on a long march. Not only would it be healthy, but "I" thought "M" was more satisfactorily engaged in camping than in writing Chinese verse about the encirclement of the enemy.

Especially since it was hard to discover who the enemy was, though he did think that perhaps thirty per cent of all individuals were enemy, or had tendencies towards being enemies.

In search of a happy context for "M", "I" thought it best to keep clear of crowds, since they might not understand, unless by happy coincidence a large group of people had decided to take up the lives of Chinese Peasantry. But that was unlikely because although highly popular as a choice, they were highly concentrated and, apart from the odd pre-packed container loaded for overseas consumption, not readily found outside of China. "M" saw nothing but struggle ahead of him as he walked amongst the corn. He heard the sheaves rustling like bayonets and saw the clouds above laden with scientific forces that seemed destined to overwhelm their poetic nature. He was in two minds about such things but somehow he had to adapt his thinking to the changed conditions. As "M" began to seek out masses of peasants and workers in order to understand the new order, "I" could not help but think, "where were the girls?" He had not bargained for the process by which the librarian turned into the supreme leader worshipped and obeyed by millions.

Somehow "I" had thought that one could make a giant leap into a life at the most memorable moment and perhaps promiscuously step out before the inevitable bad consequences of pleasure. But that was not the way life worked. It could not shoot its arrow without finding out what the target was. "M" had a mind of his own and as a good comrade, he was eager to go where the difficulties were the greater. When seeking out the oppressed, "I" caught a glimpse of his own life. It had been living off whatever it could find in rubbish skips and had taken to pushing an old supermarket trolley full of soggy cardboard. "I" tried to turn away from the ragged apparition, but "Stay!" ordered "M", as he joined "I"'s previous life in rummaging through the dustbins. He explained that to make "I"'s old life rich and strong it would need several decades of strict economy, and with modesty and prudence as watchwords, like the foolish old man, he would move the mountain, one shovel at a time. The struggle had begun.

"I" embarked upon a process of self-criticism. He called himself a useless stain upon humanity and could not see why "M" thought he could learn anything from the dissolute wretchedness that his life had sunk into. "M" said that "I" needed to modernise his outlook if he was ever to cast off his feudal perceptions and understand a scientific approach to life. He kicked "I"'s old life into action and had him shape a pointed hat out of the soggy cardboard. Then, after struggling in the mud with "I", he managed to place it on "I"'s head as a sign of his stupidity. Life was no longer the stupid one, "I" was. But since "I" was "M", when he ordered his life to kick him, the resultant dialectic brawl had left them all muddy, bleeding and exhausted.

There was no fun in this so "I" resolved the contradiction by phoning the agency for an appointment, complaining that sharing the lives of the oppressed was too hard. When he arrived, the Willow Pattern girl was horrified to see what he had done with her life. She had lived with "M" for several years and still regarded "M" with fondness. However, as she hosed the mud, blood and rotting vegetables off him, she agreed that although his positive thinking was exhilarating, and he was never at a loss as to what to do, everybody nowadays ignored him. "Dry clean only," yelled "M" in protest, only to get another squirt and kick into the tumble dryer.

Taking pity on "I", the Willow Pattern girl was still willing to enroll him on the life-training course. She thought that if "I" could coin a new slogan, all would be well. She suggested, "Power comes from the plug socket." But "I" could sense that "M" did not understand despite his approval of electrification. She suggested, "To get rich is glorious," which had "M" frothing at the mouth and banging on the dryer door. "I" was forced to sign him over before he started accusing both of them of counter-revolutionary tendencies and embarking upon another bloody struggle.

"I" walked naked through a corridor of lives kept in small cages at the back of the shop. The lives yelped at him, stamped in their feedbowls, knocked their water into the sawdust, rattled their cages and thrust their wet noses through the bars trying to sniff at him. These lives had been plucked from the streets after being thrown out by owners who thought they had grown too big and ugly. He could see that sooner or later his own would find its way here and, unlike the great lives who always found new masters, would find itself taken out the back and disposed off. Apparently once a life had found its way out of the forests into the suburbs, no matter how many times you took them back to the wilds, they returned to the dumpsters and dustbins, and often became drunken traffic hazards.

This thought horrified him. Lives being traded and cast away merely because they were inconvenient struck him as a terrible indictment of post-existence existence. He briefly contemplated picking up his old life, showering it, and shaving it, and trying to spur it into some more interesting direction. He knew from long experience that it was a hopeless task, but without a life, "I" had nowhere left to go. He would forever be naked as well as without hope.

The Willow Pattern girl, once she had pressed and folded "M", suggested that perhaps organic life was not "I"'s cup of tea. It creased easily, had uneven weaves, and you could never get the stains out. Perhaps something synthetic and washed with a wipe was more suitable for this day and age. Perhaps, he should try a fictional life. "I" was dubious. He complained about having to live among all those boring minor characters, but she continued to explain that he had misunderstood. She meant a life in fiction because at least there would be no worries about a lack of context. Writers, she told him, created their own context because the main fictional character was the author. The author wrote himself.

Being the author was tempting, but feigning the ignorance of the first person or indulging in the arrogance of the all-knowing third, made it feel like mere puppetry. Ah, said the Willow Pattern girl, maybe "I" could become the ghost behind the fiction, the fourth person, disembodied, the author of the author, the expectant audience with the finger on the remote control, and by being that he would be revitalised and free. Then she handed him the contract to sign. He looked at it and discovered that it was blank apart from a ninety-day exclusivity clause, full electronic and film distribution rights, and a first refusal on his next life. You can be anything you like, she told him and offered him a biro. Slowly, he sat down at her desk, and in an uncertain scrawl he scribbled: THE END.

REPLICAS

Jane was always frightened that she might get pregnant. She used to perform an erotic dance routine featuring rubbers, pessaries, diaphragms and distraction techniques. I thought how much easier life was when everybody was just an accident.

For someone so keen not to have an accident, she seemed pretty keen on me having one. Turn left here, she would say at the last second before a corner, and grab the steering wheel to yank it round. We would skid into startled pedestrians, policemen, articulated lorries, and apologise profusely. After which, addresses suitably exchanged and court cases pending, we would fight; great blazing rows, preferably with guests in the house or strangers in shops as witnesses so that any violence would be carefully noted and the culprit properly identified.

"One day you're going to wake up dead," she would say if I so much as took a swing at her. "Go on! Go on! Just you dare!" she would add as I relented and unclenched my fist in the hope she would let her guard down and I could catch her one on the chin.

At moments like those, the thought of having to be seen in public with a damaged wife, skull caved in, and the subsequent plastic surgery bills, did not enter into my thought processes. It would have been socially and financially inconvenient, and she would never have forgiven me, probably reverting to her ploy of slipping contaminated foodstuffs into my lunch box. But it would have been worth it.

The last time she poisoned me, she pleaded accidental attempted manslaughter, and allowed me to punish her when I recovered. Severe sex was the preferred punishment. It left no visible bruises and I allowed her to choose her own humiliation. So ardour and honour were satisfied. Though it was always me who cleaned the fridge afterwards in a frenzy of hygienic indignation.

Why our house was always so rancid I will never know. We did not keep cats, dogs, and had no particularly virulent forms of infestations, beside house spiders dying of starvation amidst great balls of fluff, and the scurf that sloughed off our bodies daily – though I never noticed it happening. In fact, neither of us were good at the noticing business. We lived in our own world, three milliseconds to the left of everyone else's, and a few photons' height above the surface. Ours was the real world whereas yours, dear reader, was and still is, the imaginary world where we might like to exist on occasions but for the most part consider a botched job hardly worth bothering with.

So we continued in our own embarrassing manner, sexually molesting each other, destroying the harmony of the other world, and wondering if one could ever make the transition from our fiction to your reality, or bring you down to our level. Somewhere in the process we suspected procreation to be at the heart of the matter. The perpetual adolescence that we indulged in kept us running on a different time scale to that of the civilians. What controlled and shaped our lives was a mysterious spiritual urge that demanded futile cultural activities. And so I restored old movies instead of procreating, and Jane worked in the Records Office for her psychological compensation. What the Freudian connection is, in both cases, I really cannot work out.

Our no children policy was a mutual indifference to the whole institution of the nuclear family rather than any real decision. Real decisions took place in the real world, which as I have said, was a purely fictional conceit as far as we were concerned. So neither of us believed in real decisions. But we did believe in omens. We believed in the workings of fate, the stars, acts of god in a godless world, and hobgoblins and gremlins that lurked in the ether. This was despite our knowing the full blown theory of special relativity, and having a more than passing insight into the peculiarities of the quantum world. We were rationalists who knew the odds, and saw them constantly working away to produce the storm of our existence.

In Hertford, Herefordshire and Hammersmith, environments in which we habitually shopped, shagged and shat, hurricanes hardly ever happened. So when Jane told me that there was going to be a hurricane, I did not believe her. There is nothing we can do about hurricanes, she told me, so in order not to create alarm, the government has decided not to tell anyone. Either that, or their supreme indifference to our suffering, left it off the map. Either way, Jane knew it was coming, but I did not believe her.

It was thus something of a shock for me to awaken to the sound of falling masonry. Under the influence of the hurricane, the chimneystack crumbled and fell through the roof onto my bed, missing me by inches. My life did not rush before my eyes in a cliché-ridden litany of missed opportunities, rather there was an unpleasant sense of waking up dead and of being no more concern to the world than a heap of inconvenient rubble. Cleared away and binned, I reckoned that not so much as a plaque on the wall would recall my passing. Despite my superior knowledge of the encroaching black hole into which all of the universe would eventually be sucked despite all the achievements of humanity, and maybe sooner because of them, this upset me. My next thought was to rescue Jane and on discovering that she was not there and had risen early to watch the wind tear up the garden fencing, and hurl trees onto parked cars, I thought it was about time I killed her. I would do her first though.

"Why didn't you wake me?" I asked, standing naked and covered in cement dust. I thought I looked tribally primitive and just ripe for some symbolic dismembering of body parts, scattering them to the winds to appease the gods of irrational nature.

"You didn't want to be woken," she replied, fully dressed, complete with make-up and the red "Marabou mules" that I had purchased from Provocateur, a Soho shop dedicated to dressing the bourgeoisie like prostitutes.

"Why didn't you insist?" I insisted.

"Because you didn't believe me."

"And that's why you left me to die?"

She thought I was being melodramatic. She did not know that the chimney would fall on me. That was an accident.

There is something very strange about accidents. Things that are quite predictable cause accidents. It was predictable that our ancient chimney was not built to withstand the ravages of hurricane-force winds and that the two things, brought together, would cause a crash and I would be beneath it because accidents happen to me. Jane knows it. She uses this law of nature to her own benefit and pleads innocence.

In the catalogue of the film-scripts that I intend to write one day, I have the following: Emilie Du Chatelet, mistress of Voltaire; far more brilliant; and the woman who literally put the square in e=mc2; on discovering herself pregnant at forty, wrote her will and prepared for death. In 1749 the odds of surviving were against her and proved as fatal as expected. She was a mean card player as well, regularly fleecing the dimwits at Versailles. For someone so smart though, why did she have so much unprotected sex and think herself immune? The question I ask here is: was this murder, suicide, or just bad luck? A dodgy husband, intellectual rivals, rival lovers, and her own disposition at the time perhaps indicate that we have more than an element of mystery. There's no need to shoot anyone when you know the odds. Nature can do it all for you.

Jane reads everything that I write. So if I have an idea, one can be certain that she would have it as well. But what is her motivation apart from a warped sense of sadistic humour?

"That chimney," I told Jane, "Is a lethal weapon!"

"Then why didn't you decide to do something about it?" she said. "After all, I told you there was going to be a hurricane."

"But I didn't believe you!"

"Then it was your own fault."

For the rest of the day I felt unwell. It is the question of motivation that is so sickening. In a world where the weapons are subtle, the motivation is often subtler. We are all being set upon by subliminal motives. If Freud suggests that a man has married a substitute for his mother, and that he secretly wants to kill his mother, then it is obvious that, despite love, lust and financial requirements, there will be a ticking terrorist lurking in his soul and his wife had better watch her back. One Freudian slip and she could be another household accident, and as everyone knows, ninety percent of accidents are in the home, and most murders are of family members.

So, what did I represent to the psychopathic depths of Jane's soul? Clearly something needed doing to cure her, or, as the shrinks put it, resolve her conflicts.

Miserably I cleared away the debris, deeply disturbed by the semiotic nature of the image. What, I thought, did the sign signify? Buggered if I knew, frankly. I skipped most of the lectures on Post-Modernism when doing my Film Studies. Editors are far more interested in the abstract movement of flat plains of colour and how they can be made to flow smoothly from one image to the next. We let the directors decide what it all means. If the director is long dead, like my avant-garde film-making Grandmother, we have great difficulty in coming to any conclusions because we know how the end-product is merely a collection of random choices by individuals with their own very different ideas about everything.

While pondering the meaning of my Grandmother and the strange truth that in my brain was a collection of connections dedicated to her shady memory, the fire service came along. Big boys in blue uniforms wearing the sort of earnest expressions that they had trained themselves to emit in the face of the tragic disruption of the lives of victims. This merely irritated rather than consoled me. I did make the effort to look as distraught as I was supposed, which, considering how depressed I was, was extremely difficult. Earnest misery is not something that comes naturally to me, though misery is normal. My expression of it is often flippant or matter-of-fact because SNAFU truly is the law of nature: system's normal, all fucked up. Strapping blue-chinned oafs in gumboots and hard hats tramping about my semi-demolished home, being efficient and serious, tapping walls and saying things like, "Well that'll have to come down," and expressing horror at the disaster zone of the kitchen, despite that having received no damage whatsoever, only served to bring out the English Spirit in me. I offered cups of tea, which after seeing the state of our cups, they declined, and then recommended that we move out of the house. However, we had nowhere else to go.

That was why we cleared out the upstairs rooms, placed our home's entire contents into various boxes, and covered them in plastic sheeting. This cannot be happening to me, I kept thinking. It must be happening to someone else. I was even more annoyed that Jane seemed to love it. The more wet and miserable it was, the better. The more wet and miserable I was, the better. Not since the three-day week and petrol rationing had Jane been happier. Everything was collapsing. The New World order would be upon us. Petrol was over. The horse and cart was back with a vengeance. No wars in the Middle East would be necessary, and flash bastards who could afford expensive cars were shafted. However, the three-day week returned to five and I was secretly pleased. Nature, as you might have gathered by now, never struck me as being a friend of mankind, especially this kind of man, and doubly especially when it blew chimneys down upon me. Nuking the whale and all it stood for sounded like good sense.

"Do you think George and Zelda's house blew down?" I asked hopefully about our friends.

"Our house did not blow down."

"I didn't say it did. I asked, did theirs?"

We had these friends who never argued. He was called George and she was called Zelda. Her mother had a Scott Fitzgerald obsession and would read his books with an electric toothbrush inserted into her vagina. Zelda was always keen to pass on these delicate details of her life. And like us, they avoided childbirth. And like us, they became involved in what I call "career hobbies". These are careers that are undertaken not for the wealth and power that they can give you, but for the immediate satisfaction that, say, something like the weaving of a raffia mat would give the mentally retarded. They start off as fascinating pursuits but there comes a point when you realise that fun is pointless. I personally think that, ultimately, sane people want to change the world rather than enjoy it. What is there to enjoy when there is so much suffering, incompetence, and general dick-headedness bounding about the landscape like demented gazelles scattered by beer-swilling rednecks in four-wheelers?

All of which firmly put George and Zelda in the insane class. They presented this solid face to the world at their dinner parties, all of which consisted of cooking up exotic dishes eaten on one of their long treks through central Asia on camel back, then showing the technically incompetent video.

"You really must give us some tips on how to make it better," Zelda would say when I gave the honest opinion they claimed to seek.

They dreamt of selling these things to some cable channel, on the theory that American Cable was full of such crap that even they could do better. So far, I had to tell them, they had failed.

"And you must properly log and annotate each sequence so that at a later date their true context can be understood," added Jane, always the archivist.

I never quite worked out why George and Zelda kept up our friendship. Perhaps nobody else would have them. Perhaps we were the last childless couples with U2 in their CD collection that had not adopted a glue-sniffing Colombian street kid. We kept them as friends largely to feel superior. That is one of the main functions of friends. I am sure Oscar Wilde once said that there is little more pleasurable in the world than the failure of ones friends. If he did not say it then he should have done because it is true. Definitely, one of the signs of greatness is that one has lots of friends and none of them like one. And for reasons, no doubt Freudian, the fact that I looked up to George and Zelda, physically, always irritated me. I am not a short man. And Jane is not a short woman. We are average in height. And I suspect George and Zelda are also very average. Only, they are more average than we are. They have exactly the right height to make me look up when talking to them, without having the pleasure of considering their statures freakish in someway. In my brain, there must be half a brain-cell dedicated to a childhood nightmare, inflicted by height differences. I must have been forced to ask some lanky girl to dance with me at "country dancing" lessons and everyone laughed at the sight. Luckily I have suppressed the memory and recall nothing more than an association with bed-wetting.

In terms of looks I cannot say I have any hang ups other than the height business. I would say I am ruggedly handsome in a tooled up no nonsense manner where Jane is exotically attractive in a dark terrier-like fashion. George and Zelda were the masturbatory fantasies of Nazi Queens: blonde and strapping – that's George – and leather-clad SS Gruppenfuerher – Zelda in the new boots she'd bought in Regent Street that very day – a source of endless mirth and risqué foursome propositions. Jane's contraceptive frenzy would have quickly dampened the novelty of such a moment, so it was a nonstarter, and maybe that is why George suggested it. Though I sensed a repressed tension in the proceedings.

"Do you know why they will never do anything important?" said Jane in the car on the way home. She was disgruntled, I suspect, by George's suggestion that she be strapped up and whipped by Zelda. "They will never do anything truly creative because they merely reinforce each other's impotence."

"Whereas we rip each other's throats out?"

"Not quite. We bicker. We pick at each other's open wounds. We nag. We..."

"...we rip each other's throats out."

"No. We have a healthy exchange of views that constantly moves us forward in life."

"Towards what?"

"Towards what has never happened before!"

To Jane, life was a march towards destiny, but for me it was all meandering loops and that was probably why I suspected she would be the one to make things happen, if ever they could be made to happen. I was Voltaire to her Emilie Du Chatelet and perhaps one day I would shag her to death and get all the kudos from much of her intellectual work.

Antonin Artaud, however, was of a closer frame of mind to Jane – perhaps a French brain cell shot up her nose and lodged itself there. One day, when particularly bored, Antonin decided that he was St Patrick and went to cast out the snakes of Ireland. This, on thinking about it, really is more Jane's cup of tea than Emilie's, pondering the trajectory of cannonballs and their impact. Artaud ended up in a lunatic asylum where he had his teeth fixed and his bowels purged.

I mention Artaud because at that time I was restoring a film of his life. Wearing my white gloves, I carefully nursed the celluloid snake back to life and could not work out why Antonin Artaud believed he was St Patrick. He could just as easily have done a Joan of Arc and set himself alight instead. He had a bit part in a film about Joan of Arc, so why not? Acting was not pretence for Antonin. It was possession. He once gave a lecture about how acting was like the bubonic plague which consisted of him crawling around the floor groaning until the audience left in bewilderment. He would have been given a Turner Prize for that today. Maybe I should have been given a Turner Prize for exhibiting my chimneyless house to the elements for nine months? The time period being merely coincidental and of no significance whatsoever, unless you want to make something out of it? Like I said, abstract plains of colour moving smoothly from one image to that of the next is all we kings of the two-dimensional really care about.

Have you noticed, by the way, how in old movies, time moves differently? People spoke slowly and the camera lingered longer. Besides the obvious technical problems they worked with, those abstract plains of colour on the two-dimensional background move slower than today's. At the time though, I bet they did not. The expanding Universe has done an awful lot of accelerating since then and two systems at differing speeds view each other as being slower. If you have not noticed this, then you are in good company. Jane never notices, no matter how many times I point out that in reruns of 1950s Road Runners, Wile E. Coyote manages to get blown up only five times compared to the six of the later cartoons.

I have notes on Wile E. Coyote going back to my notes on my first encounter with Tristram Shandy. I am not the only archivist in the family. This thought probably arrived in my mind because when Tristram Shandy was conceived, his mother gave his father an apoplectic fit by asking him at the point of climax whether he had remembered to wind the clock before coming to bed. Since then, if the author of Tristram Shandy, Laurence Sterne, is anything to go by, the boy had a problem with time as well as a problem caused by peeing from an upper floor and letting the sash window drop rather alarmingly. In Sterne's book there is a whole chapter devoted to descending the stairs while a few sentences whip through several years. Sterne was writing not that long after Emilie had discovered energy increased by the mass multiplied by the square of the velocity. Clocks, in short, were getting better, and people were beginning to notice the strange discrepancies between ones experience and objective reality. And that reality was weirder by far.

At least that is what I was thinking as the wind whipped through my house and I crept about it in my overcoat and gloves feeling much the same as I imagined Artaud did: disrupted and homeless. You might as well have thrown me off the top of a tall building and told me that I would not be falling any faster than a feather in a vacuum. The consolation was inappropriate and the sequence of events preyed upon my mind.

"It's not my fault there was a hurricane!" said Jane, but it was. I knew it was. She had called it in with some mystical incantation of hers.

"I sense that you want to tear everything down," I said to her. "You want to expose everything to the elements and let nature take its course!"

"But only so that you can put it back together again, darling."

"It's not me that keeps the lid on things. You're the one with the boxes in the basement."

"But you are the one with the murderous grandfather!"

Note this ploy. It is a classic manoeuvre. The victim is blamed for the crime. I was wearing my victimhood far too tight and just asking for it. It was not the foetid workings of my wife's dismal psychosis, but my own that called forth the wrath of the gods. It was the Grandfather Cell that toppled the chimney, swinging it through an accelerating arc where common sense would have expected a smooth toppling from top to bottom. But no, it wobbled, it crumbled, it crashed, and it crashed on me losing the suspicions like hounds from the Haringey dog track. A murderous grandfather? Could that really have been the effect that brought about my cause? A murderous grandfather whose wife was unfaithful?

I was working on the Artaud project because my Grandmother made the movie. She was a mythical creature who gave birth to my father and then ran away and was never heard of again except as rumour. She had affaires. She posed naked for painters. She made pornographic movies. But when I researched her, all I found was a box of loose clips in the archives of the Bradford School of Photography. I like to imagine a police raid, and my Grandmother running off with the valuable pornography, leaving the police behind to puzzle over the box containing the ramblings of Antonin. I imagine her in a zoetrope, forever running from a naked rozzer; his truncheon out and helmet on. Jane however, imagined my grandfather beating gran to death and feeding her to his pet rabbits. It was an interesting theory, and dear reader, you know how much I like interesting theories especially if I can prove my wife wrong.

"They're vegetarians, are rabbits!" I told her. "Eat their own shit, but don't go a bundle on a Big Mac."

"He raped her, battered her to death, then ground her up fine and mixed her in with the lettuce."

"Why?"

"Because rabbits do nothing but breed and he thought that this way, he would have many little children and be able to eat them up in a big pot. Which is why your father is the way he is, and you are the way you are."

"You have a morbid adolescent obsession with death and destruction and blaming everything on your mum and dad."

"You have an infantile belief that Santa Claus will one day bring you a present."

"If I am really good, he will!"

See? I told you that I could never express my anger and irritation in the manner that the people who become firemen and such like learn from Soap Operas. Emotions are purely culturally determined, I have decided. The secret is to spot the code. What we had there, was a blazing row accusing each other of bad blood, evil minds, and rabbitallity.

Artaud was definitely not my kind of Frenchman, though Emilie was my kind of Frenchwoman. His main crime, in my books, was that he thought films were the devil's work. They robbed the world of magic, whereas grand theatre, of the kind Jane went in for, cut through the crap and got down to the dark and dirty little secrets that haunted us all. He wanted us stunned into seeing the magical incoherence of everything that we limply rationalised and gave scientific explanations to. Emilie thought all was explainable. Artaud wanted us to be spiritually aware in order to save ourselves from putrefaction. Emilie knew it was just the way it was. And, I think, Jane wanted to drive me to murderous insanity. One day, I thought, I would rape and bludgeon her to death, then use her legs to prop up the chimney. After that, Santa would have to make a much more interesting entrance than he, or any of the reindeers, bargained for.

"Isn't there something Freudian about rooting out the snakes?" asked Jane.

"And wouldn't Freud have said something about letting chimneys fall upon husbands' heads?"

"Only if they were industrial chimneys and smoking. Ours was nothing but a stumpy brick stack last used circa nineteen fifty-six before the clean air acts killed coal consumption in city homes and set off the long chain of events that resulted in the confrontation between Margaret Thatcher and Arthur Scargill."

"I've got his cap in the wardrobe by the way. "

"Everybody's got his cap. He wore them all half a second, signed them, and sold them in *Exchange and Mart* to raise funds for his retirement. There's an as yet undisclosed government report on it."

"All the proceeds were supposed to go to a whippet hospital!"

"Patronising fascist bastard!"

"Psycho-babbling hag from hell!"

We had a bit of sex then. I won't go into the details. Suffice it to say that it was all very unsatisfactory because I could feel the chill north wind on my back. A hovering police helicopter, ready to snipe at looters, could have made a decent case for taking a pot shot at us. So I waited for Jane to glance over at the bedside clock, now situated in the living room, and the image of pizza formed in my mind. I wondered whether I had kept the voucher that gave me a free Pepsi and corncob with a king size order and hurried to climax before the offer ran out.

"What are you thinking about?" I asked in the hope that she would say "a Big Mac", and let me in on her dirty little fantasy world. But Jane always kept her secrets to herself.

"You don't want to know what I'm thinking," she said, infuriatingly.

"Those secrets that you think make you intriguing," I needled, "do not!"

"I tell you everything."

Everything she wants me to know, that is. Other than that, there was a void out there. I still do not know much about her parents. I met them once and they were not that different from my own. But I am sure they were different because everyone is different; even the most incestuous monozygotic products of the Forest of Dean.

We were the products of dull teenage years, and parents we thought were the most boring people on earth and possibly hopelessly immoral for bringing ungrateful brats like us into a sick sad world. We dressed in black a lot and if the English had ever foregone gun control, we would have been the guys up on the school roof mowing down the lunch time staff with automatic weaponry. In a way it was lucky that we discovered each other, in as much as we understood each other.

"You don't understand a word I'm saying."

"Have you ever thought of speech therapy?"

"Retard!"

"What?"

"You heard."

"Repeat. Slowly. Take your time."

The parents, plump, disgruntled and simultaneously complacent, seemed to have been born with everything determined for them. Their position was set. They lived in such and such a place, worked in such and such a capacity, gave birth, looked after children, and retired to watch television. Little lives, we thought, with tiny horizons and minds full of nonsense. Robo-Parents, we called them.

The future for us was going to be different, and I suppose it was. We did not work in factories, slave over hot irons, or even busy ourselves with jigsaws and knitting patterns. But then nobody did any more. We worked in offices and thought these good jobs until one day we awoke terrified that they were merely the same jobs and the same lives that our parents had, only sanitised. We made a pact to do something outrageous, something extraordinary, something that would change our lives. We craved the great defining moment when we could make a difference. Society would be better for us. The skirt of the old whore would be lifted and the stench would sicken enough people to send us all to the shower pronto.

"We should kill our parents," she used to say during our idealistic period. We were very moral in those days.

"But where would we go at Christmas time?" I asked.

"Mentally, idiot! We wipe them from our souls. Start from ground zero and construct ourselves without a history!"

"This from the woman whose job it is to look after the nation's archives?"

"Brecht said, all we have are our contradictions."

"No he didn't."

And so continued our dissatisfaction with everything and each other, coupled with our deep stewing in the juices of Western culture. If we never accepted each other's idiocy for just one moment, but always attacked it and confronted our deepest and most pathetic failings as human beings, then something would crack. And we would see our way through to the truth, and her destinies. So went the theory. Thus it was our revolutionary duty to be as disturbed as possible.

Before dotcoms, internet millionaires and bankruptcies distracted youthful fantasies, Jane fantasised about opening the boxes that inhabited the basement where she worked. They contained proof that British intelligence knew all about Pearl Harbour but were not telling the Americans; that Rudolf Hesse died in a plane crash and the man in Spandau prison was really a retired German schoolteacher keen on fooling Russians for the sake of the Fatherland; and Winston Churchill was certifiably bonkers for at least two terms in office. None of these startling revelations, I am sure, would have made the slightest bit of difference.

"Of course they would," said Jane, "The truth is always useful."

And this from a woman who I knew to be holding things back from me. Consequently we often argued about the nature of truth. I cannot remember the last time my parents ever argued about that. But we frequently did. She had reality in a box in her basement and I had tantalising glimpses of its passing, recorded upon clips of celluloid that I could reorganise however I wished. Whatever I came up with was affected by reality, and it was real in itself, but it was not the truth! Artaud and I perhaps agreed on this point. The experience was everything and after that it was all propaganda.

Not that Jane doubted propaganda abounded, but she harboured some faith in the truth being established sometime, someplace, for some purpose. Though why we would fall out about this matter and not about who threw the rubbish out last, like other couples, I do not know – well I do, because neither of us threw it out. Actually, other couples of our age were usually arguing about the children, so perhaps there is an innate need for all couples other than George and Zelda to argue about something and one chooses what lies nearest as a weapon.

"If the truth is always there as a weapon, then how can you say that it does not exist?"

"How else could we argue?"

"Why would I want to argue for no reason?"

At any particular time, either of us could have said those three sentences.

Jane loved maps and wars. She lovingly plotted out the positions of Sadaam Hussein's forces in Kuwait during the Gulf War. She told me there were boxes being archived right that moment that would say how it was all engineered by the CIA. And when I tut-tutted over an eye-witness report in the news about Iraqi soldiers throwing babies out of incubators. Jane grinned. "That eye witness," she said, "Is the daughter of the Kuwaiti Ambassador to the United States. She was at College while the atrocity was supposedly taking place."

I became increasingly frightened that one day she would be hauled off for the contravention of the Official Secrets act. Or, worse, she would just disappear like my Grandmother did.

I recall my Grandfather sitting in his chair at one of my family's ritual Christmas visits, smoking his pipe and reading his Zane Grey novel. I was never sure whether he ever read a different book. They all looked suspiciously the same and he rarely seemed to turn a page. I wished I had asked him now what had happened when Grandma ran off and, for that matter, I wished I had asked him how on earth they got together? He had been a shirking labourer all his life and the juxtaposition of crazy avant-garde filmmaker and this immobile old git seemed problematic to me. It was as if the only interesting thing about him had been her. And she was not around to let us in on their secret. Maybe that is why she disappeared. He was a bit of rough that she shacked up with for fashionable socialistic reasons and then quickly became bored and ran away. Maybe she changed her name so that he could not chase after her with the baby. And that was another mystery to me. How did he bring my father up?

"He wasn't brought up," said my mother, "He was dragged up."

All she meant by this, as far as I could gather, was that he picked his nose in public, belched when guests were present, and never knew in which hand to hold his knife and fork. That was about as far as his rebellious nature went. He was what they called in the labour force, a steady useful worker. He never complained and got on with the job to a satisfactory degree of competence. His father though, seemed to have been a dreamy character who spent his time going for long walks, alone.

"I'm going to see my rabbits!" he used to announce and then disappear for a day, while my father picked up a bag of fish 'n' chips from the corner chippy for what he always called his "dinner". My mother always corrected him, saying, "Lunch".

"That'll be where your grandmother is," said Jane, "She'll be fed to the rabbits piece by piece. It's always the quiet ones you know. If you go to his attic you'll find all her things carefully packed away in a box with a note saying where you can find the rest of her."

I suspect the truth was something rather more banal. She ran off with someone else and the old git decided never to mention her again. Jane was more excited by the murder scenario, naturally. And I always kept my eye open for a junk shop with a conveniently Jane sized trunk. It is hard to imagine that my father could be responsible for spousal dismemberment, but it is all connected and we are all to blame, and if I ever discovered that Jane was screwing firemen or anyone else I would probably dispose of her somehow. And maybe that was why the chimney had to fall on me.

You see, dear reader, how one thing just leads to another?

"If I was to murder you," Jane said, "I wouldn't have you disappear, I'd have you replaced. Then nobody would ever suspect."

"Then what would be the point in murdering me?"

"How interesting," she said, "You're assuming that the murderer wants everyone to know they killed someone."

"No, just that if you murdered me, what would be the point in replacing me? Surely you would want to get rid of me?"

"Not necessarily. I might simply want to get away with murder!"

Frankly, I already felt as if I was not really me. The distance I had travelled from the person I started as, seemed a long way. I could look back at the me I was and how, through my education, my career, my parents, my friends, and my deeply exhausting partner, Jane, that person had disappeared. They had murdered me and I was the replacement. When Star Trek's Scotty does the beaming up, he murders the passengers and constructs nothing more than a socially acceptable replica at a different time in a different place. Time and place, see? They might as well be interchangeable. Einstein thought they were and he was pretty smart. Seems that he was right too. From a Cosmic perspective the station leaves the train just as much as the train leaves the station. This is the place that I am in now, and I am the place. Take one quantum of energy out of the mix and I am in a different place and am a different place... I mentioned all this to Jane. I told her about my sense of disconnection from my former self and how it was all the fault of Nils Bor and Einstein, but Jane said "bollocks" and that she could see no difference.

"That's because I am a replica," I told her. "The give-away signs were that I can not quite remember everything that happened yesterday and sense that it has nothing to do with me anyway. It's the kind of fake recollection that makes me feel like the kind of person that chimneys fall on!"

"If you are a replica, how do you know? Have you ever met the person that you claim to replicate?"

I shook my head. I could not see where Jane was going with this but I thought I might as well go along for the ride. It might unleash the secrets that she harboured. Since I obviously was a different person to the one she originally shacked up with, the question of how much loyalty I could command was intriguing.

"Just as well that you never met him because you're not a replica," she said. "You are a completely different person from him. But that's all right because I'm not the person he married either."

"Were they happy though?"

"I don't know. I never met them. For that matter, I never met you until now."

"So you might be the replacement and I might just be feeling a bit odd?"

"True, and you might be lying to me," she said.

"If neither of us are lying though, who stole them away and substituted us in their place? Was it murder? Are they scrapped? Are they spare parts for repairing obsolete models? Are we the upgrades?"

"You assume that we are better?"

"We are, because we are here and they are not."

"That's fate for you," she said. "It plays tricks on us all."

"Do we dare become lovers?" I asked, "If we become too attached, will we regret it when whoever disposed of the previous people, disposes of us in the same way?"

"Why should I want you?" she said. "If it is only because she wanted you, then why should I? Don't I have any say in it? I want to have a choice in this matter."

Things seemed worse than I expected. Even so, we had a bit of sex then. We had more than a bit of sex. I slapped her face, pushed her on the floor and shagged her. She screamed and I shagged her all the more. She had not screamed before and it might have been to do with my stopping her going through her usual routine, but I thought what the hell, this is what I do now. This is who I am because she has killed the other guy. My parents too. Einstein, Newton, avant-garde frogs, randy lady mathematicians, Zane Grey, psychopathic rabbits, dinner ladies and George and Zelda, had all killed me. I thought, screw her! I thought here's one for the starving millions! Here's one for the pointless entropy of the whole kit and caboodle of existence! Here is one for my encroaching middle age! Screw her to death and dispose of the bits. Throw them to the winds. Fingers to the east. Toes to the west. Bum to the north. And mouth to the south. To know the thing, you need to destroy it. You shoot the cannonball at the gyroscope to see how all the bits fly off and then conclude that everything is comprised of those bits, which somehow do not exist unless you blow the thing apart. Then, after having my evil way, I decided not to murder her. This gave me a perverse pleasure because I knew that she wanted me to. I knew that she loved me. I knew that she had removed bricks from the chimneystack and waited her opportunity.

"Obscene Expletive!" I said, "Didn't see that wind blowing this way."

Afterwards I watched her examining her bruises in the bathroom. She did not say anything but dressed and went to work, back in the archives, leaving me to go to my editing suite and to continue piecing together the remnants of Artaud and my grandmother. There were a couple of frames of film in which I could see a vague shadow against the wall. It was someone holding the camera. They could have been anyone and I could have been anyone. I could see the liberation in disappearing and becoming a mystery. I considered walking out of the house and never returning. My old life would have had much more interest this way, except I knew that Jane would blacken the name and declare me insanity incarnate to be hunted down, sedated, and given enema treatments and thrice daily flossings. I would not be St Patrick then, but just batty.

As I pieced together the last segments of the Artaud documentary, I could see the insane husk of what had been Artaud, rather prissily serving tea to his camera-wielding visitor. He looked ill and slightly bemused and I could not hear much of what he said, except it seemed reasonably coherent French. I had it translated and fit the subtitles to his lip movements.

In one bit he said, "The murderer's anger has accomplished an act, and is released, losing contact with the power that inspired, but will no longer sustain it."

To paraphrase, he was going on about how the actor was much more murderous than the guy who did it was. At least the murderer did the deed and got it over and done with, whereas the actor had to go through the same emotions in the next performance. Sex, it struck me, would be far better if it was like murder, properly over and done with, rather than like acting.

When Jane returned from work she told me that we should invite George and Zelda over and force them to watch the final edit of Artaud. It would be our reward to them for sharing our lives.

"Be good to catch up on their latest exploits," I cheerfully said, which was the most punishing way to respond to this.

"That's right," said Jane with a smile, punishing me back. "It's going to be a good evening."

We cooked an especially banal meal and told George and Zelda how on one of our travels up the A1 to see my parents, we stopped in this exquisite Little Chef. Of course, we just had to get the recipes and bring them back to civilisation so that they may never be lost in the ever-onward march of Westernisation.

"You may joke about this," said George.

"Why may we joke about this?" I enquired.

"Just," continued George, "because this regional culture is so familiar to us, it is no less under threat than the more exotic ones that we like to feel protective towards."

"That is so right," said Jane before Zelda got a chance to say it.

We loved to play this game with them. We loved to be more them than they were.

"No," said Zelda, "It is true!"

"I'm agreeing," said Jane.

"But in such a way as to imply that it is not true."

"That's Jane all right," I said, "Irony. Sarcasm. Scepticism in the face of overwhelming evidence to the contrary."

Zelda and George were beginning to twitch by now. They had witnessed a few too many blazing rows, though I often thought that as soon as they had made their excuses and left us to it, they had slipped into the back seat of their car and had a quickie. I imagined obscenities involving matching electric toothbrushes plugged into the cigarette lighter fitting.

"This is more of your sexual bullshit thing, right?" said Zelda. She always said that and after the first glass of Australian Merlot would begin regaling us with the story of her mother and the electric toothbrush that her father had to use. "It always had these curly little blonde hairs in the brush. That was their thing."

"And Zelda, your thing is?"

"We love each other."

"Oh yes," said George, "We just love each other."

"And how are your teeth George? Are they sound?"

"Yes?"

"And your bowels? Regular? Clockwork like? I mean you look a bit puffy round the eyes."

"I'm not following your line of questioning."

"And Zelda, your father's teeth were... false?"

"That was common in his generation."

"Antonin Artaud's teeth were quite rotten and the first thing they did in the asylum was replace them with dentures. Do you think there is a relationship between sanity and good dental hygiene?"

"He was also constipated," chimed in Jane. "But not to worry, what you have just eaten will make you sane!"

There was a pause as the jokes percolated through the layers of grilled fat, wine and intense intellectual one up-manship. Then came hails of hysterical laughter as we all fell apart and rolled out of the kitchen into the living room where we could watch the video and start on the spirits.

"I hope it's porn," said George, "And that you're going to take us up on our offer."

"I'll screw Jane," said Zelda, "But the last thing I'm going to do is let *you* screw her!"

"You're much too ugly for me," said Jane.

"You're all too ugly for me," I said. "I've given up sex since the chimney fell. The imagery was so horrifying that I've felt more like bombing a small underdeveloped nation ever since."

I showed them my grandmother's film and they attentively watched and read my subtitles over the flashes of corroded images, coupled with intriguing little vignettes of a long past pretentious art scene that had in the end driven a man mad. As we sipped the Absinthe, just to get into the mood, we listened to Artaud intoning in not so gay Parisian: "The streets are choked with crumbling pyramids of the dead, the vermin gnawing at the edges. The stench rises in the air like tongues of flame. Then the houses are thrown open and raving plague victims disperse through the streets howling, their minds full of horrible visions. The disease gnawing at their vitals, running through their whole anatomy, is discharged in mental outbursts."

Afterwards George and Zelda forgot sex and analysed the video. They were more interested in that really.

"Why didn't anyone ask him the obvious question?" asked George.

"What question was that?"

George and Zelda exchanged those telepathically enhanced looks that always insinuated that I was asking stupid questions.

"The question was 'Why did he think he was St Patrick?'" said Zelda.

"She never asked," I said, "Because my grandmother probably knew the answer."

"Which was?"

"He was crazy! I mean, look at the guy? Having loon tattooed on his forehead would have looked less insane."

"I thought he merely looked troubled," said Zelda.

"Well then, there's your answer. He was troubled! And if he had not gone crazy, he would not have been interviewed. It was who he was. It would have been like asking, why are you called Zelda?"

"Because my mother had a thing about Scott Fitzgerald."

I do not know why it irritated me that they should take my work seriously enough to want to discuss its deeper motivations, but all I thought was how dare they assume that I did not ask the same questions and try to find the answers? But there were no answers and so this was what it was. It was an historical archive and nothing more. Don't blame me if history offers no conclusions. History just is and everything is its fault.

The unresolved conflicts of history were playing out in my living room. Emilie du Chatelot was floating through my walls, fondling the nether regions of all warm-blooded creatures and noting the ticking of the clock. One lover too many, one lover who had to nail her good and dead before she would ever be truly his. For a woman who knew so much, she must have known the odds. She made the choice. And Artaud, exponent of madness, could do nothing but choose to enter its realms; for there was the reality he thought was more real than anything else. And I can recall a tedious childhood visit to my grandfather, who ate bread and butter and jam, drank tea from a mug and slept soundly after lunch while the children were meant to "play quietly". And it was there, bored witless, to the sound of a ticking clock, that I found a book with my grandmother's name in it, Laurence Sterne's Tristram Shandy, beneath a stack of Zane Greys. And that led to my discovery of her film and a half-finished manuscript about Voltaire's mistress. Somehow these were all my family.

That night I noticed something. And perhaps I had noticed it many times before. There was a moment when George and Jane emerged from the kitchen with another opened bottle of wine, some coffee supposedly brewing in the background, a button half done up, a face a little redder, and the foursome joke becoming increasingly amusing for George.

"It is so good having you two as friends," said Zelda, as near to paralytically drunk as one can have without a life support machine, "Otherwise we would never know how good we were."

"Yes," said George, "We've often thought about cultivating normal people as friends, you know, just to see how the world looks from the average perspective, but our heart is not in it."

"Normal people," chortled Zelda, "are the living dead."

"They run on programmes," said George, "And never break free."

"Surely," I butted in, nursing my long empty glass, "If comparative smugness is the goal of friendship, then the normal surely would make the ideal friends? Think how superior you could feel then?"

"But it is all too easy," said George. "One would end up feeling sorry and trying to educate them by making reading lists and correcting their spelling in an attempt to jolt them out of their stupor."

"The Literary Project," added Zelda, "is the making anew of all things so that one feels the sense of novelty and wonder that one once felt, before the dead hand of education and culture and psychotic parental attitudes screwed one up."

"They fuck you up, do Mum and Dad," paraphrased George. "How does that poem by Larkin go?"

"And we aren't fucked up?" I asked, glancing towards Jane who was pursing her lips in as close to a pout that she ever got. It was strangely erotic. Why I'm conditioned to respond to that is another mystery, but there you go.

"Oh marvelously fucked up," said Zelda, "Like some third world tribe confronted by the modern world and doomed to seek solace in basket-weaving and alcohol."

"You're the one who's drunk. Your tits hang out when you're drunk."

"Put 'em away Zelda!" said George, yanking at her top to expose them further. "You'll have him telling us all about the force of gravity."

"That's just to let you know," I said, "That it is late and our time together has reached another excellent climax. And so... Piss Off until we meet again."

"An excellent moment to leave," said George, tucking his shirt in and hitching up his trousers, "It has been, as usual, highly suggestive."

Once they were safely on the ring road – with a buzz up their bum from mutually applied electric toothbrushes probably – Jane blurted out, "Robo-Friends!" and we laughed.

"Did you know that if you put Zelda and Jane together you got Zane?"

"And not Jelda?"

"Not in my universe. Zane you see is the author of the book my grandfather read."

"Most people would brag about the book that their grandfather wrote, but not you."

"He read it to compensate for the loss of his wife who ran off to make avant-garde movies that Zelda and George sixty odd years later could pass patronising comments on."

"That," declared Jane, as she unzipped my flies and knelt before me, "Is the end of all art!"

It was early the next morning when I began to feel very sick. My stomach churned, my head reeled, and I had to keep running to the toilet until finally I sat there with my head in a bucket being violently sick. After which, I crawled into the shower and lay half in half out with the hot water squirting down on me.

I thought of Artaud's description of the plague with its subversion of all morality, the breakdown of all psychology, and the sound of ones lacerated, utterly routed bodily fluids murmuring within, in a giddy wasting away of matter. The plague, said Artaud, is the manifestation of a thinking force in close contact with what we call fate. Does one die in dreams, I thought?

Normally, if that is the right word, after a bout of food poisoning, being sick was the final act and one took to ones bed weak and pathetic. Over the next twenty-four hours, one would mope about the house listing all the things one ate the day before and wondering why Jane was not also ill. One also thought, how one really should clean that fridge! But this time, I felt no better. I knew that I should drink some water but I also knew that it would come straight up again. Jane, I assumed, was sleeping and I did not know whether to call out to her, knowing she could do nothing, or brave it out.

As I lay in my delirium, I dreamt of George and Zelda gripped by similar agonies and cursing us for poisoning them. It must have reminded them of half the journeys they had taken into the wilds of the world in the name of the travel guides that employed them. They always suffered liver damaging ailments that left them at the mercy of quack doctors and herbal medicines that they assured us were not safer or more effective than Western alternatives. They had a simultaneous love and a profound contempt of the foreign, especially when – in the state of mind in which I found myself – they had to check the local bus timetable and get hold of a list of local hotel and hostel rates. It was probably their frequent distress at the inequities of the world's hygiene that gave them sufficient edge to counter our intellectual terrorism. Maybe that was why we were friends? The world had strengthened them, forged them in our mirror image, the wicked children of our imaginations that mimicked us and made fools of us, that wound us about ourselves all the more, for we thought that we were amongst others. The world, from all its angles, all its arid plains, thin-aired mountains, sultry swamps and stained hotel mattresses, could do no better than make replica upon replica of us. Granted technology and fashions changed, but ever since Ogg and Ugg got together in their nice cave and scratched some tasteful sketches of bison and their evisceration, they had Gog and Bug their best friends around to torment and join with some ritual cackling while pissed out of their brains. All in the hope that they would not end up sad and old like their parents, who seemed to have been born sad and old. Generation upon generation of replicas, all saying nothing to each other than, just you wait, just you wait! All mutually interchangeable. George was me. I was George. What difference should it make?

I lay groaning. Jane was nowhere to be found. I kept thinking why did she not notice me? Why? I imagined that she would scoop me off the bed into a packing case that would be sealed and left in the garage for posterity. She would tell my parents that I ran off with an insane Albanian woman of advanced opinions and had changed my name to Zog. She would then spend the rest of her life watching my grandmother's film over and over again as a living exhibit in The Tate.

My Grandmother, naked, running through flickering light until ground to a condiment to spice rabbit stew, my Grandfather riding the range with a fistful of lettuce, my father slathering over a parcel of fish, and my mother yelling that it is Lunch not Dinner, that we have at midday, provided me with a mental accompaniment to what I assumed was my death. To die with a parade of food and relatives seemed grossly unfair to me. If this was the manifestation of the thinking force we call fate, then I did not think much of it. And so decided not to catch the bus that day.

Two days later I awoke, still in the shower, cold, very unhealthy and crawled back to the bed.

Jane returned, dressed in a pink plastic raincoat and carrying a Boots' shopping bag full of electrolytic fluids and anti-diarrhoea pills.

"These'll make you crazy," she said, flashing the bottle of tablets at me. "They'll put a stop to all lucid thought."

"You think I think nothing but a load of crap don't you?"

"Yes. Of course."

She then casually informed me that she had telephoned George and Zelda but they were not answering.

"Why?"

"Maybe I've killed them."

"So their lives are vacant?"

"I suppose so."

"Do you want us to take possession of them? They have a Mercedes."

"And a home cinema with sensurround sound."

"Sounds like a golden opportunity to me."

"Do you want to watch me piss on this?" she asked waving a pregnancy test under my nose.

"You can tell now?"

"Well I can tell *something* right now!"

"But not anything positive?"

"That sounds fine by me. Nothing positive is just about right."

We never did take over George and Zelda's lives. We imagined that a neighbour found them in a disgusting state after having died from salmonella poisoning. We decided not to complicate the issue by letting anyone know that they last ate at our place. As for the baby, we decided to have it frozen as an embryo and place a hundred pounds in a bank account for it, with the proviso that it was not to be thawed out until the money had increased to a million pounds adjusted for inflation. That seemed the wisest thing to do, considering the state of the roof. As for Artaud, he went back in the box, nicely preserved awaiting the next student of fine arts to get a stamp on their library card and access to the mysteries of, if not life, the remnant of the grandmother that I made. And we, dear reader, lived happily ever after, amongst the archives, preparing the groundwork for our future reabsorption into the fabric of time and space when all archives, recordings and cultures will be reduced to nothingness. The experience is all there is and all there ever was. The rest is propaganda. The truth is all lies. Chimneys just fall. Probably.

LAUGHING EUNUCHS

I watched as the censor scraped frost off the inside of the window and squinted through the clearing at the grey mist that passed for Shanghai. I immediately liked him. This man knew all the stories. They lined his walls in categories. Some years he allowed more of one category, some years, more of another. I sympathise with people mired in such absurdities.

"It's the longest March ever," muttered the censor, "In order to keep everyone in step with the ticking of the Universe, last night, scientists added an extra second. If they could also throw in an extra degree of heat, or at least make the central heating work, then I would applaud them. As it is, they merely make me older and colder. But as they say, timing is everything!"

Then he turned to the thousands of documents stacked upon the shelves covering his office walls and hauled out a script. He told me that he had not read it but if a speedy conclusion to the approval process was needed, he suggested that Professor Wu of the Shanghai University History Department should vet it for accuracy.

"If it's accurate," he said, "then maybe it's acceptable, though I can't guarantee anything. But why a story about Jesuits? What possible interest could they have to Hollywood?"

"It's the star who's fuelled the interest in the project," I explained, shivering despite my black overcoat and scarf.

"A blonde blue eyed Jesuit, who also loves an imperial concubine with lotus feet?" he said, with raised eyebrows. "Spaniards and Italians are not known for being blonde. And as for loving the lotus foot…"

"If she's a concubine," I said, "Historically, she would have to have lotus feet. And some Italians are light…"

"Get Professor Wu to read it and then we'll see. In the meantime though, you might be able to do something for us."

He handed me a script with "The Long March" scribbled in ballpoint beneath the Chinese title.

"An auspicious title," I said, trying to be amusing.

"Perhaps Trek is a better translation?"

"No no. March is fine."

"If you find the English not very good, I would appreciate your corrections. But that's not the reason I'm giving this to you. We have a role for a Westerner and if your star is interested in Chinese topics then we might be able to make some accommodations."

I could see no problem in passing the script onto the star's agent, so I asked what the story was.

"Essentially "M", chased by his enemies, has to make the agonising decision to abandon his daughter leaving her to be brought up by a peasant. She enjoys an idyllic carefree childhood unaware of her inheritance. But when an East German documentary maker turns up during the Great Leap forward searching for the missing daughter, she realises that it must be her, but decides to hide her true identity. However, the German documentary maker – your star – falls in love with the beautiful girl and wants to make her an icon of heroic peasantry."

"So it's a communist propaganda movie with a big Hollywood Star?"

"Isn't everything propaganda for some value system?"

"Is it a true story?"

"It will be," said the censor with a smile. "Is yours true?"

"It will be," I replied, "Especially once your expert has looked it over."

"Excellent, we understand each other. By the way, I'm sure you will like Professor Wu. She taught oriental studies at UCLA."

So ended my first interview with the censor, which I flattered myself went rather well. Next I went to Professor Wu. She was a stern faced lady with her hair tied back and was what I would call a tight little package. My theory about handling such people was that if one can pull the right string, everything will pop out in an interesting manner.

"Do you really expect me to read this?" she asked after the initial introductions at her office.

"The censor recommended you. In fact, insisted upon you."

"He's always doing this."

As she sighed, her buttoned up jacket heaved interestingly and the subversive thought came across me that there must be a Chinese medicine shop selling her spit as an aphrodisiac.

"I don't have the time," she said, "to be reading inconsequential texts."

"Why do you have it in for the inconsequential?" I asked, detecting a weakness in the armour.

For a moment, she looked as if she had just stepped in me, but I pressed on: "Think of the people whose livelihood depends upon this project. And I'm not just talking about the grotesquely overpaid stars, I'm also talking about the technicians, the cinema ushers, the…"

Professor Wu held up her hand for me to stop.

"I've a first class honours in bullshit," I said, "How about we discus the script over dinner tonight?"

Her face froze.

"We can discuss the decline of Ming Society and the collapse of meaning in Confucian ritual," I said giving the coup de grace.

"It had better be a very expensive dinner," she mumbled.

"Then you'd better look expensive."

She hesitated and I held my breath. Had I gone too far? She did not exactly melt, but we shook gloved hands, agreed upon the time, and suddenly I felt both guilty and needing to get my body in shape at the hotel gym. Seduction has that effect upon me.

After forty-eight minutes on the treadmill contemplating how many middle-aged men killed themselves trying to impress young women, I felt reasonably righteous. Then I dressed and awaited the call from the lobby, distracting myself by lying on the bed zapping TV channels seeking the beginning of a show instead of an endless series of trailers for things of no consequence. I discovered a Hong Kong station with a Singaporean Sit-Com about some fat woman living with a fish ball salesman. So much for the Cultural Revolution, I thought, and hooted with laughter, agreeing with the censor that timing really is everything. Then I saw that a folded note had been pushed under my door.

"Is this really true?" asked the censor, steam curling from his mouth as he spoke.

"I've no idea," I told him.

"How did she send you a note if they arrested her?"

"Perhaps she asked someone to pass it on as they marched her away."

"Where did they march her away to?"

"I don't know. It's your country!"

"Was she carrying anything she shouldn't have been? Had you asked her to bring you something hidden inside the pages of something so irrelevant nobody would suspect?"

"There you people go with this irrelevance kick again! Perhaps Hotel security just thought she was a prostitute? I mean, she was hot!"

"Hot? It's twelve degrees below zero! It is freezing! I am frozen! The stupid heating system is set permanently at 1950 when it should be 2004!"

"And March at that, when all government offices have their winter heating cut off!"

"You think this is amusing?"

I could tell that the censor was not taking this well, but then neither was I.

"Now I'm going to have to read this rubbish," he groaned.

"Well, that's the way it goes sometimes. But, since you're someone reasonably in with the authorities, can't you make inquiries about Professor Wu?"

"Why should I?"

"Because Professor Wu is a friend? A colleague? A hot lay?"

"It's no concern of yours."

"It's your country, I know, but I wish you'd sometimes act that way."

"It might create more trouble."

How real his fears were I could not say, but I knew when not to push the point too far. I left to find a Pizza Hut. They had heating, as well as pizza. As I walked over Suchow Creek I looked down at the murky frozen water and could swear there was a face peering up from below the ice. I tried to decide whether it was a trick of the light or just my paranoia, but there it was, the pale frozen face of someone not long dead. I imagined explaining to those excellent linguists, the Shanghai police, that despite my association with that known traitor, Professor Wu, I had merely discovered the body and not put it there. There was no way of predicting their response so I walked on wondering why I felt so angry. I had only met Professor Wu once and for me she was just another challenge. Even if I got her drunk, she would have remained unimpressed by me. When I returned to the office, the censor had read some of the story

"This character Qu Tai Su is a mad man!"

"Well, even by the standards of his day he was a tad eccentric. He did convert to Christianity when natural attrition reduced his wives to one."

"And when the Concubine disappears you insinuate that she ends up boiled down for the essence of her eroticism and mixed into the holy water that the priest sprinkles upon Qu's head! This is absurd!"

"Where does this happen exactly?"

"Her bones are placed in a bag and thrown into the water of the Huangpo. This did not happen."

"Doesn't happen in the script either!"

The censor showed me the scene and true there was a body floating in the Huangpo but it was not little Plum Blossom. She unfortunately was thrown live into a well and last seen frantically splashing around in the dark, clawing the walls and staring up to the light at the end of the funnel where a couple of laughing eunuchs could be heard casually walking away.

"It's a metaphor for the decline of meaning that the Jesuits were attempting to exploit," I explained.

"So what is the point of her having sex with the priest?"

"She doesn't! That's a dream. It's sparked by her watching him put a key in one of the tribute clocks and winding it before presenting it to the Emperor."

I realised that the censor did not read English very well and used Professor Wu to help him. So I agreed to clarify the script to avoid any more misunderstandings and resigned myself to another week in Shanghai, hoping Professor Wu would turn up.

Back at the hotel I found a message from the studio telling me what a great job I had done on the rewrite but had turned the project into an art house picture where some unknown would play the German Documentary Maker who journeys back in time to make love to "M"'s daughter. My transforming the Qu character into "M"'s daughter was apparently a masterful, bold leap that must surely please the censors.

I immediately phoned and spoke to their answering machine: "You've either discovered irony or you're insane. If you wish to pursue that script, you need to make a deal. Otherwise, please closely read the covering letter!" Then I phoned the censor and told him how the studio was impressed with his script but thought it more art house than mainstream.

"But "M"'s daughter must be seen with a sexy westerner."

"Art house can be sexy. In fact, art house means everyone's having it off! It'll win a prize in Berlin."

"Berlin! We want Hollywood. Finding liberal intellectuals to admire our work is easy."

"Because you throw them in prison if they don't?"

There was a long silence on the other end and then the censor coldly quoted from his script: "My daughter is of no importance."

"Professor Wu?"

"She is merely under administrative detention."

"Why?"

"It is all a mistake. It will be sorted out in a few months."

"A few months!"

"This is our business not yours."

"Then make sure you do the business!"

"Timing is…"

"Bull!"

"Let's move on. Have you made the changes I require?"

I almost told the censor what he could do with his changes, but we both knew the script was a meaningless ritual. We'd make whatever movie we liked once we had the go ahead.

THE ODDS

Elizabeth was tall and thin, like a model, and Gary was robust and solid like a marine. Together they were the genetic ideal of modern western society, and as far as any dumpy, flab fighting, pasty skinned neighbour was concerned, appeared not to have to work at it. Elizabeth bought her clothes in Florence when attending annual scientific conferences, and Gary sported the kind of casual elegant style of any man who habitually drank and worked with actors. Together, in public at least, to those whose lives mundanely consisted of nine to five office jobs, they looked like they might have emerged from the pages of some celebrity-obsessed glossy magazine. That would be enough for most of their neighbours to hold ambiguous views of them; but worse, Elizabeth was a scientist who read large quantities of fiction, and Gary was a scriptwriter who read large quantities of scientific literature. Together they were The Renaissance, and woe unto anyone who crossed them, and woe unto anyone who strayed from facts to superstition and conjecture.

"We fell in love with the house," said their next-door neighbour, a podgy banker, prone to wearing a visible vest beneath his work shirt, "It was expensive though and we did some soul searching. But, we just knew that we were destined for this place."

Gary could never resist rising to the occasion: "You mean, you were divinely inspired to buy your house? It had nothing to do with a good position, a fair price or the fact that the neighbourhood was obviously prestigious?"

Anyone sitting around the Simons's dinner-table, after a couple of glasses of wine, would always step into this quagmire and find themselves roundly not taken at face value. A quick "God knows" may merely be a conversational tic, but to Gary and Elizabeth, it always raised pitying eyebrows. Consequently, dinner with the Simons's could be a trying ordeal and few people hurried to return the compliment, a fact usually taken to mean a lack of moral fibre by the Simons's who became increasingly certain that few people were worth time and effort.

They had not always been so prickly but for reasons they could never fathom, other people seemed determined to criticise them and find, despite their outward appearance, paucity and sadness in their lives. Gary worked in a cluttered little room full of books and stacks of files for the many failed projects he had worked on, as well as a couple of photographs of himself being handed prizes he had also managed to win. And Elizabeth worked twelve to fifteen-hour days in an ill-ventilated badly designed laboratory. Both facts were seen as a failure of Gary to produce enough money, and a failure of Elizabeth to act like a real wife. Real people had jobs rather than projects, were capable of boredom, and sought the company of their own sex. And real celebrities, so people seemed to believe, never had to do paper-work, wash their underpants, or work. Those who did were ersatz, if not outright failures. Therefore, the Simons's were nobodies who pretended to be somebodies, which made them worse than nothing.

And worse still, they were couch-potatoes. Even their most intellectual, career-minded friends were horrified that their living room was dominated by a huge TV set and a large sofa in which Gary and Elizabeth took great pleasure from "slobbing out" and eating large packets of crisps while watching DVDs of their near namesakes, The Simpsons. It was warm, untidy, and now that they had the garden, full of potted plants that spilled wild life of various unsavoury kinds across the floor. If it were not for their weekly cleaner, they would live in mud-splattered squalor. Outsiders found this casualness alarming, and doubly because of their extremely expensive designer clothes and their looking like a couple straight out of advertisements for luxury cars. The Simons's were people whose twisted priorities were always in need of correcting because they seemed so smug, self-contained, and happy despite their squalor and failure, despite their uppity airs, despite their scorning common prejudices, despite their hatred of bad taste and inexplicable pleasure in what they justified as merely low taste. They acted as if they were perfect and that their imperfections proved it. They never considered themselves confused and inconsistent, but everyone else did and pity was the great weapon that kept the Simons's firmly and comfortably in their place. This way, others could cope with them.

Consequently, it was with some pleasure when it was miraculously known throughout the neighbourhood that Mrs Elizabeth Simons had found a piece of soft tissue in her neck that had turned rock hard.

"You know what that means?" hummed the phone lines.

"It means they won't be so smug now!"

There was sympathy. What greater pleasure could there be than to offer ones condolences to people who thought themselves better than one, or worse, did not think themselves better than one because they were so perfect not to even consider the niceties of the communal pecking order! They did not go to church. They did not have children. They did not confide in others. They smiled and held hands in public, despite their no longer being teenagers, or anywhere near that age group, which in itself must surely rank as reason to be miserable. They did not involve themselves in any of the local events though they did visit the local public houses.

"Nothing of any value has come from any religion, no matter how ludicrous. Everything that we treasure has come about in opposition to all religious thought: freedom of conscience, freedom of speech, science and technology, sexual freedom, women's rights, men's rights for that matter, the right to vote, Rock 'n Roll, decent beer, capitalism, and even socialism, if you are so inclined. Religion has been and still is against it all!" Mr Simons paused for a quick gulp of beer before embarking upon another tirade.

"Well you can have too much of a good thing…"

"Religions all claim the exclusive truth. And are based upon nothing…"

"Whatever you say Gary, you're paying for the next round."

Even Gary's habitual smile was balanced by a hint of good-humoured cynicism, self-deprecation and the occasional tinge of imperfect glee at talking to win rather than merely converse. And he always bought his round! He was irritatingly difficult to dislike despite his self-opinionatedness and that in itself set people's teeth on edge. That was the trouble. There was no trouble with Mr and Mrs Simons!

They were city people who had moved out to the rural suburbs to find a bit more space and make it easier for Elizabeth's commute to the New University. They were used to the talk of London's Soho pubs and bars, which usually concerned media scandal and political outrage rather than dreams of Lottery wins, the sexual inclination of the local Church of England vicar – a pooftah by all accounts – and the workings of providence in general. But they accepted it with good grace despite their missing some of the juice of their Inner City life.

Even so, they could still grab some of it. When dining at The Groucho Club in Soho, Gary heard, "Cherie Blair turns up at the reception looking like she's just been rogered by her driver, and makes a bee line for the Director General and says one word to him: 'Cunt!'"

"Well, it's nice to know that this great democracy of ours is run by deep thinkers," said Gary, Armanied up for the occasion and seated next to the well-known celebrity actor, writer, broadcaster, Stephen Fry, or "Steve" as he called him.

"But the DG says, 'No thank you. But it's very kind of you to offer!'"

When Gary told her that conversation, Elizabeth laughed so much that she nearly choked to death. If she had still been a lecturer at King's College Hospital she might have been able to join him for lunch. She missed that. They both missed it, but at the same time wanted the space of their new house and had become tired of the city routine. In theory they wanted the theatres, the restaurants, the buzz, but the reality was that they spent more time in their apartment than on the London streets and all their old friends were married with demanding children and had disappeared to the suburbs themselves. They no longer felt the need to be in the middle of it all, all the time, and despite the odd gem of conversation, the initial excitement of creativity and research had turned into embittered battles for grants or slices of development funding. So, middle-aged and a little weary, they both wanted to get back to basics again, him to write the novel instead of endlessly schmoozing for film projects, and she to run her own research team even if it was with the dubious facilities of the New University.

However, now, instead of making headway with the big thumping hardback biographies they bought to read at Christmas, they were reading up the facts about lumps in the thyroid gland and learning that there were a range of possibilities, most of which were happily benign. But it did mean that Elizabeth should have the lump examined in order to assess whether it was a common lump, or something a little special. They were set up for the fall down, which Mrs Simons' sister noticed, and said to Elizabeth, "I shall pray for you."

"She said what?"

"She does it just to creep me out."

"The last thing we need to think right now is that we're so desperate we need her casting spells!"

"She just likes the drama."

"I prefer my drama on the stage, where it should be."

On closer examination the lump proved something a little special and immediately the telephone began ringing.

"I'm sorry to hear your wife's having some problems. If there's anything I can do."

"No there's nothing."

"It must all be very worrying for you."

"We don't worry, we just get on with things."

"I know how you must feel. We had a big health scare the other year. You don't want to know what we went through. It was hell. A lump as big as a melon!"

"Sounds like an ovarian cyst."

"That's right. How did you know?"

"Women get lumps that big in their ovaries. It's unpleasant, but not unknown."

"Well, my wife can tell you a few things. She thought she was dying. I mean, I turned to the bottle. Got drunk and was hitting things. Couldn't believe that we were chosen for this sort of suffering, know what I mean?"

"It's life-threatening but not fatal if treated."

"Luckily we caught it in time. Put us under a lot of strain. Tears. Arguments. I mean, she blamed me, she did. And what was I to do with it? I swear I suffered more than she did in the end. Put us right through the ringer. It changes your outlook, I tell you."

"I dare say it does."

Gary could not see why it should change anyone's outlook, but maybe it did. What concerned the Simons's more was how it was that so many people knew what was going on. It could only have been gossip from a receptionist at the doctor's. So much for confidentiality! It always irritated, though never amazed them, how corrupt and sleazy other people could be.

"We'll have to tell your parents," said Gary, "because they are bound to find out and think things are much worse."

"And your parents? There are only six degrees of separation between each individual."

"It only works if someone deliberately targets someone. We can forget about them for the time being. They live too far away and your sister would never call them."

On even closer examination, the consultant probing the lump with a fine needle and drawing off whatever fluid could be found, the lump proved to be a little more special than they had bargained for. It was not a cyst therefore it was something else. At this point the odds were looking a little less in their favour. The information they gathered on the Internet and through the doctor indicated that there was a ninety per cent chance that the lump was benign. This meant that for one in ten of people, the lump was cancerous. Ninety per cent was psychologically manageable but one in ten sounded uncomfortably bad odds. This was when the Simons's panic button began to quiver and even more e-mails and phone calls arrived from people demanding to be kept informed. How they sensed this moment was something neither Gary nor Elizabeth could understand, except that people did know a test was afoot, and perhaps they also knew Gary and Elizabeth's tendency to keep their business strictly to themselves, presenting only the most polished look to the outside world. This was their way of being polite, despite living in a culture become more and more impolite, as people appeared keener and keener on confessing indecencies before a TV camera. Gary and Elizabeth could never see the pleasure others gained from knowing their favourite celebrity was addicted to amphetamine, abused alcohol, or indulged in pitiable sexual mania, all of which came under the one problem that nobody seemed to even consider seeking a cure for: bad taste.

"Don't worry, we'll let you know when we know anything."

"If you need something..."

"We don't need anything."

"Have you asked the doctor about whether..."

"We've all the available information that we can know at the moment."

"But maybe you should talk to..."

"She had breast cancer. This is a lump in the thyroid. It is quite different."

"I can put you in touch with a real expert in these matters..."

"We have a real expert."

"You can tell me..."

"There's nothing to tell."

Gary hated the assumption that because he did not know the answer to a question he was either hiding the truth or incompetent and should be more aggressively pursuing the surgeon for more information. Did he not strive to give the impression of competence, even if he felt horribly inadequate at all times but had decided long ago not to let that blight his life? He did not mind people seeing through the façade, so long as they did not think they were any better. "Give me some credit in these matters," he thought. And because he was dealing with the local health service, everyone seemed to think that going private might be the more sensible option despite the fact that a private hospital would wait for the results of exactly the same test, probably analysed at exactly the same laboratory.

"Well, you never know do you? I mean, if you go private, they take more care of you. On the National Health though, well, they lose things don't they?"

"Private or National Health, they use the same test facilities and none of the bottles contain the words *'Private: Priority!'*"

"If it was my wife I would want the best, that's all I'm saying."

What seemed to be behind this apparent desire that he spend money on this problem was a strange assumption that men, and him being a man, had a natural tendency to put their wallet before their wife. He personally had a natural tendency to give his wallet to his wife and say, "buy whatever you want!" His failing was in the form of never being able to buy anything for her that she really liked, though she always thanked him for it before taking it back to the shop. It was one of their private jokes about themselves. It was a fact of their life that facts were hard to come by, but they did believe in facts and the last thing they needed were people trying to undermine his faith in facts. Facts gave them a sense of solidity where everything else failed.

"Have you tried alternative therapy? Non-invasive, non-toxic, a gentle and natural alternative to Western medicine?"

"It doesn't work."

"I know you have a closed mind about these matters, but these doctors don't know everything. There are a lot of spiritual factors involved in these things."

"It doesn't work."

"You have to give it a chance. There's no harm in trying and if the lump doesn't go away, then you can always go back to the doctor."

"It's a waste of time. And that could be fatal."

"But it also helps in the healing process in conjunction with conventional medicine."

"It's bollocks."

"You really should try and give these things a chance. You don't know what you are playing with here."

"I do know. The fact is that she has to undergo a nasty operation to remove part of her thyroid. The facts have it that if this were a benign growth it would probably be accompanied by low thyroid activity and she probably would not need an operation, merely hormone treatment. But since she shows no sign of low thyroid activity, and is of a risky age, and has been exposed to radiation over the course of thirty years working in laboratories, she needs to have the operation."

"But you said yourself that there is a nine out of ten chance that the lump isn't cancerous. So maybe if you tried something less drastic it would work. Operations are dangerous and they can't put back what they take out!"

Gary knew the facts were a little fuzzy, but was it worth taking a one in ten risk of leaving a deadly tumour untreated?

"Not untreated! I'm not saying leave it untreated. I'm saying, investigate some alternative treatments."

"There aren't any with any scientific credentials. There is only one way of knowing whether it is cancerous or not, and that is to take it out and slice it up and look at it under the microscope. Then we have a number of options. Not so bad if it is not cancerous. Not so good if it is."

"But scientists don't know everything. You yourself say that."

"They know when something doesn't work."

"You just think about what I'm saying, that's all."

A problem with facts for the Simons's, despite their faith in them, and apart from life being full of imponderables like whether turquoise was really blue or green, was that Elizabeth, being a scientist, knew how contingent these generalizations could be. If Professor so and so said something was a fact, Elizabeth, ever in the know, would raise her eyes and shake her head. So it had long been a rule of their lives that they avoid encouraging confused and uncritical thinking around them because it was so easy, so comforting, so disastrous and miserable to fall into it. Facts were contingent, but fantasy was not a solution, despite appealing to emotions. And the emotional who found contingency impossible and fantasy more acceptable were that way because their irrationality made their lives so miserable that all they could do was cry or laugh hysterically. Was this, they wondered, the source of the mysterious popular appeal of America's hysterical, but not in the funny sense, Jim Carey or England's remarkably bland TV hosts, Richard and Judy? Civilisation had its downs as well as its ups and for the Simons's, rationality and critical testing of facts were all that held back the barbarians.

The facts were now getting worrying. The last thing Gary or Elizabeth wanted was to be distracted from the cold, dispassionate, truth of what they confronted and so they took to monitoring all telephone calls to avoid having to listen to the advice of well-meaning people. Even so, there were some people they could not avoid.

"But on the Internet," said Elizabeth's sister, "It recommends that you have the whole thing taken out."

Their surgeon was a conservative with regards to the treatment of these lumps. Unlike some surgeons he preferred to do a partial thyroidectomy rather than carve the whole thing out.

The doctor had decided to go with the odds and hoped that another operation would not be necessary.

"American surgeons chop it all out. Maybe they get paid more for doing that."

"Of course they won't get paid more!"

"Maybe their experience is different from our surgeon's."

"Maybe they know better!"

"Maybe they treat a different group of patients living in a different area, with different environmental factors!"

"But you might have come from an area of high environmental factors!"

"A lot of factors come into making one man cautious and another man gung ho. Our man is cautious."

"Can you trust him?"

This was something that Gary did not know. His wife trusted the surgeon. Being a lecturer in a medical school meant that she knew the surgeon's reputation. But they both knew that one of her complaints about the University' scientific establishment was that they were so cautious that they could never make any decision. Which made Gary wonder whether conservatism in this matter was the proper course or merely another example of the indecisive nature of provincials. But in science, they knew that the odds meant something, even if the layman often misinterpreted them. And if one was going to latch onto a cultural stereotype to undermine ones faith, one might as well latch onto a stereotype that boosted them as well: the surgeon was a little red-faced Irishman notorious in the hospital for his love of betting on the horses. Rather than a sign of a profligate, ill-disciplined temperament, Gary and Elizabeth thought that perhaps he understood the odds not just at an intellectual level, but also an instinctual level. Their man was therefore not being timid, but just very shrewd at assessing the true odds.

"Unless of course he loses all the time?" said Elizabeth.

"Judging by the suit he's wearing, I'd say he does pretty well."

Even so, surges of panic rose up and the Simons's privately entertained many irrational thoughts, but they never allowed them to run wild outside of their own private nightmares. Gary made a point of finding out what car the surgeon drove. He asked a nurse and she told him it was a motorbike, an old Triumph which the man, so Gary imagined, must have lovingly restored. Then he saw it for himself and decided that he must have bought it very cheap from a student who rescued it from a scrap heap. Elizabeth noticed that the surgeon wore a digital watch given away free at a petrol station and hoped that Gary would not notice because Gary had a thing about digital time blanding out the very fabric of existence, let alone its indicating a man a little strapped for cash. So when speaking to each other they stuck to the facts. They made it their policy to consider the odds and await the outcome of the tests. Which meant that Elizabeth had to endure a painful operation.

"Facts are our friends," said Elizabeth to console Gary.

"These operations are routine," said Gary to console Elizabeth.

"The thyroid is not very deep under the skin and apart from a slight risk to the vocal chords and a slight risk of choking on blood, a skilled surgeon can get the whole thing over and done with in an hour," said Elizabeth cheerfully as Gary drove her to the hospital.

"You'll be up and eating within twenty-four hours," said Gary.

Elizabeth entered the hospital for the operation and despite nursing staff with rudimentary English, TV sets with no working controls, and a sad-looking food menu, none of these things worried her. Gary and Elizabeth pretended that they were camping out. They had been in far worse hotels and had felt far worse on their many varied and expensive adventure tours. Compared to a hotel room in Siberia and a bout of food poisoning in Tashkent, this was a doddle.

But it frightened Gary who hastily left Elizabeth to her fate, lest she think he even imagined it was the last time that they would see each other, and she gladly let him go because she had marking to do and what better time to find to do it when nothing else would interrupt? Gary went home, also claiming he had to get some work done and tried to deal with the many people leaving frantic messages and ungrammatical e-mails demanding to know what was happening. His parents seemed to have a sixth sense that something was up. "You seem to be very quiet. You must be very busy," said the e-mail. But Gary still did not tell them, or deal with any of the other messages, because right then the facts were fluid and he found that he could not work on anything but searching the Internet for more facts.

He woke up early in the morning, contemplated phoning his wife, and then thought maybe she was still asleep. So he had his breakfast and then phoned only to find she had already gone for the operation. It crossed his mind that that might have been his very last chance to speak to her, but he quickly reviewed the facts. If the facts had said otherwise, he would have made damn sure that he was actually at the hospital. But the facts did not say otherwise. This was merely a routine operation. Unnerving, but not to be taken out of context and blown up into anything more than say a couple of clicks beyond an impacted wisdom tooth. His calm helped her calm. Her calm helped his. And there was their entire life in a nutshell.

Gary was now under orders from Elizabeth's sister – deciding, on Gary's recommendation, to take her long-booked holiday in Miami, rather than sacrifice it in the name of irritating Elizabeth with a visit – to purchase flowers in her name for his wife. He deeply resented having to do anything for anyone but his wife, and toyed with the idea of buying the most expensive flowers he could find, sending the sister the bill and not telling his wife they came from her! But then he decided that not sending her the bill was even better, simply buying the flowers in his name, with his money, just as he intended to do anyway, despite the fear that she would not like them. He considered that if anyone else wanted to send bloody flowers they could do it themselves and not expect him to upstage himself. But were roses suitable? It was the only flower he could think of that never seemed to fail. Lilies reminded him of funerals and carnations meant weddings and those little daisy things seemed to indicate pregnancy and so roses. But were they suitable this time? Would she think him odd? Nobody else in the hospital seemed to have roses. They had big bouquets plastered with "get well" cards. He just had a dozen roses.

Somewhere in an old box in a cupboard were the mildewed remnants of the first Valentine's rose he bought and he wondered if he was the only man who had ever remembered that such things are saved, though never looked at again and if accidentally uncovered treated with amusement rather than heart warming sentiment. Photos fade, flowers fade, ornaments and clothes crack, rot, get lost in transit, and memories become garbled, jumbled messes with blanks where names and even faces are concerned. His grandmother, in her last ten years, repeatedly asked him: "Who are you to me?" Confusion was the end, no matter how one stocked the archives for some future moment when one supposedly had the time and inclination to sit and look back. One day he would wonder who that woman was in that photograph, or maybe, who that woman was sitting opposite him? And she would be just as clueless. He hoped he would remember to buy her some roses then.

The operation took a lot longer than anticipated and when Elizabeth was wheeled back into her room she did not look good. Her skin hung off her. It was a strange colour. And she had duct tape across her throat. She was crotchety. She was too hot. She felt sick. The nurses seemed bewildered by her demand to have a cold flannel put on her head to keep her cool and a plastic bag, in case of sickness, stuffed into her hand. Keeping cool and worrying about where to vomit seemed very strange concerns but Gary understood. Keep cool and know where the sick bag is, was their refrain to each other, whenever the frequent long haul flights they took hit some turbulence. It amused him to know that even while barely conscious, Elizabeth stayed true to her colours.

However, Gary had imagined this scene as the one where he went to the bedside, clutching a bunch of roses, took his wife's hand and they would both smile reassuringly at each other. But it was not quite like that. He did smile reassuringly. In reply, this wild insane glare came back at him. He was in the scene from a sci-fi movie where the hero discovers that the aliens have taken over the body of his wife. How anyone can become addicted to morphine was a mystery to Gary.

A few hours later the morphine wore off, the insane eyes softened, the sickness was replaced by pain and something more akin to his wife emerged. Gary decided to kill all the birds with one mobile phone. He phoned up her parents, sister, and friends and told them that his wife had had the operation, was OK and could say a few words to them. He gave the phone to her and she muttered a few things and they muttered the sort of depressing things that one never wants to hear but so many people mutter on cue.

"I'm so sorry that you're not feeling well..."

Why they were sorry, he did not know. It was not their fault. But that was the way people reacted. They wanted a role in the drama but had no idea what the drama was all about so they played their part badly. And the fact that Elizabeth had managed to speak on the phone reassured him that there she was and everything was right.

Gary had anticipated that he would spend the morning checking that she was fine and then go home and try to do some work, but no matter that he knew she was functioning, there was no way that he was going to leave her alone in that state in that bleak place. Perhaps going private would have been better? At least the TV set in the room would have worked.

He stayed and read some women's magazines, looked out of the window, paced up and down a bit and gave Elizabeth a few sips of decent coffee that he had brought in a flask. He fell into making the sort of conversation that other people find horrendously pretentious when in earshot of the Simons's. He discussed the nature of late Ming society and the role Jesuits were trying to play in it and cheered her up when he checked her e-mail and found that she had another paper accepted for publication. These were the things that occupied their lives. Other people had pets, children, interior-decoration or tango lessons, but the Simons's thrived on creating new facts or telling new fictions. This way they had some conception of the true odds they had to deal with. Gary's business-as-usual good cheer was hard work, being largely one-sided, with Elizabeth drifting in and out of the nothingness that remains when the personality switches off, and Gary wondered if there was better value in just breaking down and screaming and shouting and leaving all responsibility to other people. The noise would fill the emptiness, would bring those who heard within the cycle of life and suffering that so many people believed was all there was. Then he reasoned that the only reason others did that, was because they were too stupid to be able to make the right decisions and needed to signal for others to take over. Could he really trust others to know better than he did? From what he knew of other people, they were prone to irrationality and allowing emotions to make their decisions regardless of the facts of any matter. They seemed to think this made them somehow lovable, whereas most of the time it just made them irritating, and at worse despicable. The daily news was full of the explosions of the irrational, while all that was good grew from the workings of the reasonable, the arguers, those who worked over their thoughts until they moved smoothly from premise to conclusion.

Eventually the surgeon arrived to tell his hopefully factual story. The operation had gone on for so long because they had found things in the lymph nodes that they did not wish to find. They had to test these and decide whether to go for the full dissection or stick with the current plan. They did a test and decided to stick with the plan. But now they had to wait for the biopsy on the thyroid itself.

Gary recalled a piece of information that said that if there was cancer it was likely to affect the lymph nodes as well. It did not say, "every time," but the implication was that it would be rare if it did not. However, there are rare kinds of cancer that would not show up this way. And these were of the kind that one wanted to avoid at all costs. So the facts that Google indicated gave Gary two conflicting pieces of information. It was very likely that the lump was benign, but there was now a chance that if it were not benign, it might not be easily treatable.

Elizabeth took the dismal view of the information believing it must be cancer otherwise the lymph nodes would not have looked suspect and Gary kept quiet about his position feeling that this was not the moment to be going into the details of his wife's failure of logic. He opted for distraction techniques; after all he did not know the facts for a fact! Good home-made coffee, more chocolate biscuits and a promise to go home and return with some home-cooked pasta instead of leaving Elizabeth to the fate of the Hospital's kitchens, did wonders for the morale even if the last thing Elizabeth wanted to do was eat.

She had hit a low point. She still felt sick. She felt weak. And all the prospects of another operation and an uncertain future of radiation therapy preyed upon her mind. For distraction she allowed herself thoughts of past glories, childhood moments of joy or pain, memories of the strange journey made with Gary, who was such a downbeat character when she met him. And she was such a misfit. The two had miraculously met when neither had a future, when her PhD was unfinishable as far as she was concerned, and he was a desperate young man in a bed-sit with a typewriter. They clung together and the world became controllable. On seeing Gary arrive the next day, she perked up. At that point their whole relationship was stripped down to the raw desire to be with each other. All the clutter of life had fallen away, and they were left with the fact that for whatever reason, they simply liked each other and the presence of the other made them feel better. Which was far more than they could say for the presence of other people, who either ignored them entirely, which irritated, or seemed determined to discover cracks in the edifice that they had constructed to protect themselves, and make them feel worse. The two of them together created a wall behind which they could hide and be happy.

"Everyone has their ups and downs!" said infuriating, but smiling dinner guests, when the conversation bounced off the lack of children in the Simons's life – a pity apparently – onto the nature of the marriage relationship.

"We never have our ups and downs," said the Elizabeth, "We don't argue. Never have. We cannot see the attraction of a life of divorces and trying to date like teenagers into your fifties. What makes people so fickle? Why don't they do things with each other? Why don't they discuss things? Plan projects together?"

"You have to be able to live your own life! You can't be in each other's pockets all the time!"

"We look at the separate lives supposedly married people lead and cannot understand why they want to be alone so much. We never want "our space". We always want to be together. Our constant battle with hotels is the battle for a double bed instead of the twin beds they insist that we should have."

"Oh I love a single bed for a change!"

"We're confused by the complications of other people's relationships. Don't you actually like each other? If you don't, whatever brought you together? And if you do, why do you organize your lives in such a way to keep you apart?"

"We don't organise our lives. This is just what happens!"

"Then why don't you organise your lives? You make them sound so miserable."

"There's nothing dismal about our lives. Is there? We're fine! We like it this way."

"There is a forty-three per cent chance of divorce for all couples," said Gary, spotting blood and going in for the kill. "Though obviously, separate activities increase the opportunity for adultery, which is the cause of twenty-nine per cent of divorces. A hefty forty-five per cent of them are caused by the behaviour of one or the other and I suppose that means there are more downs than ups in their case."

"Well, we're not a statistic!"

"Everyone is. Nobody bucks the trend. Everyone creates it. Everyone has to adjust to it. Everyone must strike their bargain with it. Everyone must adjust their behaviour either to swing with trends they approve of or to slip themselves into one of the thinner tail ends of the bell curve. So when you say, 'Like everyone we have our ups and downs,' you are saying, 'Like everyone, we stand a forty-three per cent chance of divorcing.'"

As the day in the hospital progressed, Elizabeth began feeling better. They ate chocolate, drank coffee, discussed their books, wrote e-mails promising to get the illustrations for her paper to the printers, arranged meetings about film projects, told people about visiting times, and worked out when they might take an extra holiday to recover from the ordeal. They fancied Sydney for the food, weather, friendly Australians, and the presence of the great outdoors and most of all, the lack of everyone they had to deal with in London. And they discussed what might happen if the biopsy showed that she had to have the other operation.

The odds were that seventy percent of these thyroid cancers were curable. Those were good odds. Seventy percent of the one percent means that you have to be very unlucky indeed to be in that nasty thirty percent of the one percent. But it is a small population, and there is more room for error in the figures, and surgeons, so they reasoned, must go by the feel for the situation. Their surgeon was conservative because, in his experience, the odds were even better than the official ones. Or was it merely because he was a dull, cautious sort of man?

Beyond the rumours of him being a gambling Irishman, it was hard to tell what sort of man the surgeon really was. He was definitely a hard-working man. He got up early. He worked late at night. And he was ruthlessly efficient. Everything about him apart from his digital watch and old motorbike spelt business. His suit was sharp. His manner was brusque and though a bit shy in Gary's overbearing presence, he joked with Elizabeth in his charming Irish manner about VIP problems suggesting that she was being given special treatment. He probably told everyone that they were VIPs. But it worked for the Simons's. And he gave facts and nothing more, then quickly left the room before anyone could draw him into long discussions that could easily spiral out of control as fear grips people.

There followed a couple of days of uncertainty but Elizabeth recovered from the anaesthetic and they persuaded the surgeon to let them go home where she could have a weekend of rest and recreation with some decent DVDs, a soft sofa, a bar of Fruit 'n Nut and a Spit Roast Chicken from the deli. They decided to restart their ever-promised fitness regime after the ordeal but until then, whatever they liked, they would eat.

Elizabeth's appetite indicated to Gary that cancer was even more unlikely an outcome, but every now and then a wave of terror emerged until the phone call came.

"You'll be happy to know," said the Surgeon, "that there'll be no need for a second operation. The biopsy shows much as we expected. Nothing malignant but you have a fine example of Hashmoto's disease. Make an appointment for next week and we'll start you on your medication."

The surgeon seemed quite cheerful about it and Elizabeth felt almost relieved that she did actually have some kind of ailment. She would have hated to have wasted his time for purely cosmetic reasons, but thankfully all she was facing then was the inconvenience of monitoring hormonal functions and taking a few pills. The worst of the crisis was over and a warm glow of relief quickly dissipated the tension and they found themselves back with their life. It was something of an anti-climax, but they looked at each other and nodded and said that everything was as they knew it would be all along.

"Well, I don't know. These things are never really cleared up," grumbled the neighbourhood watch on their phones.

"They're in denial! That's what the Americans would say."

"Wouldn't be surprised if we found them dead in their beds. They are just the sort of people to top themselves. They are never out of each other's sight. That's probably what put her in there in the first place."

"Probably found the only bit of her that wasn't malignant!"

"They've always been pleasant to me. A bit superior perhaps, but they're always laughing about something."

"Probably about you! They have some private joke that irritates the hell out of me whenever I see them."

That night they discussed how they had reached an age when the prospect of their death had become real. Beforehand, death happened to ones grandparents and friends in accidents, but as far as oneself was concerned, death seemed impossibly remote. Now it was not. The facts were that despite longevity being pushed up, they would die thirty or forty odd years from now. The facts that constantly comforted them and kept the worst nightmares at bay, would one day run the other way, and the Simons's wondered if they would find them quite so friendly?

However, with the facts, good or otherwise, they could make real plans for the future, even if they knew the future was short. They had obligations that they felt had to be fulfilled. They would like to leave their things in order, though they also relished the thought of some of the chaos they could leave behind. There were people who they could be generous to without fearing they would think the Simons's wished to spend time with them. There were also people they would no longer need to suck up to. They could get rid of time wasters they presently suffered for fear they might have a need of them at some future date. They could drop everything for that rainbow out of the window, or that moment when all they would want is to be with each other.

As it was, the odds were on the Simons's side right from the word go. They knew they were. There were no miracles, merely professionalism, rationality, and them being their usual selves. And now their little brush with mortality made them far less tolerant of the murky insanity of others. They closed their doors. Time was running out. They had work to do, and they had each other.

"Why didn't you tell us," said Gary's parents when he finally told them.

"I wanted to tell you the facts when we knew them."

"But you should have told us!"

"Why?"

"Because we're old!"

"So? You might have died old and happy knowing that we were all right whether we were or we weren't."

"But that wouldn't have been true."

"But it would have been. We just didn't know it. And, besides, you're not dead and you will see the scar this Christmas."

The neighbours smiled.

"Feeling better?"

"Oh yes."

"That's nice."

"If you need anything, let us know."

"We will."

They won't.

THE CHINESE FARCE

S am Gold felt rather befuddled as he staggered out of the elevator and searched his pockets for his door keys. He had just returned from a visit to a psychic Shenzhen masseuse recommended to him by his maid as a cure for insomnia. He had not known that insomnia was a problem until his maid told him it was. He just thought that he liked to go to bed late and get up early and be very tense all day. Being tense and sleeping four hours a night marked him out as an alpha male.

"Mark you out for heart attack," was the maid's diagnosis.

"Perhaps you only dream that you don't sleep and you really only awake for four hours," was the masseuse's diagnosis. He could tell that she did not really believe what he told her, but she took his money nonetheless and assured him that the Chinese medicine she gave him would help him relax.

As she therapeutically hammered the soles of his feet, he took the pill and dreamt that he was Napoleon the Third and had discovered the Empress, amidst a swirl of incense, worshipping a trouserless Chinese man who sang the famous song – or at least famous amongst Chinese scholars – "We part, we go on our way, naked without a tie in the world." Sam had not cared much for the experience. He thought he would rather stay awake and keep a rational eye upon his wife instead of letting his imagination get carried away.

As he turned the key in the door he heard a high-pitched screech sounding like sex with a cat, which he assumed was sex with Mrs Gold. He listened a moment for the mantra of the Fire Breath Orgasm – Mrs Gold's specialty – but only the screeching continued. He burst in and found Mr Tian singing, his face covered by a red mask with white eyes and a painted curling black moustache. He wore it with a yellow gown that had large flowing sleeves. Tian explained that tonight's Chinese lesson concerned "The Peony Pavilion."

Sam took a deep breath, fetched himself a gin, and since he paid good money for his tutor, he calmed down and proceeded to take on the role of the diligent student.

"After this," asked Sam, "will I know how to tell a taxi driver where to go?"

"Ah," said Tian, "You drive Mercedes, so not a problem."

The lesson was strenuous, especially when all Sam wanted to do was seek out his Ching Yi, a name that Tian had used in reference to young beauties, and make sure that she need not seek satisfaction elsewhere. But he supposed that a smattering of Chinese would come in handy since he lived in China. However, despite being able to read prodigious amounts of it, he still could not hold the simplest conversation with the average Hong Kong man.

"They're ignorant people," explained Tian, "They have nothing worth listening to anyway."

Tian was oblivious to Sam's weariness as he coached him through a few lines of the opera and had Sam play the female part of Li Ni Ang.

In perfect classical Chinese, Sam précised the story, explaining that Li dismissed the advice of her tutor and instead of studying, escaped into the heady atmosphere of the perfumed garden where she dreamt of sex so perfect that she died for fear that she might never get it for real.

"That's not quite the story," explained Tian. "That's your Western thinking. Think Chinese."

Sam tried again: "The fake dream lover takes advantage of an innocent girl and she kills herself because she liked it too much. Then, when the lover she thought was a dream is revealed as real, she returns from the grave to seduce him. Which nearly gets him executed because everyone thinks he's lying. Then they all go to Hangzhou and live happily ever after."

By the look on Tian's face, Sam could tell that he was somehow wrong.

"Why don't the Chinese have farces?" asked Sam.

"We have face."

"Farce."

Tian was not familiar with the concept.

"When the person you least want to see bursts through a door, that's a farce," explained Sam. "The French do it very well."

Tian thought for a moment. "Ah," he said, "We have an un-farce. In Chinese stories the person you most want to see, walks out of the door and is never seen again."

"Unless they're dead."

Tian sighed, "I think today's lesson is over," and then he packed his mask and left, still in his gown. Tian's spindly trouserless legs poking out of the end made Sam suspect something. He almost ran after him to say so, but his maid marched in announcing that dinner was about to be served. She shuddered on seeing Sam who was still wearing the mask of Li Ni Ang.

"You look like a ghost," she exclaimed and crossed herself.

"If you believe," said Sam in his best Chinese, "There will be ghosts, but if you don't, there will not." A Song Dynasty scholar was reputed to have said that, and now Sam had said it. He felt rather pleased with himself. His maid did not understand a word. She was from the Philippines. She understood even less his penchant for amateur dramatics and how it had taken him into an alarmingly intense interest in Chinese Opera. Its high-pitched delivery, banging gongs and interminable plot lines were the obvious products of insomniacs who wished to inflict their perpetual half-baked state upon the rest of the world. But, for Sam, a language was meaningless without the stories that it told and in lieu of a Chinese wife, otherwise known as a sleeping dictionary among linguaphiles, opera was his key to the mysterious landscape of the Chinese soul.

Ghosts had been seen that summer, though only hysterical teenage girls hunted down by *The Apple Daily* saw them. This was not that unusual in Hong Kong. Even the most reputable newspapers ran stories on haunted toilets, Mass Transit Railway Stations, and hotels notorious for attracting clientele who light charcoal fuelled barbecues in their rooms and "Smoke themselves to death." Despite the Chinese not believing in anything in particular they took great delight in conjuring up ghostly apparitions. In this instance, they were first seen playing on the stairwells of housing estates and then frolicking on New Territories' tyre dumps. It was a bad sign, as all but the most special ghosts tend to be, and doubly so because the gates of hell were not supposed to be open until the seventh lunar month and the mid-autumn festival.

For Sam, despite his obsessive attention to Chinese details, or maybe because of it, the fact that ghosts liked to spend inordinate amounts of time in unsanitary conditions during very high temperatures proved their non-existence. Nothing in Hong Kong could exist without air-conditioning. His wife, for instance, existed only because she was a genie of the air-conditioner, living in perpetual pursuit of congenial masters. Just set her to cool and dry and she was yours.

But during the seventh lunar month, Sam was driving slowly down Queens Road. He was close on the bumper of a Lexus and having premonitions that, inside the Lexus, his wife was meeting her lover – or, at least, that a Lexus was the sort of car that would be driven by the sort of man who would take his wife as a mistress – when he thought he caught a glimpse of either a ghostly procession, or a swirl of pollution. He drove through it, turning it into swirling eddies of grey ectoplasmic shadows that spattered upon passersby.

"The ghosts are the voices of the city," announced Tian from the car radio – a man who owned a Lexus, and besides being Sam's Chinese teacher, was also the all round expert on all things Chinese that English language radio dragged to their studios to entertain the ex-pats with his simultaneously astute and bizarre feng shui fuelled political commentary. "Yes," he continued, "They march because they protest what we have done to the world!"

Sam shouted back at his car radio: "Voix de ville!" This was the mantra he used during Fire Breath Sex! His wife had explained the technique and how he had to yell something at the point of orgasm in order to intensify it. So he chose the French for the voices of the city: "Voix de ville!" Was it a coincidence that Tian had called the ghosts the "voices of the city"? He turned off the radio in disgust at anyone taking ghosts seriously. Especially if that person was rogering his wife! To steady his nerves and put aside all such paranoid thoughts of Mr Tian, his Lexus, and his wife giving new meaning to the term "eating Chinese," he sank into a reverie on the origins of the name "Vaudeville".

He had spent four years studying French Literature, writing a thesis deconstructing the influence of Napoleon the Third upon French theatrical tradition – based solely upon the semiotic relationships conjured up by the possibility that Georges Feydeau was The Emperor's illegitimate son, thus writing, "as Leonard Pronko has suggested, lurking beneath the frenetically joyous surface of Feydeau's farces is a vision of the world in explosion". He rapidly became disillusioned with academia because, as he informed his tutor, "Who gives a damn?" The clincher was that the tiny world of University Literature Departments was unable to enjoy a good laugh without asking whether the portrayal of a speech impediment – a comic device much loved by farceurs – was morally reprehensible. So, much to the disgust of the exquisite and largely homosexual intelligentsia that he called his friends, he took a corporate position. Naturally his company sent him to Asia. And not even Francophone Asia, not that he would have relished the Ho Chi Minh City office, but at least the Vietnamese could make decent pastries and coffee.

Ten years in Japan, ten years in Korea, and now he was in Hong Kong where he expected to end up like most ex-pats of his kind, marrying his Filipina maid. Then one day the future Mrs Gold appeared at his door with a backpack and a scrap of purple paper bearing the address scribbled across a Buddhist Swastika. She walked in, took one look at the wealthy immensity of the living room, another look at the thin, stooped, middle-aged risk assessor, and said, "You're older than your photo. I assumed it was a fake." And she pushed her way through the door. She said she was twenty years old, liked pineapple and was called Mayflower, after the Pilgrims, and she had a tattoo on her arm saying: Essex Born. "People often read it as Eastbourne," she chirped.

She was not the sort of girl to say no to, so despite her obviously being at the wrong address and really searching for "Hong Kong Dick", the Broadband chat room beast of Mid-Levels who probably had several backpacker skins decorating his walls, he said yes to her staying a few days – it seemed the humane thing to do – and magically his prostate trouble cleared up and he proposed within a week. The Fire Breath Orgasm was a powerful beast.

"You're sort of like my soul lover," she said. "I feel like you're the first person I ever loved."

She believed in karma and never admitted she was at the wrong address but his maid kept reminding him that Mrs Gold seemed to spend all her time looking for the right one.

"She paints her face," she said, "and fools you."

"By removing the mask, we conceal," said Sam, ever the theatre buff, "But by wearing it, we reveal our true selves."

He loved the theatre and the way one forgot the artifice and lived in the dream. He thought that if the entire world was an illusion, what was the point of seeing through it? And so spent an inordinate amount of time thrashing about with the prehensile Mrs Gold and feeling satisfyingly wasted for the rest of the time.

"You kill yourself carrying on like this," said his Maid. "You got good life insurance or something?"

"Excellent," said Sam the risk assessor, "I optimize all risk return ratios in everything I do."

The mysterious Lexus that could have been Tian's, could have been Hong Kong Dick's, or might never have existed and was but a product of sleep deprivation, disappeared amidst rattling trams, glistening umbrellas and rain that fell like willow branches. Sam switched the radio back on and found Tian was still waffling on about angry spirits demanding the right of representation in a world that was being destroyed without concern for their infinitely possible future and explicably, Sam felt very tired. He hoped that his vision in Shenzhen had been the result of chemically induced insanity rather than insight, but he was not sure because the psychic had also predicted that buildings would tumble like waterfalls, temperatures would soar, islands would sink, and we had all better prepare ourselves because the veil of illusion was about to be ripped from our eyes. All that seemed horrifyingly prescient, but he decided that he would either have to rid himself of his fears by taking a holiday and sleeping for a week, or confront his wife and risk offending her – or worse, seeding the adulterous idea in her marvelously chaotic but deeply erotic mind and regretting it so much that he might purchase a Rip'N'Burn Barbecue Pack and have done with it.

Back home he was greeted by nothing but his array of Chinese Opera masks exhibited upon the dining room wall. He could remember some of their names: Huang Pang, Zhang Fei, Cao Cao. He opened a cupboard door and removed the make-up box that Tian had presented to him for being his most loyal student, and set to painting his face. He painted his lips red, and then around his eyes he smeared a greasy pink. Finally he painted in thick black eyebrows. His epicine friends at the Sorbonne would have approved far too deeply for his own comfort, but he was now a randy young aristocratic scholar about to exhume the body of the beautiful maiden he loved. Dead girls were always the most insatiable lovers in Chinese stories and randy lads were never adverse to digging up a good corpse and putting it through its paces. He would in such a state conjure up his wife and there would be much yab yum, or at least a bit until dinner was served.

He went to the bedroom so that he might see himself in the full-length mirror but hesitated by the door. The moans that he heard spoke of one thing: sex. The die was cast. He had always known. It had disturbed his equilibrium. But a moment's thought and he could have deconstructed the signs right from the beginning. It had been destined. The drama had moved through all the required developments. The entire universe, even the collective consciousness of the Chinese, had conspired to create this cycle of events. He now had no choice but to move to the denouement and so burst in through the door to find Mrs Gold naked but for a navel ring, lying on the satin sheets of their king size bed, hyperventilating as the Fire Breath Orgasm engulfed her.

Sam quickly looked beneath the bed, flung open the wardrobe, then checked to see if Tian was naked and dangling by his fingertips from the windowsills of their twelfth floor apartment.

"I am opening my chakras," explained Mrs Gold in a long exhalation.

Sam was suspicious.

"You will receive the benefit," she explained.

"Is there any left for me now?"

Apparently there was not and she proceeded to take a shower.

"I am practicing my orgasm for you," she shouted from behind the shower curtain. Then she began a deep breathing exercise while soaping herself.

"I hope you are thinking of me," shouted Sam.

There was no reply, merely the gurgling of suds down the drain. Sam felt all the adrenalin that had been pumping through his veins gurgle down the drain with the suds. He felt a little ridiculous. He was a skinny, round-shouldered purveyor of probabilities with a fetish for make-up and oriental poetry, and definitely undeserving of the affection of anything so fresh, so juicy, as Miss Essex Born, 1984.

"Did you know," he ventured upon a subject he knew his wife would be interested in, "that ghosts have been demonstrating in Statue Square?"

Mrs Gold emerged from the steam, glowing. She kissed Sam lightly upon the lips smearing his red lipstick.

"Who were these ghosts?" she asked.

"I don't know!" said Sam, "Chinese ghosts tend to be anonymous. Western Ghosts are always Francis Drake or Elvis. They're always someone."

"Am I someone?" asked Mrs Gold.

"Of course you are."

"Someone to you?"

"You're the only one!"

"That's nice. I've heard lots of stories about how rich men in Hong Kong have one wife in Hong Kong and another in Shenzhen."

"When would I find the time?"

"If the day comes when I can't satisfy your needs, you will give me fair warning?"

"I'll try and be satisfied with what I have."

"You're too sweet. Now I must get ready. I have to meet someone who might want to use me in a modeling assignment."

"My wife, the model! I'm a lucky man."

Then he heard the maid announcing dinner. He left Mrs Gold and joined his maid who glared at his smudged make-up and told him that Mr Tian had phoned to say that he had left his trousers in Mrs Gold's wardrobe.

"Why on earth did he do that?" asked Sam as he sat at the single place set for him.

His maid was about to explain that she knew exactly why, but Mrs Gold entered, wearing a T-shirt cut to below her breasts and a skirt slung at the bikini-line.

"I'll be back," she said, as she walked out of the front door.

"We part, we go on our way, naked without a tie in the world," said Sam, translating a Ming poet.

"But you have some very nice ties," whispered the maid as she kneaded away the tension in his neck. "You have lots of nice clothes."

FIVE YEARS ON

So I say to the Fortune Teller, "When I'm really bored time hangs heavy. I'm conscious of every single second ticking away. Five hours can seem like five years. And my mind searches desperately for something to do. I look out for novelty excursions and events and toys. All just to fill in the moment. And when I fill in the moment, time flies, I become engrossed and just don't know what I'm doing. And then five years can seem like five hours. And I wonder what happened to my life!"

The old guy acts like he's heard it all before. No doubt fat sweaty gweilos like me often wash up in Temple Street burbling about being unloved and unappreciated, as if he was a bargain basement psychiatrist and not a predictor of the fates.

"Show me the palms of your hands," he says.

"Not yet," I says, "I want to tell you about something that happened five years ago."

"I'm only interested in the future," he says, "The past can look after itself."

This is like a red rag to a bull. He's shooting me a line and I know it, so I get on with it. "In the freezer compartment," I tell him, "I got this..."

Now I don't like to say nothing with all the tourist geeks hanging about but I was there so I was there to square, right? So I reach across the little wooden table and pull the old guy by his shirt front down to a more private level. "I got this branch," I say.

He sees what he takes to be food stains down my shirt and gets smart arse. "Did I mis-hear and you said brunch?"

"No!" I say, coming over all innocent and disarming, letting him think I'm a bit dumb you know, like its best to with these Chinese guys. "A tree type branch!" I tell him, "I brought it down from the New Territories the day Soo Lin discovered icicles. Not a lot of icicles and if you want to get pedantic about it, not really icicles at all but just a bit of frost. Even so, Soo Lin..."

"Soo Lin?" he says, as if this is like some great crime, "This is your Chinese girl friend?"

"Yeh, all that," I says, ignoring this racist slur, "And it was she who plucked the twig I shoved into the eski. Bloody cold day that day. Not what you would have expected. Stupid bringing the eski really. But in the chill there were compensations: the romantic view; my arm round her shoulders; the twig with its icicles."

"And sexual intercourse?" he says, his legs twitching with excitement.

"No," I says. And he says how he suspected as much and then says the twig is Freudian and the frost is her passion which I symbolically put on hold by dunking it in the ice box.

"Uncanny," I says, stunned by the mention of Freud. But then I suppose if he can read palms he can read books too. Anyway, I goes on: "One day I was staring into the fridge. Ostensibly to stare down a burger, contemplate the twig and live in the instantaneous moment of consciousness. I mean, it was a day when nothing of significance was happening. Nothing! Zilch! So I made plans."

"That's right," he says, all knowing like, "You gweilos have got to make it happen! Instead of just letting it happen."

"If you like," I says, I mean he's probably right so I let him get away with it. "You see I enrolled on this course in personal relationships. There I got into a grapple with this anorexic who turned out to be Soo Lin who also needed to work on her personal relationships. We learned how to talk to the right hand side of the brain and then how to talk to the left hand side.

"That can come in very handy," he says, "Some days I'm talking to someone and I think I must be talking to the wrong ear."

"Yeh," I says, twigging he's jerking me about. So thinking in for a penny in for a pound, I says, "Well, we decided who was a big chunk person and who a little chunker."

"You're a big chunker, I can tell," he says, all but calling me a fat slob. No matter, he had wisdom I wanted, so I take the shit hoping to get to the smooth. I continue: "Yeh. And she was a little chunker, hence her continual obsession with getting home early. But not the night of the freezer! I had plans."

"So you met her at this therapy thing and you had your plans for reviving interest in your life," he says and goes on about me wasting time chasing after problems. "How very Western," he says. As if I could be anything else! "You act before you have the right thoughts," he says. Probably true. Who knows what half baked subconscious dreams run my programme?

"Nothing worse," he says, "Believe me. We call this Incorrect Thinking. And that comes from not knowing the correct order of things. It can only result in turmoil."

"Christ!" I says, and I mean it, "I should have come here instead of going on that course!"

"Just show me the palms of your hands," he says, reaching forward. But I'm not ready so I pull back. I want to tell him things first.

"If I listen," he says, typical Hong Kong, "You have to pay more. So why not let me do the work and pay less?"

I tell him I'll pay whatever. So he shrugs his shoulders and lets me get on with it. Of course I don't know if he's listening or what, but he keeps his mouth open and eyes shut making some kind of show of concentrating. I tell him how Soo said her mind was all wrong. Her life going nowhere. And when she saw the ad and it said, is your mind wrong, your life going nowhere, she thought wow! Like it was aimed directly at her. And she knew there was ESP involved. Which impressed me, because I mean, there is like this big world out there and a bigger universe around it and then what? Like it must be even bigger out there and ESP comes right in and turns it all round inside out. So time stops and is all time. And distance shrinks and expands and you are in all places. Everything is one and ESP like tunes in, right? But if everything is one, what is it? I mean, and so I said to her, guess where I'm going to take you and what I'm going to do and I pick you up tomorrow and we expand our dimensions, uh huh?

Suddenly he opens his eyes. I can see him looking at his rolex and going red in the face. "OK!" he says, "If you do not let me see your hands, I cannot tell your fate! So either we do it, or we don't!"

"Calm down granddad," I says, "You'll get to the punch-line soon enough." So I tries to tell him how after announcing my spiritual search and how, after all, she told me she lived on Lamma Island where her brothers played water organs... I mean, I was the flesh in search of the spirit and she was the spirit in search of the flesh! And he goes apeshit! Blurts out that this creative logical dualism business can drive a man nuts! He starts shaking and wagging his finger saying, "Right side, left side, don't matter. Topside, downside only counts. Transferring the fancies down into the loins, that's where the action is!"

"Now we're talking," I says. "You're my man!"

"She was thin?" he asks.

"Very," I says, feeling the guy is on a roll.

"Thought sex was food?"

"She said she thought food was fattening."

"Oooh," he says sucking his teeth, "Food fattening. Sex fattening. Fear of pregnancy, of femininity, vulnerability, giving herself to another. Oooh, tch tch... Nasty. What did you do then?"

So I tells him how I once yelled at her: "Attack me! Break down my resistance! Release me from my mental prison! Tear down the wall that separates me from others!" And how she just told me not to be selfish. And I told her sex is the meaning of all relationships. It is what gives them significance. It is a commitment to life. It is the loss of oneself in the singularity. It is diving deep into the wholeness of everything. It is the answer to the unformable question. The entry into nirvana. The BIG YES!

I mean, I was really living. I felt that was the moment. The moment of total unification. I just had to express myself symbolically. That was all there was too it. I pulled open the freezer and dragged out the twig and waved it before Soo Lin's nose. "Look," I said, "Remember when you picked this for me?" And as she studied it, the frost thawed. Big omen I thought. Big Omen! "It's the frost we picked," I said to her, "I've kept it all this time! Now look at it. It's time for it to melt."

"And did it melt?" says my man.

"Well," I says, preparing him for a downer, "Then she tells me she's married and it's her husband does the water organ recitals and that I was only a fantasy fling that can go no further.

She only went on the course to help with her marriage. Which it did. Due to me. The thrill of the hidden secret releasing the monsters of the Id and all that."

"The thrill of the hidden secret," says the old guy with such relish, buzzing with wisdom. And I knew he had the power. The bald guys in vests and tattoos stopped playing cards on the pavement to eavesdrop. Only once in a hundred years did this kind of cosmic awe explode with witnesses.

"Go for it," I says, and he gives me in a single breath all this stuff about the symbolism of the twig being, that it represents, amongst other things, secret knowledge, and of course the secret was me. I had locked myself in a freezer, perfectly frozen in time, in the big now, neither future nor past, and she, knowing that I had the knowledge that she sought, knowing that everything was solved, answered, and represented by me and my deep freeze, she could get on with her life, excited by the presence of someone who knows. In short she was now thrilled by her husband now that she no longer relied upon him for anything other than the thrill!

"Yeh?" I says, sensing that he's holding out on me.

"By taking her up that hill," he says, lowering his voice to a whisper, "You set yourself up as God. She saw you as pure spirit. With you love was transcendental. The purist. The most perfect a woman could ask for. Now pay me five hundred dollars."

"What about my palms," I says, showing him the blood stains. "What's my fate then? What's my fate?"

GOING GWEILO

Chief Inspector Standing, greying, wired, a little too well dressed, one of the few gweilos left in the Hong Kong police force stood before the old Chinese man, who for obvious reasons, he knew as "The Blind Man." Beside him was his friend, Lee Qu, a little powerhouse of a man known for his ability as a fortune teller, a talent that had failed him this day.

"It will make you rich," said the blind man, "A retirement fund. You just make a meeting. Use the tools you are given. Kill this target of no consequence to you or we destroy you. This service to us, is the punishment for your crime."

Chief Inspector Standing's crime was what? A wasted life, an indifferent life, without love, without anything other than the daily stripping away of everything he thought he ever stood for, a life without any achievement other than sucking his way up to Chief Inspector? What was his crime? It did not matter. The only crime there ever was, was not getting away with it but he could still feel his rage mounting.

He looked around the room at all the witnesses to this. They were "the brothers," as they liked to be known, dressed in their red silk pyjamas, mopping the sweat from their red pudgy faces. They formed a cordon around the Inspector. There was no escape. Many years before, the brothers would have been youngsters on the fringes of the Triad, skilled in nothing much more than looking fearsome and wielding choppers and knives when called upon.

"Blood needs to be spilt!" declared Chief Inspector Standing.

"Hou!" grunted all the Cantonese-speaking brothers in approval, "Hou! Hou!"

The Blind Man cocked his head to one side. The Chief Inspector sensed the approval. Blood did need to be spilt. That was their way of sealing a bargain and showing that everything had been understood. Blood needed to be spilt!

Lee Qu, officiating at the ritual, handed the Chief Inspector a long knife, drawn slowly from a sheath hanging in a rack beside the altar to Guan Yu, the God of War, Policemen, and because he did not go cross eyed reading a whole page of Confucius, the God of literature as well, a butcher's rack of implements that was always there for these occasions.

"This is the right way," said Lee Qu, "You've learnt."

"I have," said Chief Inspector Standing, "I've listened hard over the years and learnt as much as I can at your feet."

Lee Qu, the master, stood proud. His protégé had finally become useful. No longer merely a fixer of parking tickets, no longer a source of information about who was running which investigation, and which judge could be counted upon. No longer merely a man who gave one an edge over the rivals. The Chief Inspector had come of age and after a lifetime of indulgence, now would make the final payment, and take the final risk. If he got away with it, he would be free.

Chief Inspector Standing quickly grabbed the blind man and fish hooked his mouth with his bony fingers. The blind man astounded, struggled feebly as the Chief Inspector reached in his hand, grasped the tongue with his thumb and forefinger and sliced across the flap. The tongue instantly came away with little blood, a pathetic lump of meat, and the blind man, now gasping and choking fell to his knees. Lee Qu and the brothers stared at the Chief Inspector, astounded by the act. This was not supposed to happen. This was not what he was meant to do.

Then the Chief Inspector drew the knife across the palm of his hand and slapped the blind man across the face sending him sprawling before the altar. He held up his hand to show that their blood had mingled.

"We're brothers!" he announced.

He had gone gweilo, as the Chief Inspector called sudden outbursts of intolerance, but the Chief Inspector knew that he had given everyone face and that was all that mattered. And the brothers led the blind man away: a surprising sacrifice. He would be dismembered and scattered as tradition demanded, each piece to each association, as a sign that among them was now another man who was bound by no laws, a man with no home, a man who could not turn back and so, the one in whose mental drama they all would willingly play their roles. And he too would unknowingly call upon his own assassin one day.

"We are one," declared Lee Qu, his voice quivering, "The past is gone and we will have our future!"

"And what's that going to be?" asked Chief Inspector Standing wiping the blood from his hands upon the altar cloth.

"It is written in our past," replied Lee Qu. "We are but the weapons of our ancestors and they are past shame."

***

Earlier that week the Chief Inspector had arrived at a crime scene. It had been a shambles. He had smiled, mustered his police Cantonese, had a few words with the scene of crime officers and discovered nobody was doing much. Everyone was sat around with their lunchboxes eating their noodles, chatting, smoking, and making wild speculations about how the headless skeleton arrived on the roof of the Hui Xun Building. It must have been naked, they scoffed, naked and without a head! Surely, someone would have noticed it climbing up the service staircase like that? But they reckoned it was years ago and so an incident hardly worth pursuing.

"Hardly worth pursuing!" blustered the Chief Inspector, going gweilo on them, "This was someone's son or daughter! This was someone's lover! This was someone who might have contributed to society and you tell me it is not worth pursuing?"

Chief Inspector Standing started blustering about treating the crime scene with respect, about gathering all the evidence, taking photographs, picking over every single speck of dust, and submitting it to laboratory analysis. Then he went on about plain old plod work gathering information as to who was in the building, who regularly had access to the area, and what sort of staff turnover was there? Some one, somewhere, some time would have heard or seen some thing! Then he regained control. He had been allowing himself to go shamelessly gweilo recently. After years of control, his imminent retirement reduced his desire to repress it.

He was on the brink of a nice pension and a respected place in society for a lifetime of service under colonial and Chinese rule. He should have been Commander! He should have been up for a knighthood! He should have gone a lot further! To say that Chief Inspector Standing resented his situation was an understatement but it was just his luck that one-country two-systems, the slogan of the handover, had not quite meant the old colonial government being left to its own devices. A throw back to colonialism he might well be, but he had his plan: one last great bust before retirement just to show them what they were missing! The clock was ticking and so to speed things on he would solve this case, the old-fashioned gweilo way, without the tiresome need to manoeuvre his way around the new order. He would talk to his snout.

"I've got something for you," he said to Lee Qu. "Headless. Stuffed behind an airconditioner on a roof. Was put there recently. Very little soft tissue. Probably boiled off or picked over by animals. Unlikely that DNA will pull up anything at all. And I want it all sorted out before the plug's pulled on me."

Lee Qu had been an old friend from when the Chief Inspector first arrived in Hong Kong. Years ago, gun at his side, strolling the vegetable and gut strewn passages between the wet market stalls, smelling the ordure, high on the clatter of Cantonese haggling, he had felt himself to be a great adventurer. He had also felt ashamed of his ignorance and had genuinely worried about how to police and be fair under the circumstances. Somehow he had to be one of them, and Lee Qu had offered to be his guide into this world. He knew things; he was a fortune-teller with a stall in Temple Street. He not only told fortunes but acted as a post office for special packages of a certain white powder. The Chief Inspector had never quite worked out whether he would have been better off arresting him, but he had been advised that if he wanted to survive in Hong Kong he had better find someone to help him; in those days a policeman was only as good as his informer and Lee Qu became his prime source of information about the underworld.

"I think someone is sending a message to someone," said Lee Qu.

"In what sense?"

"Why did someone look on the roof and look behind the air-conditioner?"

"Because the air-conditioner broke down."

"Not a coincidence! Someone wanted the skeleton found. It was not being hidden. It was being revealed."

"Who to?"

"Someone who would hear of its existence."

This was the sort of fortune-teller reply half of his conversations with Lee Qu ended in. But there was some sense in what he said. A message was being sent. Someone would know whom the skeleton belonged to. And someone would feel a gun was being pointed at their head. Maybe there was a connection with a public figure? The Chief Inspector hoped so. A demonstration of impartial justice was just the ticket to leave his image pure and clean, a truly British sort of legacy.

As expected, the crime scene yielded no clues. The discovery sequence went thus: the air-conditioner broke and eventually was noticed; the engineer finally went to repair the machine, found the skeleton, phoned the police, went home for lunch. There were no prints, no weapons, no pieces of clothing, nothing to identify the skeleton other than the medical officer's supposition that it was female, probably about twenty-five years old, and maybe dead for quite some time, and that was it. It looked like the case would be filed away, though the Chief Inspector was expected to field any press enquiries with the usual anodyne statements that investigations were under way and that foul play was not ruled out.

It was a mystery, but he scoured the newspapers, convinced that this old crime had some contemporaneous connections. He had his secretary clip and translate things from the Chinese language press that smacked of scandal. There were kidnappings and tragedies, but he could not see the sort of thing that would produce a message of this nature. Looking through the files of missing persons he could see many potential victims. Fillipina maids arrived in Hong Kong and disappeared without their families knowing where. Perhaps they just ran away? Or perhaps, as their families always thought, something terrible had happened and that their employer had fed them to the dog. Backpackers, Indian brides, and an abnormal number of mentally ill women disappeared over the years, but nothing leapt out at him. The dates seemed wrong. The sort of person seemed wrong. The message that could be sent seemed wrong. And he only had another day to work it all out. After that, life would be pointless:

a bungalow in Brisbane or a shotgun under the chin, both had their charms. If he solved the crime, he thought he would take the bungalow. If not, then it would be the shotgun. That seemed fair.

As on many previous occasions, Chief Inspector Standing climbed into Lee Qu's Mercedes, big and stately, a car for gliding among the crowded over-busy streets and making believe all was opulence, pleasure, and calm and nothing unrespectable was taking place. The locks clunked solidly and the seat belt effortlessly slipped into place. Chief Inspector Standing made himself comfortable.

"You're wrong about this message," he told Lee Qu. "This is merely house clearing. Someone had an old body lying around and wanted to get rid of it."

"No," said Lee Qu. "Why just strip it clean? Why not grind it to powder? Why not break it up entirely?"

"It's a skeleton used by a Chinese Medicine Man! It's been bought illegally and it's made up of boiled down Sri Lankan. Costs sixty dollars instead of a thousand. And that's the crime solved. And I'm the genius that did it."

"But I think you know the truth."

Lee Qu and Chief Inspector Standing laughed. They laughed a lot together. They had grown old together. When they first met, Lee Qu had nervously read the Chief Inspector's palm, expecting to be arrested, and so predicted a great and glorious future for him. The Chief Inspector had believed him too, after all, lifelines, heart lines, noses and earlobes were all part of us, and so why should they not tell us our character? And why should not our character dictate our destiny? And in Hong Kong it took a very special kind of character, one that could bend with the wind, and accept certain aspects of the local culture that made all too many go intolerantly gweilo.

The Chief Inspector did a little bit of tolerating at his retirement party that evening. The girls, all well paid, well coked, well stacked, oozed whatever it was they perfumed themselves with. Chief Inspector Standing never quite worked out what it was and wished his Filipina wife still stank of it. It was a special smell, a hot sex sort of smell that came after a few drinks, after a few joints. And the Mamasan was all over him, the older woman pimping for the younger, lying to him about what a nice man he was and how she had a nice girl needing a gentle introduction to the craft. He was doing her a great favour. He liked to do these favours.

"Any of your girls disappeared, Mamasan?"

"All my girls disappear sooner or later."

This was true. They never gave forwarding addresses. They never gave real names. It was a blessing of a sort. You knew that sooner or later they would stop calling you and blow away as if they never existed. That was the pact one made with them. You bought them a drink; you cracked stupid jokes, slapped their bums and grinned in their faces. Two at a time, three at a time, he had had all permutations, all possible pornographic postures and half the time he was too drunk to do anything so he would watch them fake it. Maybe they did not fake it? He did not care. Now and then there were those that he felt a strange paternal concern for. Better that they be with the likes of him than the likes of half the people that would visit them. But he was glad when they were gone and now he was even more certain of what was happening and the shotgun under the chin was looking preferable to the bungalow. He had complained once, perhaps a little too loudly, about a troublesome woman.

"Troublesome women!" he muttered to Lee Qu, steaming in the bathhouse. Always the best way of finishing a night and ridding one of the smell.

"It is always troublesome women," said Lee Qu, naked and being oiled by a masseuse in a bikini who knew not to ask the question about the full body rub. It was too late. They wanted to relax, forget the game, return home to bed clean and pure. She would get a large tip.

"Who makes them go away?" asked the Chief Inspector. "Someone might have failed to pay the price…"

"Yes."

"But this is a very old message. And a very old debt surely forgotten?"

In the stupor of the massage, the Chief Inspector pondered the nature of crime. He wondered how slowly did some one have to be killed for it not to be murder? If someone slipped strychnine into his sandwich then the sudden onslaught on his system would be attempted murder at the very least, but if someone slipped in some extra high fat mayonnaise repeatedly until obesity killed him, who was the culprit then? Slow down a crime and somehow it is not a crime. Take a cent a year, and who cares? A little favour here, a little favour there, and where is the corruption? Or let slip a few small misdemeanours in order to catch a bigger fish, and you become a hero rather than an accomplice. And doesn't everyone reap rewards from others' unknown crimes? And they accumulate no guilt, even when the crimes are discovered. They call that discovery, history, and it had sent him a message.

"Who needs to do the next generation a favour?" he asked Lee Qu. "Who is calling in all the debts, absorbing the crimes, and passing on the power and wealth derived from the crime to the next generation? What old man will take responsibility for a crime so that others can get off scot free with all the rewards?"

Lee Qu and the Chief Inspector laughed. They knew the answer all along. The answer was always the same. Everything they had in Hong Kong had derived from the one source and they knew he would take their soul in return.

"Do you really want to see him?"

"Yes. I think now would be a good time to see the blind man. Because he'll see me whether I want him to or not."

"You could walk away free. Or dead... Or neither."

"I won't say my goodbyes though. I never say goodbye."

***

The Mercedes glided through the gates of the underground car park, past the yellow and black stripes of bollards battered and bent by careless drivers. The concrete depths, hot as hell, had plastic coated concrete floors that squealed like pigs in an abattoir as the tyres rolled over them. Here in the subdued light, stinking of exhaust fumes, un-airconditioned, the blind man's organisation had its office. It disguised itself as a car wash though nobody ever saw a car being washed by these men. They sat in the glass booth, watching TV, picking their teeth, gnawing on chicken bones.

Chief Inspector Standing knew the men by sight but not by name. He merely acknowledged them and let Lee Qu shake their hands. The Chief Inspector often affected ignorance of Cantonese, which in this case was largely true for they spoke in their own special code impenetrable even to themselves as misunderstandings among this crowd often led to severed limbs and bodies bleeding to death in crowded places. Nobody noticed of course. That was how headless corpses could find their way through crowded streets, up busy stairs, to tops of buildings.

Lee Qu and the Chief Inspector went through the office in through the metal doors at the back, built with metal wheels and great bolts to hold back fires or strangers, whichever came first. Stepping across the metal threshold, Chief Inspector Standing was in the corridor leading down towards the heady pounding machinery that pumped the water, pumped the juice into the shopping mall above them. The rest of humanity lived in the skin whereas Lee Qu and the Chief Inspector lived in the bowels.

These visits to the blind man always put a demonic cast of mind upon the Chief Inspector. Sliced, diced, thriced, cut to the bone, then boned and still aware, he recited to himself the punishments that greeted those who fell foul of the Triad's elaborate faith in the right of might. The guilty transgressor would be taken to task in the dark to the sound of thrashing metal, rumbling drums. As he walked he could hear the music of hell: The Bomb! The Gun! The War! The Poor! The School! The drains! Late trains! Lame brains! And the chorus, howled by off key sneering harpies: This is the way the world works! This is the way the world works! The younger Triads had abandoned their Cantonese Opera for the Gangsta Rap of LA.

With Lee Qu beside him he knew no harm would befall him, merely another compromise. Was he willing to pay the price? In return for Hong Kong, a city created by drug smugglers, you paid the price.

He heard a toilet flush way above him and he could hear the contents hurtling down through the pipes. He looked up and thought how appropriate. Then he arrived. A door was flung open, Lee Qu ushered him through and there in the grey room, lit with hazy carelessness by neon lights screwed to the concrete walls, was Guan Yu's altar.

There were a few battered red hassocks for kneeling on and the ashy stench of old incense reddened the eyes. The harvest festivals of Chief Inspector Standing's home village church were never far from his mind whenever he saw these shrines laden with their slabs of meat, mouldering fruits, and burnt out joss sticks. It was a long time ago, a long way away, and here it was almost a parody. Or perhaps it was the Home Counties version that was the parody?

Chief Inspector Standing turned around to acknowledge a blind old man, a squint for a face, being led in by several brothers, their faces red with heat, dripping as they mopped themselves with the sleeves of their silk pyjamas. After all these years, where Lee Qu fitted in the hierarchy, the Chief Inspector did not really understand. Perhaps he was the only one who knew the ceremonies and traditions that made them think that they were more than a bunch of thugs but rather patriots? Perhaps he was the real boss and the Blind Man merely a figurehead?

The old blind man, thin, dressed poorly, his fingernails well kept and polished, calmly sat on a chair brought to him and crossed his legs and listened as Lee Qu announced, as he had on many occasions, the presence of the famous detective. The flattering irony of the Chinese always made Chief Inspector Standing nervous.

"I was wondering," began the Chief Inspector, "about bothersome women."

Alarmingly the old man reached up and felt his face. His hands smelt of chicken and cigarettes.

"It's alright," said Lee Qu, "He just wants to make sure you are who you are."

"Sometimes I'm not sure of that myself," said the Chief Inspector.

"So you go that restaurant?" asked the old man, his Cantonese strange and difficult for the Chief Inspector.

"What restaurant are we talking about?"

"One of the many problems I solve for you. Remember the table you booked, how it already been used. You already eat and pay bill. You in a hurry. You check your credit card; got cable subscriptions; clubs you belong to that you never attend. The amounts mount up. Someone else using your account. Then it stop. Before it get too much. Before you get really into problem."

Chief Inspector Standing listened to the monologue. He thought he understood and then thought perhaps he did not but was merely guessing its meaning. Trying to deal with anything in Cantonese was always fraught with this problem. But he recently had had a dining reservation usurped by someone else. And there were strange anomalies on his credit card that he thought for a moment meant another was using his number, but then it stopped and he forgot about it. These things happened all the time in Hong Kong: a little glitch in the bank account, a little extra off the credit card, a square metre less than the lease stipulated, a little give on the taxi's receipt.

"I'm not here about Credit Card fraud," said the Chief Inspector.

"I thought you were here to thank me for stopping them robbing you?"

The Chief Inspector tried to ignore him.

"That's not what I'm here for."

"Huh! Lucky we look after you. Lucky we know everything."

"Very lucky. But I'm on more important business."

"Let's reminisce a little," said the old man, "Was it fifteen year ago?"

The old man grinned and grasped Chief Inspector Standing's hand.

"You in love with that woman you found in bar," he whispered. "One day you were there with the girl, who had the child. Was it yours? Looked like yours. But you would not pay for that girl's child!"

"He's done you many favours," whispered Lee Qu. "Stopped many scandals. Protected your family."

The Chief Inspector and Lee Qu laughed.

"As always," said the Chief Inspector, "You know everything but never quite tell me everything."

"You know how it works," said Lee Qu, "You only need to know what you need to know."

There had been a girl in Chief Inspector Standing's life, or several, beside his Filipina wife, but there was that one who wanted to live rent-free in one of the many apartments he hoped would provide him with a comfortable retirement. She had threatened to tell his wife and then, strangely, he never heard from her again and hoped he never would. Now it seemed that he had.

The Chief Inspector began looking for the exit. The incense smoke thickened. And in the reddish glow, the smoky haze, Lee

Qu no longer looked like his old friend, but more the enemy he always knew him to be, the man who introduced the girls, the man who helped supply them with whatever they needed, the man who knew his weaknesses.

"Our bodies," continued the blind man, "dug from shallow graves after our murders, have teeth to give away our identity. And they will tell their tale."

The blind man smiled and showed that he had no teeth in his head.

"We have more!" he announced. "Her hair. So nice. Her ears. So beautiful. And her eyes. You look into her eyes?"

The God of Hell, eyes red, blazing with justice, fumed before the Chief Inspector, finger pointing and reaching for the judgement stick. He would hurl it any minute and have the Chief Inspector spread over the guillotine and sliced in two. His fingers would be removed; his tongue; his ears; his legs and arms would be hacked off. Every part of him would be scattered to the corners of all creation, bringing fortune or frightening the monkeys, he did not know which. He looked for the exit but in Hell there was nowhere for him to go.

"He has the skull," added Lee Qu, "He solved your problem. No-one need know anything unless he say so and he wants you to be very grateful, for now is the time for you to make your final payment for your final reward."

"Final reward?" blurted out the Chief Inspector, "What rewards have I had?"

"You know what rewards."

Lee Qu had once told him, "You will have great power and authority over the lives of many. Use this power wisely and you will be remembered well."

The recollection made him boil. He had had little power, though what he had he thought he used wisely. He had done no wrong, merely made a few mistakes. And the problems had gone away. He did not know why or how, but he was glad of it. But now, here was a problem that was back! A pang of regret passed over him. But there was nothing that could be held against him for doing what anyone else would have done, and not returned the phone call of an over-demanding woman! That was not murder! Not understanding the messages that had been left was no crime! Being ignorant of others interfering in his private life was… He did not know what that was! It certainly did not oblige him to anyone. And then, as the Blind Man ordered a murder at his command, imagining the gun beneath his own chin, he went gweilo!

"Blood needs to be spilt!"

"Hou!" grunted all the brothers in approval, "Hou! Hou!"

The knife! The tongue! The blood! This is the way his world worked!

***

The deed was done and the blind man was dragged away and Lee Qu stared into Chief Inspector Standing's eyes, as he had all those years before and grinned.

"I see a great future for us all. A great future! Justice is the crime, and always has been. And we are the only people who really understand. We are the judges and now we will judge."

The world was renewed, the contract signed; Chief Inspector Standing had with blood taken the final step. He emerged from the darkness into the light, walking and wondering who had done this, who had led him to this, and why? But now, he had an army with him, and all he need do was to say the word and from where he was, from where he stood beyond recognition, beyond being known, or found out, he could see that he had achieved his future. What would be the next stage he did not know, what would be the future, he had no idea, but the past was now erased. He was where he was and this was what he was. He had paid his dues and now there was nothing else but to reap the harvest.

Below the shopping malls, outside the air-conditioning, deep in the drains, in the warehouses, in the sweatshops and brothels, the base of the pyramid would be firmly ruled so that all others could live in harmony. It had been a long education, a long removal of restraints, for now he was one with the brotherhood. He felt proud as he ordered the skeleton from behind the air-conditioner to be accidentally incinerated in a mysterious fire that would take place at midnight in the morgue. No one ever performed a crime that did not exist, and he decreed what existed or not.

THE PUSSY MAN BLOG

In Singapore's bookshops there were cartoons about the likes of George, the Ang Mo, the crude, rude, klutzy wallet with a beer gut. By rights he should lead around a skinny Indonesian girl three foot shorter than himself in tight jeans with diamante beading on her denim jeans. But he had his pride, and liked a gal who could fill out a spreadsheet and work her Asia Miles.

Consequently, he worked out. He wore Armani. He played mahjong and watched the latest Korean soap dubbed into Mandarin with English Subtitles. He shaved his chest to rid himself of grey hairs. He plucked his nose, plucked his ears, his eyebrows, and even trimmed the hairs on his knuckles, which grew at an alarming rate. He had once waxed his back except for the next twelve months in this heat the stubble caught up on his shirt and left him with a horrible rash. The back, he decided, made him a Silverback. That was what he was, a Silverback, the king of the jungle, the best of the beasts, and until some younger stud had the guts to kick him out of the troop he would have his pick of the women, shaved women! He drooled at the thought. He would blog the pros and cons at his office desk on Saturdays, much better than hanging about his pokey apartment off Orchard Road, within sight of four floors of whores, as they called one of the entertainment malls it backed onto.

He still had not fully unpacked. His new clothes he laid on the floor and allowed the humidity to iron them. Ironing was women's work but Pudding, his Chinese girlfriend, whom he made love to on a bedless mattress twice a week, never ironed anything. She had a maid back at her apartment. She had a career, another life, but twice a week she was Pudding because George called her that. She offered to send the maid round to iron for him and George thought how cool it would be to make love to the maid as well. He did not know the maid was fifty-eight years old; he assumed all Singapore girls were twenty-three. In ignorance, he agreed that Pudding's maid could pay a visit and deal with his washing and ironing until he acquired his own maid, though that seemed a very permanent kind of decision to make. Anything permanent, since his divorce, was not on his agenda.

George liked the girls. Which was why he liked Singapore for there it was all so easy. He revelled in the happy conjunction of Chinese and Malay genes, steeped in a hot steamy brew of tropical humidity and soy sauce, creating complexions that went on for ever: milky coffee, blemish free, and well upholstered, beautifully finished, with on occasions MBA included. These girls were good to go and got all the better for the going. Surprisingly, George seemed to figure in the equation. Go figure!

For George was no hunk. He was slight, slightly successful, slightly happy, slightly bald on his head, less on his back, slightly overweight, and often slightly drunk: the ex-pat par excellence, lusting after young Asian flesh. He was a lust accountant with a column of opening lines carefully annotated with a percentage success rating: if you were sushi, which kind would you be? He was not so middle-aged that he could not be cute, but he knew his limitations. He could still be attractive by playing the line and letting them do all the talking. Nothing a woman likes more than talking about herself and nothing a man likes more than watching her, so he wrote in his blog, The Pussy Man Blog.

Which is how Pudding came across him. She knew where to find him and told him how fascinated she became by the thought of meeting a stranger who had exposed all his wildest fantasies to the world. She knew exactly what she had to do to drive him insane. He liked that and he knew it excited her. He could smell it on her as soon as she joined him at his favourite seat at Hooters, over beer, ribs and coleslaw. The game was perfect. He wrote his blog and then along she came to make it true, after the event. A diary that foretold the future! The effect was turned into the cause and his life was running backwards and he could feel himself getting younger.

As Pudding yelled, screamed, groaned, gurgled, pulled wild faces as her breasts flayed the air, during their twice-weekly sessions, he became younger and stronger and the condoms became weaker. It was the Year of Living Dangerously and he was Mel Gibson and she was the woman, the love interest, who was played by the actress that was not a dwarf. His memory failed him at times.

Despite the amount of noise Pudding made, she began complaining about other noises in the apartment. George heard nothing, which was hardly surprising. Nor did he sense that something was watching them, as she assured him there was. There were no cameras, he told her, no strangers lurking in a cupboard, no cupboards in fact. But she heard scuttling scratching sounds, somewhere beneath them, or above, or within the fabric of the building. He listened and maybe it was true something was there and it excited both of them all the more. There would be a hole in the ceiling with an eye watching them wrestling themselves into a lather that not even the most ferocious Singaporean airconditioning could dowse. This was nothing more than further proof that Pudding, half his age, at least, shared the same disease as he did, a gaping hole in the psyche.

He filled the hole by reading the Chinese subtitles to the dullest American blockbusters, but it allowed him always to say how he read Chinese. This was his best opening gambit with girls who really needed no opening gambit. He would turn up at Hooters, chat up the little waitresses in their industrial strength bras and tight silk shorts, and pick over his BBQ ribs, licking his fingers, worrying about the smear of fat and barbecue sauce that always gathered in the creases of his mouth, in the creases with the little grey stubble he could never shave without cutting himself.

Pudding filled her psychic hole cruising Clarke Quay catching the eyes of his like and sparking a conversation. He would reply in Mandarin and be heralded as not only a brilliant man, but a stud too. His Mandarin was sexy, pronounced like a purring cat licking up the milk: pussy talk from the pussy man. Are you barbecue sauce or pesto? He always got a smile, always got a conversation, and then Pussy Man's purring pussy talk got him into cahoots with Singapore Party Girl number eighteen, otherwise known as Pudding, a careless cleavage and a large smiling red lipped mouth who lived at home still. In short,

George, running from the suburbs, collided with Pudding, aka Jenny Lee, determined not to be like her parents.

Run back in time a little and you find Jenny Lee, dutiful daughter, working in a bank, meeting no-one but shy Chinese boys worried about having to go for two years army service, or worse, after army service and desperate to catch up on their career and with little skill with women. How could one have a future with mere boys playing catch up with the girls? And the Chinese boys, so all her friends complained, did not kiss. The Ang Mo though, mature, moneyed, experienced, besmitten with even the dumpiest and hairiest and most uncouth, uncultured, unattractive of girls, stuck his tongue in all the strangest places. They could even be your ticket out of Singapore, the dullest town on the planet!

If you clicked backwards through George's Blog, way passed the dead links, to the remnants of his divorce blog, you could find the fossil of suburban man: last coherent entry: "She even took the dog!" After that, blankness upon blankness, filled in with an all consuming two years of studying Chinese in order to blank out his mind, until one trip to Singapore and the night he never did get to Geylang where the legal brothels were, because what need was there? The girls came screaming into his arms. They leered at him in elevators. They wore next to nothing in the cool of the hotel lobbies. They paraded in little tight hot pants, navels bejewelled, cleavages exposed, long legs and high heels and ready smiles. Call me Big, George Big, he said, offering his hand by way of introduction. So was born The Pussy Man, his new non-boring self, his Pudding lure. If you were a pudding, which would you be? Ginger Sponge and Custard? Mango Pudding and Black Rice? Spotted Dick? Whoever said Singapore was boring was not a middle-aged Englishman.

One through to seventeen were a middle aged man's folly, wet dreams when he had long forgotten what a wet dream was, and better than a day at the gym: a cardiovascular work out, an elixir of youth. He even began remembering people's names again. Do you like deserts or the sea? Number eighteen preferred eating cheesecake to going on boats, confused as to what exactly he was asking her. And much to her bewilderment he called her Pudding thereafter. Ah, Pudding, he would say, take me shopping for some clothes for you to take off. His wife, ex-wife, would be jealous if she ever read about his shopping trips with Pudding in her pants, navel ring, butterfly tattoo, slave bangles, and high high-heels. For George it was rebirth and for her it was liberation.

Scroll forward through the nights of passion, the gymnastics, the role playing, the dirty talk, the toys, the quickies in strange places, the slow weekends in a spa on Sentosa Island – So Expensive, Nothing To See Anyway, as the Singaporean cynic had it – and then Pudding's maid arrived. She was under strict orders to destroy the thing that lurked behind the walls. So she brought a huge tube of Be Gone spray and blasted the corners of George's infested room. She tutted as she prowled about the semi-inhabited apartment, stomping the floors, banging the walls, and picking at the peeling paintwork. Everything would have to come off. That was all that could be done. The plaster should be removed and then everything sprayed and vacuumed for lurking within were animals, insects, or worse, something much worse! She sensed ghosts, spirits, and evil forces.

Pudding's maid was from Malaysia, a true daughter of the soil, and had a magic wart that she rubbed and made a wish on. George shuddered at the thought of his fantasy where he and Pudding had a superheated threesome with the maid. He deleted that from the Blog just in case the rather dumpy fifty-eight year old slapped on a hormone patch and went berserk one day. Instead, she complained that George was ruining her mistress and could not understand how a man like him could live in such disgusting circumstances. She filled four bin bags with old newspapers and magazines and the odd box of half-finished pizza, and instead of ironing his underpants, threw them out and ordered him to purchase new ones. His shirts she thought were cheap and similarly should be disposed of and the only item in his suitcase she approved of was the Armani suit, because it was expensive. She also disapproved of it because it creased in the humidity of Singapore and made him look like a British Footballer, which for her was a lowly beast and not suitable for her mistress. He would, if he was to continue this folly, have to smarten up and not look like the third rate overpaid accountant he probably was, no offence sir!

She was rather fascinating in a weird hairy-footed hobbit like way. Her wart was all the more wondrous for being magical! It was magic, she told him, because it was heart shaped. It was her protection in this evil world and Allah obviously wanted to keep her pure. He had also wanted to keep her mistress pure but George had unleashed her vanity and she could not fight it as she had no wart and a penchant for renovation work. Then Pudding's maid offered to tattoo him, which was another skill beside mass slaughter, ironing, and interior design, which she was blessed with. It was her that had tattooed Pudding's butterfly in place, an act she regretted as it was meant to destroy evil but only seem to fuel it. Pudding, she said, had lost all self-respect since meeting George. She had been such a sensible girl, an office girl with an all too charitable nature. Allah would punish him for taking advantage, unless she tattooed him. Then he and Pudding would be as one and this, apparently, was OK by Allah, for marriage would surely follow. It would be a heathen marriage though because Pudding was an idolater, who would pop into a Buddhist temple now and then, and George was an accountant, but even so, marriage would be some protection against the evil spirits, no offence sir!

Now he had an insight into the other life of Pudding. She was an office girl! He had wondered if she worked the escort agencies, or even the Geylang Brothels, but no, she was a Singapore Office Girl, the sort of girl that the Singapore Government's Social Development Unit tried to loosen up and get close and personal with the clueless geeky guys straight out of national service. So Damned Ugly, was the usual joke about the SDU and its clients. Except George had met the office girls and yes, tight they were, tightly packaged, black jacketed, sensible tight, hair tied back tight, often born again Christian tight, spouting a love of the Blessed Mother Teresa, but eyes ablaze and alert for whatever was happening: tight but fit to bust. And Pudding had busted, so George discovered, most likely under the influence of her maid reading her the collected works of the Brontë Sisters as a child. All of which made sense of Pudding's strange conviction that George's ex-wife must have been mad.

In Singapore, Pussy Man wrote, he was no alien, no intruder, no extra in the drama but a player, playing the role long assigned to all male, middle aged ex-pats with hypertension and fat wallets. This was no England, this was no dull suburb with husbands grunting and snoring before the telly, kids resentful and spoilt, wives believing men to be jokes, boys, children, pets, or pests. Pussy Man might have more chips on his shoulders than those of a Tesco's delivery boy, but here in the tropics they melted and so here he would stay! Here for the first time he found love, true love, the love that knows no bounds, love agape, love passionate, love spiritual, love lustful, lewd, loud and ridiculous, love actually, cute love, rough love, blind and blissful and indiscriminate, and most certainly not the watery whimpering dog love of the commuter belt. He would marry every Singaporean girl, everyone different, everyone delicious, everyone his best friend, simultaneously!

Pudding read it of course and asked him, if he could decorate his soul, what colour would he paint it? He had no idea and so Pudding suggest the colour of the moon! Pudding was a published poetess, published on the Internet that is, by herself. But a poet writes poetry and she wrote it, accompanied by animated smileys because she knew poets used a lot of similes. Poets were also sensitive to their environments and Pudding could no longer make love in a room surrounded by evil spirits, even if she did not believe in them. So, as his home should reflect his soul, what colour would he paint it? George hummed, haahed, harrumphed and eventually agreed that moon was a good colour.

Consequently George and she would have to forego all carnal pleasure until her maid ripped off the plasterwork – another talent of hers – cleared the infestation, and then redecorated. Instead of sex they now pored over design catalogues and colour charts. If you were a furnishings catalogue which would you be? IKEA? Habitat? G.O.D?

George realised why his marriage had been shortened once the children started going out on their own. His wife was dull! She would never have dreamed of painting anything the colour of the moon. It would have just been plain yellow to her. She was so dull that she ran off with another guy who was an exact replica of himself and married him. No interesting woman would do anything as pointless. An interesting woman would get a tattoo, a Brazilian wax, and hire a professional Sex Goddess to orchestrate a hot night of nooky. (He had read that a woman in Camden had set up a consultancy.) How he became interested in his wife in the first place was a mystery. It happened somewhere between finals and qualifying as an accountant. They dated, she moved in, he met her parents and her parents met his and it went through the house unopposed and she became pregnant and that was that. Damp cold mud, piles of mulching leaves, smoky garden bonfires, sunless drizzly skies, and the smell of paint from the endless B and Q-ing came to mind at the very thought of his wife, his life, her life. That was it! He lived her life and not his. Her Indoors dictated everything. What do you want to eat, she would ask, and he would say, I don't know, I'm not hungry yet. But what do you want, she would say. Well, he said, I could get a takeaway. And she would say, we've got a chicken pie in the freezer that has to be used up. And he would say, I suppose we'd better use it then. And that would be their big conversation of the day.

But now: it was ribs at Hooters and call me Big, George Big. Ni hao! He was liberated. He could not understand why he had never left England before. At least his adventure had started, no longer a chronicle of Warholish, Pooterish, Adrian Molish banality, a list of the contents of his fridge, a list of what he liked and did not like, a list of his favourite bands, and dream football team, instead, rip roaring piratical adventures in swampy seas of dusky women: Love and Lust in Singapore! Tremendous stuff! Publishers, real publishers who did books and stuff, would spot his blog and turn him into a household name. If you were a household appliance, which would you be? How could he fail with a big Hoover?

For some reason the maid was slow ripping out the plaster. Pudding would turn up, always looking ready for sex, though carrying her catalogues and tape measures, and then the Maid would come and rub her wart to see if the spirits were angry. The two of them would then knock on the walls, listen, and confirm what the colour scheme would be and what kind of man George was. Was he a black leather upholstery man or a cushion man? Did he want the feminine touch or would the gleaming chrome and wide screen TV of the bachelor pad suit him? George would brew up a bowl of soupy noodles for everyone, eat it while pretending to listen, and then attempt a nuzzle hoping the maid would turn a blind a eye, but apparently even this was forbidden by the magic mole, unless he had the tattoo. He was still thinking about it.

Unfortunately, Pudding did not seem to read his blog any more. When he declared it was the most auspicious time of the year for Singapore Party Girls to wear short skirts and parade through the streets without their knickers, Pudding wore her jeans and delivered a box of paint rollers. This was sacrilege. Singapore Party Girls and Pussy Man do not decorate apartments, they trash them! On cue Pudding's maid slipped on a mask, white overalls, raised a jackhammer and began hammering the plaster off the walls. As the plaster fell, the wart twitched and Pudding was ready with the Be Gone! Any mad wife walled up would be chased away and Mr Rochester, dear reader, would have to tuck in his batik shirt.

George backed away, defeated by the clouds of dust, and then the souls of the dead appeared to be released along with a howl and a shriek as Pudding let loose with the spray. Around George's feet the cockroaches clustered, as if trying to find sanctuary beneath his protective shadow. Fine specimens they were too. Gloriously brown, shiny, and very family orientated. There was something commendable about their glorious beauty and astonishing staying power.

The maid ripped the walls and the floors off, her biceps bulging amidst the clouds of poison and white gypsum. Roaches flew everywhere. George had never seen Roaches flying before. Shambling, untidy wings, that once extended could not return beneath their brown canopies without reference to an instruction manual, flapped, fluttered, and beat about his face. Somehow, this was not what Pussy Man was all about. This was plain George and very disturbing it was too. He had to grab his laptop and run in search of a margarita, which he found at the Iguana across the Singapore River, opposite Hooters, not far from where the bungee jumping machine was – you can't miss it. When girls failed George, only drink could restore his equilibrium. He blamed English literature.

The SPG, he wrote, got him! The Singapore Party Girl got the Pussy Man, or at least did not care whether they got him or not because essentially they paraded him as a trophy at plush restaurants, hotels, and deafening clubs where they danced with their girlfriends and he got drunk watching them all. They would surround him, ooze over him, soak in the finest margaritas, stew in the outside heat, grab a bite at Boat Quay, spidery crabs, skate and ray, clams and prawns, picking fingers, sucking out the brains, cracking a joke and a crab claw all in one movement. He was in there, hand on one thigh, tongue in another's ear, flirting with all and them discussing the price per square foot of Singaporean property, the Straits Times pretending to be a newspaper, bureaucracy, news on the Internet, censorship and its uselessness for they all travelled, knew what was happening. Despite, or maybe because of the Government's nannying, tough stances, refusal to allow racial abuse, public debate on religious differences, security issues of a tiny island in a sea of potentially hostile countries, they were smart. The savvy awareness of the SPG compared to the bored and desperate housewives of Croydon, who think Big Brother merely a stupid TV program, gave him a perpetual hard on.

He ate and drank his fill and waited for Pudding. He waited and hoped for Pudding to Party but he knew the truth. The Pussy Man was just George. He tried writing more of his blog but started writing about how bad his back had been lately. He started writing about how the pain to pleasure ratio slipped a little in the wrong direction and how he largely forewent the more energetic forms of sexual activity, trusting to the good nature of the girl, her underwear, and expert mouth. George was still Pussy Man, but suffering pangs of age and Pussy began to mean something entirely different. Doubt flooded his mind. How long would it be before the Singapore Party Girl tired of him? Would he be a joke, a pet, a convenience to be used as a manipulator of paint brushes, a disposer of rubbish bags, a cash cow, the guy who had to complain to the neighbours, discipline the children if he ever saw them, and be the stranger in the house unable to relate, unable to talk to anyone but the dog? And would she take the bloody dog! Her indoors, far away, now with another who had a pension plan, had said she loved him. No SPG uttered such words and they were George's pension plan.

The girls at the Iguana smiled, served him margaritas in a jug, and warily danced around pussy man who no longer seemed so intent on working on his laptop. In the steam of the night, he watched the model aircraft flown by the children across the river, remotely flying, lights on their wings, like big glow worms. He felt controlled by invisible forces, flying in what he assumed was a free and easy manner, but always twitched back away from crossing the river where if he did, he would crash, and be eaten by the Singapore crocodile that cleaned the canals of the bodies of suicidal over-worked students and rejected old men. He felt a long way from nowhere. No pudding for him, he thought. And Pussy Man died. Another scheme for re-invention drying up and failing to make the breakthrough he deserved. The girls would be bored with him. He would have no history with them, no point of contact, no cultural resonance, no shared CD collection. If you were an iPod, which ten tracks would be most frequently played? It made no sense. The lines were down. The bandwidth too small and nobody would ever understand because the middle-aged, clapped-out, hairy-backed, pot-bellied blokes from the suburbs with mediocre minds, mediocre careers, trying to grab a little bit of glory, adventure, and passion were despised jokes that young blades could never imagine themselves becoming.

Twelve margaritas later he returned to his apartment, sans floor, sans plaster, still being sucked clean by an industrial cleaner wielded by Pudding's maid. She would finish the plastering first and then do his tattoo, to match the Trompe L'Oiel design that she had decided would make a true feature wall in his new living environment.

There was nothing else for him. He would have to allow Pudding's maid to tattoo him. She was a traditionalist, she explained, and that pain was all part of the ritual. The tattoo was a magical one, as her wart was, and he would be protected from all manner of evil thoughts let alone evil spirits and she began the process of pricking in the ink using a sharpened bamboo stick and a little mallet. As far as he could work out she was tattooing something that looked like a blood clot into his arm. It would, she told him, settle down and become a component in the overall design of his life, making him as one with his environment. His soul would thus be restful and he and Pudding would be forever joined together in a spiritual mystical bond no matter wherever they were in the world. If some horrible flesh eating infection managed to get in, he should contact her immediately, as she had an array of antibiotics available on the off chance of such an occurrence. It was rare, but she was prepared with a supply bought in Thailand as they manufactured generics there at a tenth of the price you would have to pay at the doctors in Singapore. But don't worry, sir.

Pudding and her maid moved into his apartment, leaving her mother and father. George was told that he would have to meet her parents and he would not be allowed to call her Pudding in their presence. He had also better bring along his CV and photocopies of his qualifying certificates, as her father would interrogate him, especially as he was so much older. He would have to leave a large amount of money to keep his young widow going for some time, and pay for the college education of his children. Pudding patted her stomach and her maid explained that for the best results this Pudding had to be kept cool. She outlined a course of windswept moors, cold blasting rain, Wellington boots full of mud and the smell of cows in a barn munching hay. She had read the collected works of the Brontë sisters to Pudding when she was a child, and so the northern climes were implanted in her soul and needed now to make the connection. The maid would also like a trip to Howarth and it would be most useful for her to accompany them as she would organise the details of the trip and let them develop a good relationship with their new baby, which had to be born in Yorkshire. The Wart never lied. And Pudding thought all this extremely exciting and exotic. It would be like stepping into the pages of a fairy tale, or at least the set of guidebooks on tours of Great Britain that she had recently purchased.

George was from Watford, which was about as far north as he cared to go, but the predilections of the Londoner were probably lost on Pudding, and so he resigned himself to going along with whatever she had planned. If she wanted wind swept heaths, then that is what she would get. This, he mused, was the inevitable punishment for lust and decided to call it love. She would put a collar on him and look after him, feed him, water him, put a nice blanket in his bed and one day, old and decrepit, hair falling out, incontinent, and too tired to go for a run, she would have him painlessly put down. His tattoo reminded him of a dog once the swelling had gone down, though it was supposedly a Sun and Moon. He decided it was more like a Wolf though. And so began work on his new Blog: The Wolf Man Blog.

THE DEVIL'S WORK

When Donny Tsang was twelve years old he came across an old piece of guitar music by Robert Johnson, a black blues singer of the 1930s and quickly mastered the piece. His mother thought him very clever; and when he began winning school prizes for music, his father began showing his brandy-swigging business associates photographs of his talented son. Better still, when Donny reached puberty, he discovered that being able to apply his guitar skills to the pop songs of the day went down very well with the girls at his mother's church. The Devil's Music, as the blues was known in the American South, was in a very real sense, heaven for Donny.

However, much like the old bluesmen, one day he came to a crossroads where he had to choose between music and a good honest living. He knew which road he would have chosen if it was a choice between picking cotton in some backwoods of nowhere and travelling a road strewn with cheap women, cheaper alcohol, and maybe a bit of glory on the way. But he lived in Hong Kong and his road to nowhere was a road to an American university to study law, which at the time did not seem to exclude even expensive women, alcohol or his guitar! Apparently one could have everything if one came from Hong Kong.

He formed a band and played gigs around the university's neighbourhood and turned into a super cool lawyer. Handsome, with a sharp faced tartar look, he would have looked at home on horseback riding the steppes with Genghis Khan and would have been catnip to the ladies as it was, but his blues guitar put some very serious icing on his cake, several nights a week for five years.

Then Donny returned home to bluesless Hong Kong, and married Amy Ng, the kind of girl Genghis would have burnt down a city to get. An early exponent of the navel ring, she gave the Canto-Pop Pout as good as any Hong Kong singing sensation, and was all movement. It had been love at first sight, at least for him, and she could not help but think that a designer-suited slick lawyer, who sang songs to her with a sexy voice, was the perfect accompaniment for such a superior specimen of Chinese womankind as herself. The wedding was a hoot. His old law-school band flew over from America, re-united and grooved for the reception party. To have Hong Kong's stiff and formal legals suited up and jiving to Donny's rendition of *One Step At A Time* was proof enough that life was good, that everyone was a rebel at heart, and young forever.

"She steps to the left, she steps to the right, she walks all day and makes me run all night!" sang Donny.

And watching his bride getting in the groove, he knew that he was living what blues aficionados called "The Life!"

"I'm going down to Louisiana to get me a mojo hand," he sang, "I'm gonna have all you women right here at my command!"

Donny had his mojo working. He thought that he had the best of both worlds but his wife was more ambivalent about it, and not merely because she knew he used his guitar to attract women. She was very aware of her own capabilities and would keep him very busy. But why did he play the blues? Just how could a guy with his looks, his money, his opportunities, his future, sing tunes by people like Muddy Waters?

> Well if I feel tomorrow, like I feel today
> I'm gonna pack my suitcase
> And make my getaway
> Lord I'm troubled, I'm all worried in mind
> And I'm never bein' satisfied,
> And I just can't keep from cryin'

Now what did Donny know about being so troubled? What did he know about being worried in mind? What had he got to cry about? Not too much, as far as Amy could see, but as his career became serious and the guitar playing fell away, he settled down to making money out of human frailty and greed, and to her irritation, became a troubled man.

"It is a sin to be rich," sang Lightning John Hopkins;

"An' you know that it's a low down shame to be poor.
A rich man ain't got a chance to go to heaven,
an' a poor man done got a hard way to go."

Donny had to admit that nobody in Hong Kong ever thought like that, and for that matter neither did he. The blues were cool but maybe he never really was a bluesman at heart? Maybe with his background he never would be, never could, and it was an insult to the old bluesmen anyway! In short, Donny the lawyer had become a whole lot less cool and he knew it and, given the amount of money he was making, he knew that it should not be a problem. Except that his work bored him and he never seemed to have time for anything else.

Amy in the meantime did a bit of modelling, opened a chintzy fake antique shop, and featured as pouty girlfriend of a two-gun gangster in one of Hong Kong's "Seven Day" movies – that being the number of days it took to write, cast, shoot and get onto a DVD. She became Donny's main claim on all round coolness. She was the reason he wore the designer suits and she was the reason why everyone wanted him as their legal advisor. This was the dream team. Through her he became embroiled in many lucrative disputes over contracts in the entertainments industry. These guys, he kept thinking, are so lax in their legal arrangements, that they will always get screwed and always need him. Their ignorance was his ticket to a long lucrative career.

His involvement with entertainments' law gave him an excuse to dust off his guitar and at least hang it up in his office as a kind of prop to let his clients know that he knew a bit about the artistic side of things. He was not completely soulless. But the work he did was so dull, nobody could possibly pay him enough. The only way out of having to close-read thousands of pages of ill-conceived contracts and agreements was to become a partner and delegate that to the lower downs. Then he dreamt that by becoming the boss he would give himself some time for his music.

When the firm decided they could do with another partner, they did not consider Donny. Instead they went for someone from outside. The man wore a bowtie, was married to an ex-Miss Taipei, and most importantly, was accompanied by some heavy duty corporate clients, so what other choice could the partners make? It was a business after all. Still, Donny complained that he had been under the delusion that loyalty to the firm counted for something.

"Donny," said his boss, "We have given careful consideration to your status. We have examined your efforts over the years and although we are very satisfied with your diligent work, unfortunately you're just not enthusiastic enough. We don't want someone who thinks this is just a job!"

Donny could not help muttering what Brownie McGhee once said,

> "B'lieve I'm most done travellin',
> Lord at my journey's end,
> I been lookin' for me a good partner,
> but it seem bad luck is my best friend."

That was why Donny began thinking about giving up the law for his guitar. He knew no-one else in Hong Kong would have thought of the semi-literate lines some black guy once sang in Chicago. They would, if they thought at all, have reached out to some Chinese proverb, but the truth was, he did not know any Chinese proverbs. His education had been exclusively English. His father had made sure of that. That was where the money was. And the bit that had been purely a result of his own willpower, was his guitar.

A Cantonese-learning English friend once complained to him about the difficulty of starting up a Cantonese conversation with anyone. Donny told him that there was nothing in Cantonese that could be remotely interesting to his friend. The average Hong Kong person had nothing to talk about; his education was pitiful compared to more developed countries like Singapore and Japan. He just worked, watched stupid TV soap operas featuring Donny's wife, went out to dinner with relatives on Sundays, and went to bed early to get up and go to work again. They did not have any interests outside of that. They had no hobbies and only looked at the pictures in the news papers. If they read any literature it would be Kung Fu Comics. If they listened to music, they probably did not even notice what kind it was or that there were many different kinds. "So do not think you are missing out," he told him. "There is nothing to miss out on and you are better off not mingling with them!"

Donny would call himself a banana except he felt that inside his yellow skin, he was not white, but black. Well, a little bit black. He would not stretch the point too far because being passed over by the law firm filled him with a very Chinese sense of shame.

"Wah, go tell them go to hell!" said Amy, "Branch out on your own. That's how you become partner! First you become rival!"

Donny did not see it like that. He decided that the Devil had been playing with him, preparing him for the realisation of where his true destiny lay.

They call it stormy Monday, yes but Tuesday's just as bad.
Wednesday's even worse, Thursday's awful sad.
The Eagle flies on Friday, Saturday I go out to play,
Sunday I go to church, where I kneel down and pray."

Aaron Thibeaux Walker – T-Bone to his fans – said it all. It was three chords and the truth and nothing but the truth, except of course that Stormy Monday is a notoriously tricky piece featuring ninths rather than the usual blues trick of sevenths. Only a blues man would think that worth mentioning. Or that is, only a certain kind of latter-day blues man would think it worth mentioning. The originals just did what they did and never did go much on giving it too much thought.

"I'm never going to work again," Donny announced to his wife. "From now on, I'm just going to play."

"If you make it pay," she said, thinking this a momentary burst of frustration, "No problem. But…"

And then she began thumbing through his extensive CD collection, all racked up against a whole wall of their apartment.

"Blind Lemon Jefferson, Big Bill Broonzy, Too Tight Henry," she muttered as she ran her fingers along the shelves.

"What are you doing?"

"Where you got Deaf Melon Wong? Where Lame Idiot Wu? Where Dim Sum Chang? No Chinese Blues Singers? Nobody want to hear them?"

"Americans don't want to. There's thousands of home grown blues singers there. There I'd be nobody! But this is Hong Kong! Here I would be someone. People have little choice but to listen to Canto-crap. So why not give them something decent to listen to?"

"Because," Amy pointed out, "This is Hong Kong! You know who live here? Chinese!"

"So? I'm not asking them to think, just sit in a bar, throw some dice, drink some beer, and let me play!"

Amy had to admit that he had a point. Hong Kong worked in a cultural bubble all of its own. Here actresses, as she freely admitted herself, without training or talent could make movies. Singers who could only mime to recordings could become stars. And quite a few famous writers employed others to write for them and nobody cared. As it was, that month she was going to get fifty thousand dollars for a two day shoot and all she would have to do was scream when the demon ripped open her dress and tore her heart out. So maybe a guy who really could play the guitar, could earn something in a place where the money flowed so easily? And, it was not so much that Donny planned to earn a living playing the blues, but more a living running an exclusive club. Clubs, she understood.

Donny wanted Hong Kong to get into the jive of the 1950s Chicago blues clubs. He wanted to give Hong Kong the experience of those dark cellars, where the black guys sang of their women and, in the manner of speech he alarmingly began trying out, "iffen they wuz good they had the meanest of dogs, and iffen they wuz bad, they wuz so bad they wuz good!" If he opened a place like that, conjured up the ghosts, made everyone wear the clothes of the era, tight frocks and baggy suits, and then party all night, he would be the blues man of Hong Kong! He would call himself Donny Blue. There would be no competition. How could he go wrong? He knew all too well how he could go wrong! Hong Kong was such a stuffy place. And bars and clubs were difficult beasts to handle. His wife would be crucial in this enterprise. He would have to make sure that she brought along a few of her associates from the film industry. He would also staff the bar with models between assignments. If that did not assure some good free spending customers, nothing would.

Immediately he found a place and put in a bid for the lease. It was in Mong Kok, what Hong Kongers would call a grass roots area, with massage parlours, mah jong clubs and plenty of cheap restaurants and prostitutes. It was the kind of place, he reasoned, where it did not matter if the music was a bit too loud or the drinkers spilled out onto the road in front of the door. And although the Chinese liked their vice in bright lights with tinsel, Donny would teach them the darker, slower arts, lowering the lights and slowing the tempo so that it shuffled along like an old steam train.

"Not very trendy!" said his wife when she saw it. She could not imagine any of her friends being seen dead in this part of town.

"That's the point," explained Donny, "It'll give it authenticity. The Blues is where the demi-monde meet the fashionable set. It's the dutchess getting screwed by the janitor. It's that kind of thing."

"Maybe better if you do jazz club instead?"

"Nobody likes jazz!"

"More exclusive. Charge more. And do less."

"No, the blues will work for us here. I get the sense that this is a place that needs the blues."

Amy had picked up a few blues lyrics and pointed out that perhaps Hong Kong was not as ready for the blues as he would like it to be. She recalled a certain Brownie McGhee song that went:

"I'm crazy 'bout my whiskey, crazy 'bout my gin
But you know a yellow woman is crazy 'bout outside men
Yellow women's are mean and they're evil, crooked on
                                                every hand
Why don't you take my advice now boys, and be a black
                                                woman's man.

It was a favourite song of Donny's, often brought out as a prelude to sex, proving there were some Hong Kong women who reacted to such music in rather interesting ways. But Donny took her point. The low-brow nature of the area meant he would have to try and find some way of creating a more up-town atmosphere to bring in people with money.

He took the lease and hunted down the few local amateur musicians who played the blues. And for the first month, they played their sets, drank, listened, and had a party. The joint was jumping. It was smoke-laden, crowded, sweaty, had women in tight skirts, slick guys rolling joints, funky guitarists showing off their licks, musclebound drummers giving the skins some stick, and all it lacked were a few blind pianists tapping the ivories with one hand while running crafty fingers up the legs of obliging underage girls. Amy was pleasantly surprised and had to admit that she was wrong and that it was a big hit like their wedding all over again.

"Wah, so many people!" she told him, thinking that he must be pulling in a reasonable amount of money.

"And I can still tell my parents that I'm at the bar!" he joked.

It was a good opening few months but eventually the amateur musicians with their limited repertoires tired of giving each other their support. One can only listen to *Stormy Monday* once a month, no matter how well played. And the glitterati never materialised, despite the sexy bar girls, probably because they owed more to the Mong Kok streets than the cat walks of fashion salons. Worse, as far as Donny was concerned, by the second half of the year, given the shortage of blues singers in Hong Kong, he was reduced to allowing rock bands to take the stage. At this point there came too many frenetic versions of *Born to Be Wild* and *Sunshine of Your Love*.

By then he was not seeing many new faces and seemed to be losing the old ones, especially as the less competent rock bands blitzed the place with interminably long out of tune guitar solos. Then the accounts began showing that the beer sales and cover charges were not covering costs. The bar could not support itself unless it was full for most of the evening. As it was, often the only customers were the band and their personal friends.

Even Amy stopped coming, her enthusiasm for blues guitar having waned long ago. As she ran on the treadmill at the California Gym, her iPod was more likely to be playing Jennifer Lopez than B.B. King. In order to restore her floundering film career she was perfecting a very hard body under the guidance of a personal trainer, whom, she assured Donny, was gay, as evidenced by his habit of patting males on the buttocks as a mode of encouragement. "I do all this for you," she told Donny, "So I have energy to make you feel good."

Donny had to do something to stop the slide and decided to take the music more up-town and jazzy. Although he was not a great jazz fan, he thought that he would attract the high spending designer suits if he got rid of the shabby rock bands. And nothing could clear a room of rockers faster than a chromatic scale.

Donny handed more and more of the management work over to the bar staff and began practicing new pieces. Every week he wanted to impress the customer with a new pyrotechnical display of fretwork. He paid for a bassist and a jazz drummer and rehearsed them in up-tempo, high-precision pieces full of crowd-pleasing moments. He stretched himself, contorting his fingers into configurations that were no longer natural. The devil's music was superficially simple, but buried within its strict formulas was a lawlessness that opened up undreamt of musical worlds but only for those who took the pains to travel in that difficult territory. Donny was ready to break the law and find his own style, even if it meant stretching the definition of the blues into the more dubious territory of jazz. The thought made Donny shudder, but when he found his groove, he knew the bluesmen would have been proud of him and that took away all his uneasiness.

"I want you all now to get together,
I want you all now to take some time,
I want you all to get to know each other,
you can't keep working that daily grind..."

Those were Donny's lyrics. He had written songs before but he had never devoted a whole set to nothing but his own music. It was risky because there was magic in the old tunes and anything new had a habit of leaving puzzled expressions on people's faces, no matter how much it fit in with the old routines. But he ditched the shuffle beat, ditched the twelve-bar, and started introducing something more fashion-model friendly and encouraging to a clientele more inclined to drink cocktails with enormous mark ups on the price. It was the perfect fusion of Hong Kong and The Blues!

He now felt that the club's musical policy was on track, except that he had to play every night and he had to replace amateur enthusiasm with calculated professionalism. He even stopped drinking, just to make sure he only ever hit the most extraordinary notes.

"Oh that's ugly!" yelled the bass player when Donny hit his stride.

The old bluesmen treated their gigs as one long party with sex in the intervals, drink and drugs on the stage, and had an uncanny ability to do without sleep several days in a row. "Woke up in the morning!" sings the bluesman, but Donny began to realise that was a lie. They never woke up in the morning and when he woke at four in the afternoon, he would set to rehearsing and arranging new pieces for the evening's performance. By eight o'clock he would have to check another band and try to negotiate the club's schedules. Then he would check in with the bar's manager and find out the previous evening's takings. Somewhere in there he would try and catch a glimpse of Amy who was complaining that he came home at eight in the morning stinking of smoke and disturbing her sleep, and that was all she ever saw of him.

"Why you say you feel so much better!" she said. "You're worse than you ever were when you worked!"

He noticed Amy now had seven studs in her ear. She seemed to be living a life that he was quite unaware of. And just who she was living it with, he had no idea.

"My baby's sick of me," sang Donny on a BB King kick:
"She wants the doctor in,
but ev'n if she was dying,
I wouldn't let her get no medicine…"

Then the daylight hours began filling in. Those working vampire hours wonder if the daylight people see it as a challenge to them. Outside no road could be repaired without an eight A.M. bout of drilling. No van could be loaded without twelve people yelling and sliding and shutting van doors. And then he would have to visit the accountant. He had to hand-deliver cheques to drinks suppliers who refused to supply him unless he paid in advance.

He had to deal with the repairs to the toilets, and then there was the family who were feeling neglected and wanting to see him. There were weddings to attend, funerals, birthdays, and festivals that ate into the daylight hours that he needed for sleeping and often he would fall asleep at the banquet table. This, he thought, was why there were never any great Chinese guitarists. And normally, if asked to perform at a wedding or birthday, he would have obliged but now he had no patience for that. If they wanted to see him play, he told them, come to the bar! He was there every night!

"You expect them come to bar? You crazy?" said Amy.

"Why not? If I'm supposed to support the family, it should support me in return."

"No! So stupid."

"If I had to cancel meeting the family because I had an important case to deal with, they would think me all the more important. But since I just run a bar, it's always me that has to give up my time for them."

"Your job is to show respect. Why you expect anything from them?"

She was right. The obligation was always from the bottom up. It was why he chose law in the first place. It showed respect for his family's wishes. His father, now retired and spending his time in Macao's Casinos, was muttering how his son had been ruined by his mother's church and music. And his mother was muttering how her son was just like his father, preferring to hang around in bars than do any real work. So why should he expect anything from them when he stopped complying with their wishes?

"R–E–S–P–E–C–T,

find out what it means to me!"

He thought at least the audience at the Blues Bar might give him some respect. He wanted them to idolise him, not just treat him as Donny the lawyer who packed it in to run a bar and play a bit of amateurish guitar. Especially now that he was playing better than ever. But these guys in their designer suits with their designer girl friends thought they had the right to answer their mobile phones while he played.

"It's Hong Kong," the bass player told him.

"Yeah!" the drummer added.

"These bozos here will never appreciate real music," said the bass player.

"Never!" added the drummer.

The bassist knew of an opportunity to tour Japan's clubs where he was sure their blues would be a big hit.

"We are the bomb! I'm telling you!"

"Da Bomb!" agreed the drummer.

Donny was touched by his band's enthusiasm. They were his real family, he thought.

"No," said Amy, "They just some dick heads you pay to play with you. You want a real family? Then we make one. Get you respect then."

How she managed to miss getting pregnant during the following weeks of respect is a mystery. She even consulted a Feng Shui expert who, on seeing the darkened apartment and its mess of tangled wires, microphones, guitars and amplifiers informed her that no child would feel safe surrounded by so many sharp and potentially shocking objects. He even dismissed the boudoir and its red satin sheets and fluffy cushions as too reminiscent of a bordello for an innocent child to conceive of conception. He suggested something more pastel and soothing. What she wore to excite her husband was one thing, but the living environment had to be more like a nursery. This would mean they were serious. "Perhaps," he suggested, "you're more career orientated than homely and that's the problem." It cost her five thousand dollars for that piece of advice.

"Aiyah! Typical man saying it all my fault!" she muttered as she let Donny off the hook that afternoon, thus ending her momentary craving for a child. She had never been that keen, but right then there had been a moment when she wanted to do her family duty. Especially since she had no more offers of any acting jobs.

Donny had no idea what was going through Amy's mind and took the opportunity for a few hours sleep before he got back to the club.

"When you got a good friend," sang Amy, "that will stay right by your side

Give her all of your spare time, try to love and treat her right!"

"What you say?"

"That's what it say on cover of this CD of yours."

"What?"

"Robert Johnson. He sang that."

"Hey, Amy, I've got to be back at the club in an hour. Give me a break will you."

Then his accountant informed him that if he really wanted to make the bar work, he would have to get rid of the music, reduce the staff, add a sports feed for the TV and try to bring in lunch time crowds as well as a solid drinking crowd for the evening. The blues, it seems, did not sell enough beer to pay the rent. In short, he would have to return the bar to the sort of establishment it was before he took it over. It made a steady income in those days.

"It's a very traditional Chinese sort of district," explained his Indian accountant.

"You mean they want traditional football games on the traditional TV while drinking traditional German lager?"

"They want what they want," said his accountant, smiling and shrugging, "A bar's a bar and that's what business is all about. You do whatever makes the money and don't do what doesn't."

"Screw the bar," said the bass player.

"Yeah!" said the drummer, helpfully.

They had worked hard to develop a fiery set and they did not want to lose their guitarist. It was easy to find good guitarists who thought that drummers and bassists were essentially interchangeable idiots, but it was hard to find good guitarists who knew how a band worked and how every note mattered. They were not just backing for Donny's guitar sound, they were the sound! And they wanted to take their up-tempo wide-awake jazz-blues fusion music to a bigger audience. And here was another big plus about working with Donny: he was a lawyer and would not let the band get screwed.

"Make the band the business!" the bass player said succinctly.

Donny made up his mind. He would close the bar and then go on tour.

"You can take a couple of weeks off and join us!" he told his wife, thinking she would approve. She would get to be Rock Chick and the whole nightmare of running the club was out of the way. They would have more time together and could live on the road and be wild and free and forget Hong Kong, forget the whole Chinese family thing, and become real cosmopolitans, rootless in place, but attached to the music, which of course was "The Truth and Nothing But The Truth!"

"Wah, who you think I am?" she said.

She saw herself sitting in some sweaty club until her husband finished his set and then hanging around, looking sexy despite being ignored, while he drank with the band, schmoozed promoters, or crashed out for the rest of the night. Then she would spend a day travelling in a mini-bus with a couple of chain smoking roadies and three snoring musicians. This did not strike her as being any fun at all. It struck her as being demeaning, and besides, she was thirty years old and despite the studs in her ears, she was seriously considering bringing in the decorators and having the whole apartment done out in pastel shades. She was even going to suggest he put all his equipment in storage so that their home looked less like an industrial plant.

"You play guitar so long now and it look more like work than fun. Why not just make the bar earn money and forget the guitar? You don't like the bar no more, then go back to the law!"

"But the band! I can't let them down."

"Screw the band!"

"But the music!"

"It won't miss you."

"Oh babe! Without it, there is nothing going on in my life!"

All blueswomen are called "Babe".

"Where you think you are? Mississippi? Chicago? You think you are Elvis Impersonator? Elvis Wong? You think that funny? Well what difference you?"

"I don't impersonate nobody baby!"

"This is China! Play when you a baby, work when you a man."

"That's almost a song."

"Maybe it should be."

Donny could have pointed out that he did not have the seven studs in the ear, the navel ring, the tattoo, or a string of DVD performances featuring bits of his anatomy. And he did not spend half his time being rubbed down by some expensive clown spouting mumbo jumbo about centring his kundalini. He worked! He created things! He made things happen! He did not just hang around waiting for other people to make things happen. He got organised. He was thorough. He was not lazy. And the only reason she was telling him to grow up was because he now could not afford to pay for her so called career!

Donny woke up in the morning. He had a plane to catch. He was heading to Tokyo to arrange the tour. When he looked at the dining room table he noticed a scribbled note and on closer inspection it was from Amy. Then he recalled that she had not been in the bed when he had crawled in that night. He began to sing as he read the note:

> Just give me one more kiss,
> Just before I go,
> 'Cause when I leave this time
> I won't be back no more."
> The note said, "I'd say go to hell, but you just say cool!

"Cool," growled Donny, reaching for some aspirin. "I just love this girl. Her timing is perfect."

The band naturally commiserated and even more so when he told them that she had cleared out all the joint accounts and a solicitor was advising him to sell the apartment and give her half the proceeds.

"It goes with the job," said Donny, who hoped that having his woman done gone and left him was so bluesy it could only help the music. And there would be other women. Bluesmen were never short of women. What they were short of on his hectic Japan tour, was someone to organise travelling from the hotels to the gigs and set up the equipment. He had hoped that Amy with her talent for taking taxis and bossing people around would take care of that for him. Consequently, it was touch and go whether they would arrive at any venue in a fit state to play. Black coffee and amphetamine fuelled their gigs, not necessarily to the detriment of the music, but definitely to the detriment of Donny's fraught nerves. But that was all part of the job.

An earthquake in Sapporo cut short the tour, but that also went with the job. So did the demands for mortgage repayments and the pile of solicitor's letters from creditors left over from the bar that greeted him when he returned home. And so did the drummer joining a Japanese band doing Beatles covers and the bass player getting a job playing keyboards in a hotel in Phuket for three Filipinas doing Supremes songs. As Donny lay upon the bed now stripped of all bedding, he could not get to sleep. He kept replaying all the music he had played, all the notes he had missed, all the tunes he had half-finished, the riffs he had not yet mastered, the lyrics he had jotted down for later development, and over and over again the music ran in his head. There was no room for anything else. This music was hell and there was nowhere in Hong Kong to go with any of it. If he was ever to pay off his debts, he thought, he really would have to get a job as an Elvis impersonator. There was no market for the blues. If he was to carry on, he would have to accept that every band would be short lived; every new musical outburst would be greeted with enthusiasm by a small number of people who would soon tire and move onto the next thing. Life would be precarious and mostly concerned with playing music that did not move him. He had no home in this world. And the thought of returning to the law made him all the sicker. It was as if nobody wanted him! They just wanted a man in a good suit.

In the middle of the night he phoned up Amy and sang the old Robert Johnson song that he learnt all those years ago into her answering machine:

When you got a good friend
that will stay by your side
Give her all your spare time
Love and treat her right.

He knew she was a sucker for a good song. And he knew no body else would encourage her career like he could, though he could not recall whether she had a career right that moment. For that matter he did not know whether he had a career either, so it only seemed fair.

"I've been writing some songs all about you," he added. "You're what my music's all about."

Now that really is doing the devil's work, he thought. He just hoped his mojo was working and that Amy's personal trainer really was gay, and that there was some glory down this road.

Me and the devil, we're walking side by side.
I'm gonna beat my woman, until I get satisfied.

That was another Robert Johnson song that he knew he would be singing if she did not phone back. The blues covered every possibility. It was all there was. Everything else was just a job, like every woman was just a woman. But he would give Amy one more chance to show she was not like everyone else. He would give Hong Kong one more chance to show it had some soul. Everything, he decided, would have one more chance. And if there were no more chances?

Blues falling down like hail,
and the day keeps worryin' me
There's a hell hound on my trail.

XANADU

India alarmed Joe the moment he trundled his trolley into the chaotic airport arrivals. He imagined a land of poetry and although he did not have great hopes for an international airport, he found the scruffy brown mess of fractious people that descended upon him offering hotels, taxis, luggage handling, money exchange, and demands for charitable donations, instantly disenchanting. He vowed to stay as close to his five-star hotel as possible.

"Hello Mr Lampton," said Krishna, the assistant sent to collect him. "Good flight?"

"Oh yeah. It didn't crash. Always a good sign," said Joe, still confused by the uproar of the arrivals and catching only a good look at the back of Krishna's head as he led the way.

Yes. Always a good sign. You didn't bring your wife? You could go to the Taj Mahal with her once business is done."

"I'm not married."

"Then we'll have to set you up with a fine Indian girl. You will discover that our women are the best. We train them well in the arts of the bedroom."

"Terrifying."

"No, not terrifying! Dangerous! Just what a man wants from a woman."

"I meant it was a terrifying thought having other people set you up with a woman."

"Oh no. We do it all the time in India. Our friends do it. Our cousins do it. Our parents are always doing it. And I tell them, get me a dangerous woman! And they say, huh, you're crazy! And I say, yes! Crazy! A crazy man needs a crazy bitch!"

"I'm not sure I need anything at the moment, other than to get out of this place."

Following Krishna, his head bowed in the hope of avoiding the beggars and free lance baggage handlers, he tried to collect his thoughts about the computer game his company was designing and what he must tell the awaiting meeting. Five hours by plane was nothing to worry about; he had previously done seventeen and still made a conference key note speech. All he had to do today was give a brief morale-boosting introduction to the game concept, a shake of everyone's hands and then sign the contracts.

"Alph is the sacred river that runs through caverns measureless to man down to a sunless sea," explained Joe to Krishna as the private mini-bus that collected them jolted and honked through the swarms of people spilling out over the roads oblivious to the chaotic interweaving trucks and three-wheelers. "And in that deep romantic chasm, which slants down the green hill athwart a cedarn cover, beneath a waning moon, a woman wails for her demon lover."

"A demon lover! Yaar! Now you're talking. Everyone is going to try really hard to get through to that level!"

That was exactly what Joe wanted to hear. He continued: "Alph would begin as the river, and Betty the wailing woman would arouse it so that it must transform into a man."

"Alphabet! I get it boss."

"That's right. And their demon progeny would be Alpha Betty and this would trigger a graphics encounter and the realisation that the copy of Coleridge's poem, Xanadu, on the inside of the packaging, is more than just a piece of literature, it is a hint sheet!"

"Xanadu! Whoa man, I know that one. In Xanadu did Kublai Khan a pleasure dome erect!"

"Well, that's the Frankie Goes To Hollywood version of it," said Joe, "But I think a lot of Indians will know this. They love English literature."

"Do they? Do we?"

"So I'm told."

"We will once we've played this game!"

"Hopefully."

"Cool. You know much Indian literature?"

"How long, how long, in infinite pursuit of this and that endeavour and dispute?"

"What's that?"

"Persian. Omar Khayam. But I suppose that classes as Indian."

"Oh yeah. How about, They beg and they lie and they suck for your vote, but once they're in power they treat you like a goat?"

"I don't know that one."

"Baba Sehgal man! He's a rapper!"

"A rapper. Well. I'll have to look out for him."

"You want to work some of his stuff in there. Make the game really funky."

The goal of Xanadu was to achieve maximum happiness within the confines of Kublai Khan's pleasure dome; and in the end would be the beginning: an exhortation to move away from the computer screen, and bearing in mind the lessons of the game, seduce ones own demon lover.

"Beware! Beware! His flashing eyes! His floating hair! Weave a circle round him thrice, and close your eyes with holy dread! For he on honey-dew hath fed, and drunk the milk of Paradise," quoted Joe when giving the presentation to the Indian programmers. He finished with a flourish, pinning the concept down: "Men quote poetry. Women dance. This is the surest way of everyone getting what everyone wants!"

There was a faint ripple of applause as the audience slowly recognised the quote, or pretended to do so. Everyone could now get down to work, thrash out the details, turn ideas into numbers, and numbers into pictures. Another project would be under steam and Joe would prove to be the man who stepped outside the box and discovered a new genre with a new market. Joe was legendary for his ability to make complicated concepts succeed.

"First class speech, boss," said Krishna, "We've a little entertainment lined up for you now."

"I just want to go back to my hotel."

"Oh yes, you get freshened up. Then I collect you and take you out. All the boys want to meet you in person."

"Do they really?"

"Oh yes, you're their hero. You make it big man. They all want to be like you."

"What? A middle-aged man still playing children's games for a living?"

"But a rich middle-aged man! We can all learn from that."

"There's no poverty in youth."

"Is that another piece of English poetry, boss?"

"Time, the destroyer of worlds, annihilator of all sides. That's definitely Indian."

"You are a walking encyclopaedia of poetry."

"Young men write it, but you get old before you understand it."

"That's why we want to learn from you, boss."

Joe tried to meet Krishna's eyes but Krishna was glancing elsewhere, looking for people in the departing crowd. He waved and gave a mysterious thumbs-up.

"It's all settled. He's cool!" shouted Krishna to nobody that Joe could recognise. Then he patted Joe on the back and pushed him forward ahead of him. "There you go boss. Everyone happy. We get you ready now. We have lots of suggestions to make."

"About what?"

"The game! You need plenty of sex in it but nothing filthy-dirty. A Westerner can show their tits but no Indian woman."

"Nobody shows anything in the game."

"Oh but they should, just not everything. There are ways of conveying wicked and filthy thoughts. This is Bollywood after all."

"The game isn't about wicked filthy thoughts."

"Oh no, of course not. Of course not. Little town fantasies, that's what works here. Work in America too. Sex and shopping. The whole world is the same."

Joe peered out of the grimy window of the Morris Oxford taxi that seemed to him more like a big blue-bottle than a car. It buzzed and dodged in and out of cows, lumbering trucks that belched diesel fumes, dilapidated double decker buses, suicidal bikers, and various dead things. The India of the economic miracle was all very fine but to be part of it was to be marooned amongst this explosion in a rag and bone factory. Bombay in daylight was a sick ensemble of grimy blocks, shabby shack shops, uneven pavements, pot-holes, and the stunning faded glory of old colonial buildings with perfectly manicured patches of greenery amid squalor. And as the light dimmed and the neon advertisement of the new shopping malls began lighting up and the traffic seemed to ease, something magical began to emerge:

the Bollywood imagined by all the dreaming beggars asleep on the piles of discarded film magazines.

"One thing puzzles me boss," said Krishna, "The happiness algorithm is desires obtained divided by desires. So you score highest if you have no desires. Thus, if you have no desire to even play the game, you score infinitely high. Is that what you believe?"

"No. If you have no desire, then you cannot achieve any desire, so the mathematics produces a zero score. Therefore your first step to happiness is to purchase the game."

"Ah," said Krishna, the back of his head rattling above the front seat expressionless, "Cool. Much better than anything the Buddha had to say about it."

"I don't think the Buddha had much to say about computer games."

"Happiness, boss! He said a lot about happiness."

"I'm sure it would make us all happy if people bought the game."

"Oh yes, but people pay good money to hear something more spiritual."

"Well I don't think people will think too closely about the philosophical niceties of the algorithm running the game's scoring system."

"Probably not. You're the one who knows these things."

"That's right."

"Oh yes, you are the expert in games. But India is a big market boss, and, as the HSBC Bank advertisement says, quite poetically I think, a little local knowledge can go a long way."

Joe stepped from the taxi and briefly had to breathe the dank air with its stench of smoke, exhaust fumes, and cooking oil. Krishna quickly whisked him past the jostling shoe-shine boys with scabby lips, runny eyes, and scrawny dirty hands that demanded five dollars for "same colour polish." "Shoes very dirty boss. And I'm very hungry." He was wrestled through a cordon of grizzly-chinned shot-gunned security guards, and then through the glittering hording, flashing with electronic displays of exploding stars and inside one of Mumbai's hottest of hot spots: The Pillhouse, named after Bombay's red light district. A woman in the sheerest of saris, damp with perspiration, a gold tikka upon her forehead, namasted as they entered, the gilt silk wrapped around her body making her look more naked than naked.

Armanied millionaires, nero-jacketed politicians, starlets tightly pinked in pants and transparent high-heels, mingled with the curries, caviar, mountains of pineapples, dates and guavas. The A-list filled the foreground, a private reception taking place in the courtyards trampling over shampooed gravel, watched from a tree by what he thought must be a leper. Joe perked up momentarily; the glitterati without a pen and Philips screwdriver in their shirt pocket looked a little more like a good time and they would surely not want to tell him how he should be doing his job! But Joe was whisked passed them –   "Private   party, don't stare," said Krishna, "Their security will beat you up." His destination was the discothèque inside, at the end of the complex where the wannabe A-list resided for the time being. Here the young dot-com men he employed played.

"Midnight is when the real action starts," said one of the young men who now jostled with Krishna for the pleasure of leading Joe into their world.

Black-faced waiters in starched-white suits silver-trayed purple cocktails to Joe and Krishna. Before them young men in sweat-soaked shirts danced while mango breasted women, draped in red, green, blue chiffon scarves, drank, talked and ignored them. "All these women," explained Krishna, "Want jewels on their fingers, Chanel on their back, Mercedes on their bums, Tigers in their beds and husbands stupid enough to pay for it all."

"Not too many Tigers here then."

"Maybe they find husbands stupid enough to pay for it though."

"Are you stupid enough?"

"First I've got to be rich enough."

The music changed and a thumping bass shook the ground. "They keep party-hopping left and right," barked a rapper, "But they never get to party on a Saturday night!" The men in their sweaty shirts stomped and threw out their arms in LA Gang signs, mouthing the words along with the song. Joe backed himself into a corner which only served to encourage the more earnest of his programmers to step off the dance floor and come forwards with the look of people who had long pondered deep questions.

"In from that chasm, with ceaseless turmoil we see things," quoted Joe, "As if this Earth in fast thick pants were breathing, a mighty fountain momently was forced, amid whose swift half-intermitted burst, huge fragments vaulted like rebounding hail, or chaffy grain beneath the thresher's flail, and 'mid these dancing rocks at once and ever, it flung up momently the sacred river."

"No need to keep working boss!" said Krishna, "We get it. Sacred rivers are big in India. Sacred rivers, fishy women, perpetual virgins, you name it, we got it, so we get it."

"I was referring to the dancing and pointing out the curious aptness of the fantasies of the Lakeland poets in describing the writhings in a Bombay discotheque."

"Oh yes, those Lakeland Poets. Hey, we should teach you the bhangra! Very sexy dance, man. Show off that big chest to all the ladies, yaar..."

Joe grinned and tried to assess if learning the bhangra was better than fending off any more questions.

"He's not married," Krishna told the boys, "So I promised to set him up."

"With someone looking for a rich and stupid husband? Is that it?"

"No boss. You're the Tiger!"

"By midnight," said one of the other young men as he pointed to a dark door at the rear of the club, "All the ladies are like animals out there!"

"Animals?"

"Yaar man, they are on all fours!"

"They get real nasty," said another identical young man-boy, keen to be near the guru of games.

"Nasty?"

"Yeah, man. Anal is the new Oral!"

"You don't talk to the boss like that!" said Krishna, giving the young man a quick slap on the back of his head. A flash of bitten-down fingernails caught Joe's attention. "Anal! New Oral! What is that?"

"That's alright," said Joe, not wanting to be at the heart of an argument. "How's this Bhangra thing go then?"

Joe learnt the Bhangra, not very well, but well enough for everyone to practice their sycophancy on him. Sycophancy was a skill he noted came naturally and perhaps ironically. He could not tell.

"These Punjabi's they got rhythm!" explained Krishna, "All DJ's in Bombay are Punjabi! They mix the discs. They control the flow. They take us up high, then get us real low..."

"That's almost poetry."

"You heard of Baba Sehgal?"

"You mentioned him."

"Hindi Rap, man! First Sikh Rapper. Big star a few years back. An inspiration to us all boss. This is why we get it!"

Krishna grabbed his crutch and ground his hips like his hero from the latest Bollywood movie. "Whoo!" he squealed and licked his crooked lips at a couple of girls oblivious to him. The cocktails seemed to be having an effect upon him.

A strobe light flashed and Joe watched the dancing men, thinking how the droplets of sweat spraying jerkily into the air were like explosions in a comic book. He was forty-two, a significant age for everyone working in the games industry, and everyone in his field of vision seemed to be twenty-two, boundlessly energetic, and hopelessly foolish. That was at least something, he thought.

"One things puzzles me," said one of the gathered programmers, sweat dripping down his arm as he drank from a beer bottle. He looked very earnest and Joe could barely stifle a groan.

"And what puzzles you?" said Joe, weary of these doubts that he detected.

"All this poetry in the game. I mean, it's a role-player and you pick up points interacting with characters. But it's all conversation. And not all very understandable. Too much typing and reading. People just want to click."

"They can click if they want and just watch the graphics."

"Yaar, but they want to click and have things explode, not have some stuffy Englishman spouting stuff. It's so colonial man!"

"Load in the Hindi version then. Have some Indian spouting stuff. We use Bollywood stars to do a local version. And we use some Shanghainese stars to do the Chinese version. And... I don't know, Omar Sharif, if he isn't dead, to do the Egyptian version."

"Things don't explode though."

"It's a dating game! You learn how to pick up women, or you can play it with your spotty, flat-chested and clueless fourteen-year-old girl-friend who wants to be in love!"

"All Indian girls are hot! With enormous tits. And they don't make you work for it!"

"I thought this was the land of double-locked bedrooms, chaperones and virgin middle-managers?"

"No man, that'd be too tragic even for India!"

Joe looked around in the hope of catching Krishna's eye and have him rescue him. At the back of the room, the dark doorway offered a quiet retreat and so he staggered forward, patted a few of the boys on their back, muttered he needed to take a breather. When it was obvious he was moving towards the back room, he could hear grunts of approval.

"Yaar, he's cool," said Krishna, as Joe escaped. "Top of his game, and still hungry. He's the man to beat all right."

Joe immediately felt relief as the temperature dropped and the volume of noise fell to a low thump. Ears numb, he stepped through the door. A mosquito sizzled in a blaze of blue from the ultra-violet insect-catcher. Every sound was muffled; every sight hazy in the smoke of some narcotic. He met a gathering of pot-bellied men in kurta pajama, smelling of turmeric, their greasy fat fingers counting out rolls of high denominational rupees, one eye on the money, another on the interloper, a Westerner, a walking wallet: Joe.

He reeled backwards as a face pushed towards him stinking of bad teeth and purring: "One hundred dollars?"

"I didn't know you had to pay?"

"Of course you pay."

"I haven't got any money on me. I don't carry money," said Joe sensing a hand patting him down.

"Oh man, you gotta pay if you want to play!"

"I'm with those guys out there."

Krishna shouted something from beside the door and that seemed to settle all the payment problems. Then Joe felt a hand pull him down to the ground where in the haze of smoke lay a dark, naked woman, who spooned out florescent white powder onto her stomach, piling it high in her navel. He pulled away and bad breath came to his nostrils again.

"Relax man! Let her do all the work. She's a professional virgin. Everything she offers is pure."

He heard singing. But the song was in a strange language. Even so, he could make out between the cyclical hum of the air-conditioner, the words: "And now 'twas like all instruments, now like a lonely flute, and now it is an angel's song, that makes the heavens be mute..."

"Are you one of those cut'n'paste boys?" whispered a voice in his ear.

He recovered a moment and turned over to wrestle with a red silk cushion, then victorious, he emerged between the oiled thighs of a dark woman with arms full of silvery bangles.

"Here," she said, slipping a silver pipe into Joe's nostril and giving a gentle blow. "Now don't sneeze!"

He held his breathe, his eyes streaming, and his throat numbed.

"Oh Jesus!"

And then all was love and beauty and she was doing all the work, removing his clothes, oozing over his chest, breathing heavily into his ear: "You shag like a porn star," she groaned, her long straight black hair engulfing him. She slid off, propped him up and began fingering dribbling honey-coated pastries into his mouth.

"You American boys must be eating all that growth hormone..."

"English, I'm English actually."

"Oh well, all that dairy cream must give you the edge."

This was obviously the girl that Krishna had fixed him up with.

"One moment in annihiliation's wastes, one moment the well of life to taste, infinitely I would have lived in bliss for taking no more than just a kiss."

"What?"

He could feel the honey dribbling down his chin and then he sensed his head banging up and down on the back seat of a noisy vehicle. He smelt carbon monoxide belching up through the rust holes of the floor and thought he would suffocate until he was being doused in a cold shower wearing nothing but a kurta. For some reason his suit had gone missing.

"You don't marry them," said Krishna. "Not even if they are sweet smelling pregnant virgins."

"I'm not married am I?" came his voice, as if from far away, "Get me her address before it is too late! We have to sort this out."

"Yeah yeah boss. You sleep. We find her tomorrow."

"Tomorrow. Yes. Tomorrow and tomorrow and... I'm not married am I?"

"You said you wanted to marry her."

"Did I? I should marry her…"

"Go to sleep boss."

"I'm a tiger."

"That's right boss."

In the depths of his five-star bed, rocking to the rhythm of trolleys trundling the long corridors, bells on doors ringing, grunts of alarm at his presence, and then mysterious scurryings and doors closing. There was no sense of urgency, just drifting flashes of consciousness, lists of things to do, Alph and Bet slowly calculating all of pi, the number 3.14159265 endlessly lengthening and endlessly fading into nothingness. "A circle, a circle," he muttered as he woke and saw the light through the crack in his curtains and heard the Mumbai cacophony beyond the double-glazing.

He shaved and examined his face in the mirror. He looked as he felt: eyes black, skin pale and liver sick, his hair with more grey than he recalled, and his wardrobe with fewer clothes than he brought, except for the kurta which he slipped on over a pair of jeans, then put on a pair of flip-flops and left his room. In the hotel foyer he stared through the plate glass doors at the mess of yellow air being buffeted by a downfall of July rain.The concierge in his black suit with a white handkerchief in his top pocket fussed over a group of bewildered Germans trying to stop the staff from helping them with their luggage. They feared they would not see it again. Joe stepped around them and went through the revolving doors into the rain where its brown streaks glued his kurta to his skin. He pushed further out into the teeming streets, torrents of filthy water ankle-deep running off the pavements into swirling storm drains. Cars and motorcycles stalled and called forth a plethora of helping hands to push them to the side of the road and keep the world flowing by.

"Five miles meandering with a mazy motion," muttered Joe, "Through wood and dale the sacred river ran. Then reach'd the caverns measureless to man, and sank in tumult to a lifeless ocean."

Joe stepped off the pavement and found the waters swirling about his knees. He would be bound to catch something, he thought, but it was probably too late to worry about that, so a bit of putrid water should not worry him. He waded across the road attracting young men and boys who called out to him.

"Hey Boss, you want to buy a watch? Suit? Carpet? Come to my shop. I give you good discount."

"No, bugger off!"

"I give you bugger off then!"

"I'm not a tourist."

"You need a guide? I speak good English."

"I'm Serbo-Croat. No understand English!"

"You making fun of me boss?"

"Piss off."

Hands grabbed his arms, tugged at his kurta, "Rupee! Rupee!" wined some emaciated child with skinny knocking knees and no face, just two watery eyes and a gaping suppurating hole.

"Piss off!"

Hands thrust bangles, beads, biros, bananas, bicycle mirrors, before his eyes for his purchase. He tried to push them away, the barrier, the bombardment of fleas that infected the tourist. But he was a businessman bringing business not a tourist shopping, and he wanted to avoid the cars and buses that transported him to places full of people he did not want to meet, full of people challenging his ideas and marrying him to what? This place? And now here he was sinking in more people he did not want to meet. He longed for the arms of the dark woman in the dark night, a neon lit night, blackness hiding the squalor, perfume hiding the stench, narcotics drowning the horror of his own existence, the poetry! He longed for the poetry. Had he truly reached the final level and there was nowhere to go? Had his programme ran its course? Had his algorithm produced infinity or zero? Was he a tiger? Where was his demon lover?

A hand grabbed his arm and pulled him through the crowd, miraculously parting, forgetting he existed, melting away into the hubbub of the drowning town.

"Good afternoon boss. I'm here to pick you up and take you to the airport before it is too late."

Joe remembered the flight and suddenly his schedule flashed before his eyes. An umbrella was held above his head as he was led back into the hotel.

"The monsoon is really bad this year boss," said Krishna, "And every year it gets worse. We say we're going to have the drains fixed, have the walkways put in, but in the end nobody takes responsibility in this town."

Krishna shook the umbrella dry, handed it to one of the hotel staff and then began rubbing Joe down with a threadbare towel produced from inside his shirt.

"Good trip? Get all your business done? Everyone happy?"

Joe nodded as the towel whipped about him.

"That woman last night," asked Joe, "You fixed that?"

"What woman?"

Joe tried to focus on Krishna's face: neat black hair, grinning eyes, a slightly ironic turn of fist-cracked lips, long earlobes… unknowable.

"This town's really buzzing," said Krishna, "Next time you come, we'll plan something really special. Something really wild! We'll try get Baba Sehgal to put on a show. Then you can see what a great guy he'd be to do the voice over. And write the copy. Here's a magazine article on him."

Joe gingerly took hold of a crumpled, damp Hindustani magazine featuring a photograph of a fat little man dressed in drag, vaguely reminiscent of Madonna.

"Baba Sehgal is a great admirer of Madonna."

"And 'mid this tumult Kublai heard from afar, ancestral voices prophesying war!"

"What was that boss?"

"Nothing. Just nothing."

"Nothing. Oh, yeah. I get it boss. Now, you get a good rest on your flight. You earned it. Now, it's up to us. Baba Sehgal, he's the man though. He's the man."

SOFT BOILED EGG

The package delivered to Mr Jones David, contained DVDs. He signed for them as David Jones, and the Chinese delivery man read the signature as Jones David, seeing only what he wanted to see and David, long term Hong Kong resident, no longer bothered to correct this all too typical error.

He ripped open the packaging, discovered plastic covers and no labels, and could understand why they had been so cheap. The DVDs he ordered were usually the latest English sitcoms. The jokes nowadays fell flat but he relished the words despite their satirizing a world that he now knew little of. Buried in the boondocks of Shatin City Plaza Three, he buzzed about the six hundred square feet of flattage like a bluebottle in a beer mug – not that one got bluebottles in Hong Kong. He wondered if real life was elsewhere. Maybe Jones David lived it? As David Jones froze in the air-conditioned shopping malls he imagined Jones David, international playboy, living a life of languid elegance featuring French Chateaus, halls of sunlit marble and gold statues, where dinner-jacketed men raised their champagne glasses to the pale totty in the flowing gown and teetering heels. David Jones, school teacher, however had to put up with clanking lifts, brown water out of the shower, bags of rubbish in the corridors, and security grills locked tight before the doors as if they were in a top security prison rather than a housing estate.

"Drama," proclaimed David, "Holds a mirror to the world. Discuss!"

He loved to throw in the word "Discuss." His class were bemused teenage Chinese, whispering to each other hoping one or the other would translate Sir into Cantonese.

"Come on now, this is what we do in school, we discuss things."

This was not what they did in school. They learnt things. Give them a list of facts, or not facts, it mattered little which, and they would recite it.

He had never been particularly racist. When working in a Peckham comprehensive, black, white, Muslim, Jedi, it was all the same to him. Fourteen separate languages were spoken in his London Comprehensive, among them Ethiopian, and he had thought it amazing; such diversity, such a wide range of cultures and experiences to draw upon.

Swapping that for Hong Kong was supposed to be no more than another multi-cultural experience proving his superior liberality, only better. Except David came for the girls, or at least one girl, who happened to be Chinese, and for some reason felt there were more opportunities in Hong Kong. What she meant was there were more relatives in Hong Kong. In the UK she had been an exotic and pugnacious little sex machine. She was living pornography: "Oooh, you gweilo, so big!" He had never been a racially stereotyped sex object before – or any kind of sex object for that matter. It worked for him. He was smitten, and would follow her anywhere. So here he was, in his six hundred square feet with the girl, the four year old daughter, a parade of sisters, brothers, cousins, and other people's babies, while he worked in the local secondary school. And his Porn Queen became Bitch Wife Number One, controlling the bank accounts, doling out the pocket money, plotting school enrolment for the daughter and insisting he give her a son – only now she said: "I'm ready. Be quick." And forgot all the erotic niceties.

They, them, the Chinese, had Shanghaied him, enslaved him, put him to task. He was required to give his genes to the pool and receive nothing in return. The money was slightly more than at home, but a con essentially: living conditions were crap; pensions were non-existent; political rights a joke even for the Chinese. Perhaps in the good old days when the white man ruled, David might have felt some pleasure. His role as devil man or white ghost, depending on who translated "gweilo" for you, would have included a sense of power even if it had only been an illusion. Now, however, he was merely an immigrant, a minority, afforded little respect, given little leeway by a community where multi-culturalism was nothing more than a meaningless bullet point in some Civil Service department's PowerPoint presentation, a left over from British rule and suspiciously a Western plot.

"Wah, you marry dictionary and still speak so bad!" joked his in-laws at his attempts to speak Cantonese. He spoke it as well as they spoke English but they dispirited him. "You become boiled egg now, white outside, yellow inside, ha ha haaa!" The Chinese ended every sentence with an embarrassed giggle... He could not say that. His "Racism Awareness Training", RAT for short, made him say, "The Chinese that I know, end every sentence with an embarrassed giggle."

"Come on! Drama! The mirror reflecting our experiences. Is this true?"

"It like a dream!" came the one quietly mumbled reply. A full ten minutes of coaxing had produced this one short sentence from one shy girl in white socks, spectacles, with a pink Hello Kitty barrette in her hair.

"Very well. Give me examples."

Back in the UK, even among the Chinese in the class, there would have been a fight over this distinction. Someone would have said, "Bollocks". Another would have yelled out that The Matrix – much favoured teen film incomprehensible to adults – was spot on, like we all live in this big computer, programmed to feed the bastards who run the place. Someone would have done some funny voice about having a "cunning plan" – at least they would have ten years ago when the sit-com that that catch phrase came from ran. Now, they would probably be yelling "I'm the only gay in the village," the catch phrase from the latest award winning BBC comedy that David had just caught up with.

Here in Hong Kong, there was silence. "Come on, give me examples of drama as a dream and explain why this is not a reflection of reality and what it is a reflection of?"

"Just a dream, that all."

"Is that all? Then why do people write it? Why do people fight for it? Why are we inspired, enthralled, impassioned by it? Why do we take our identities from it?"

Amidst the deadly silence he slumped down into his chair and muttered, "Why do I waste my life like this?"

"No one go to theatre, no one watch Hong Kong TV, they read only comic book, play only computer game, never get out the shopping mall," explained his wife every three months for the past ten years when this happened, "That all they know about drama."

"They've read Shakespeare! We've just done King Lear!"

"What that got to do with them?"

If the shenanigans over his father-in-law were anything to go by, Lear had everything to do with them! Chinese families, or at least this one, had rapacious daughters plotting the plundering of the estate, charting the insanity of the old man, and with true filial piety, making sure that he got his portion of salty cholesterol laden soups every day.

"He's an old man," they told the mother, "We need to make sure we all get a fair share."

The sons plotted too, and the sons of the other "wife", and then the "uncles" of the home village waited to pillage the old man's clan-assigned properties.

If none of this was Lear then what was? But they would not see, they would not make the leap of imagination, and he did not know whether he should care. But it would make his work less dull if they took to Shakespeare, though in Hong Kong nobody believed work should be interesting. In fact, why should anything be interesting? East met West and, as his wife might have said while in London studying for a degree in mathematics, cancelled the terms. She never finished that degree, swapping to an accountancy course after the first year.

"You work, make money," said his wife, unable to understand his dissatisfaction.

"Stay after class," he demanded of the one person who attempted to answer his unanswerable question. This proved that to answer a question was to court disaster; the gods would notice you and you would be in trouble.

"I just want to give you this," he explained, hoping the gesture would encourage her, "You might find it interesting: English comedy show. Next lesson we are going to discuss the difference between Comedy and Drama. So here's something funny to watch. And you can tell us all about it."

Sue Peng, Little Peng as the Cantonese had it, seemed to regard it as punishment rather than preferred treatment. It was contamination. But then that was what education was all about: contamination. They were to be contaminated with English, prepared for a world dominated by Chinese forced to pay lip service to the need for dialogue with the powerful neighbour across the Pacific, which in reality they could ignore.

The weekend came with its usual hectic lull. A list of chores was handed to David: go to their parking garage – which of course was no where near the apartment – and get the people mover; use it to pick up two sisters, one brother, the mother; then ferry all of them over to the hospital where Old Wong lay – gagga at sixty-five, a stroke having rendered him incoherent, though, so his family worried, not enough to stop him from moving money to the various overseas accounts that his "other wife" had access to. Nobody had actually met the second wife, but she was believed to have an apartment in Shenzhen. David thought there was probably a very cheap prostitute, if not several, that saw to Old Wong's needs, but Wong found it more prestigious to let everyone believe in the "other wife". It made him a big man.

While the horde spent their time attempting to get the old guy to sign a contract, David was to deliver everyone's children to the various piano teachers, maths crammers, and language schools that every three to four year old needed if they stood a chance of enrolment at a convenient school. All the dull faces that stumbled through David's classes had been pre-educated like this, though David rather considered it more an inoculation than an education.

"Let them play, let them have fun," said David.

"No time," said his wife. "Can play have fun when they got money and no responsibility."

"Like your father?"

"He selfish man. Never had education. That why we still have to work so hard."

David never tired of wondering on just how many levels his wife totally misunderstood him. He dreamed of being like his father in-law, but knew that one step in that direction would also land him in a hospital bed, murdered by dimsum, or worse, stripped of all assets, and cast out without any idea where the money was hidden.

If he gave her a son then perhaps, stud duties performed, he would be allowed a little slack. She would lavish her attentions on the boy, beat him into submission and make it impossible for him to forget his old mother and leave her destitute. David could then make more visits home to wallow in the conviviality of The Pub and its endless attack on New Labour, the death of English league football, and the bloody Americans.

"You can never go home," she told him.

"But you came home!"

"I come home and they say I'm false Chinese."

"False Chinese?"

"And you now a boiled egg. No-one back home interested in you. They think you been in coma for ten year."

"I have been!"

"Then what they think of me, coming back here, going back there, and you want Children be like that?"

Contaminated: the dirty little secret of the gweilo is that he, or she, too is contaminated. Diversity of experience has turned to perversity. What was so exhilarating has become exhausting.

"Chart say I'm ready. Rush back this lunch time."

"O, horrible! O, horrible! Most horrible!"

"What you say?"

"Hamlet's father."

"What that got to do with making a son?"

"Sorry. Mind elsewhere."

"You hear what I say then?"

"Oh yes. Lunch time shag. It's in my palm pilot."

The class were laughing when Sir walked in. And they did not quieten; restless and evil. A little more like those English comprehensive pupils he now thought of as lively and enquiring. Suddenly he recalled why he really escaped to Hong Kong.

"So, I see you are all prepared for our discussion?"

Sue Peng was not there. He was counting on her.

"And Miss Peng is where?"

More giggles, more whispers.

"Come on now! Tell me where she is? She hasn't ducked out of this class because I gave her an assignment? Is that it? Is that it? What on earth is wrong with you people?"

He nearly said, "You Chinese!"

"Are you a Gay Lou, sir?"

"What?"

The similarity between "gweilo", the tiresome name of the Westerner, and "gaylo", the not so Cantonese slang for homosexual, never failed to fascinate the teenage mind. Every year someone would crack this joke.

"Is this part of our discussion on humour?"

More sniggers.

Aah, thought David. He knew the source of the current line of thinking, the catch phrase: "The only gay in the village."

"Excellent. I see you have been studying the source materials. In English we call this kind of humour, camp. It has a long and honourable tradition. Just as Chinese Drama required men to play the women's roles, so did English drama. The first Juliet was a boy. Though one should not rush to announce As You Like It a Camp Comedy..."

David looked at the fidgeting, bored, uneasy children. He had enjoyed himself for a moment.

"But of course, all this is a bit complicated for you to understand. So, you tell me the difference between comedy and drama?"

A long fidgety silence was followed by a spotty boy, yawning and murmuring: "Comedy is funny. Drama isn't."

David wrote that down on the board and waited as the class pulled out their notebooks.

"And comedy is funny because: one, it has jokes; two, outrageous characters; three, absurd situations..."

Lunch time, he rushed home.

"Hurry up, trousers off," she said, as he came through the door. "Not got long."

"I can't just do it! I have to gather my mental imagery, summon the whores in fishnets, picture the welts of the whips across the slut's back... "

"I thought of that."

She picked up the remote control of the DVD player, hit play, dropped her pants and got down on all fours in front of the TV.

"You can see screen from there. Come on. Must be back at work in half hour."

The theme tune of the latest award winning comedy from the BBC, began to play. "You see," said fat little bald albino comedian, as the theme music subsided, "I'm the only gay in the village." The laughter track cackled insanely at such wit and

David lost all interest in his wife's rump as he wondered what had become of the pornographic DVD she had ordered.

Disgrace beckoned, and he rather welcomed it. He could be drummed out of Hong Kong as a supplier of pornography to children. It did not have the kudos of deportation because of political activism but it would make it impossible for him to stay in Hong Kong. Perhaps a comic memoir of his days corrupting youth could make him a celebrity? Everything was an opportunity if it did not kill you. That was his motto.

"You finish?"

"I haven't even started yet!"

"Wah, you useless. I got no time. You better be back early tonight before everyone home."

"Can I go then?"

"No use you staying here."

It was strangely liberating to return to work where, Adolf, the headmaster, Adolf Cheng, was waiting to see him. He asked David about the rumour that he was distributing gay pornography. There had been a complaint from the parents of Sue Peng.

"Gay pornography?"

"A lot of naked men."

"All a misunderstanding," he improvised, wondering if his wife, in all her Chinese perversity, had imagined that filling his head full of erect penises would somehow improve her chances of a boy, "I passed on a British sit-com for them to look at as part of our discussion of the differences between drama and comedy. Apparently there were a few off colour jokes that would probably have been bleeped out on local TV..."

"Comedy?"

"Oh yes. You know, Full Monty sort of stuff. Very famous British Comedy film about male strippers."

"Wah," said the Headmaster, "You not suppose to be funny. Just do the course work."

"It is relevant."

"No. Humour not good for the classroom. If her parents understood English, we would all be in real trouble. I tell them you probably buy pirate DVD and didn't know real content. Next time you only give them serious homework."

"They believe you?"

"Of course they believe me, I'm Headmaster!"

How disappointing, he thought, that the Chinese respect for authority meant that he could get away with anything short of buggering Adolf. But even that could not be counted on. He would probably end up deputy head.

"You stupid trying to impress little girls!" said his wife.

"I was not trying to impress anyone."

"And you succeed."

"I was broadening the curriculum."

"And they think you want to get in pants of their daughter."

"On the contrary they think I don't."

"Maybe that why you not have son. Not enough hormone."

"I have hormone." (How easy it is to slip into the pigeon of everyday.) "But not enough Whore Moans!" he added, just to assert his right of native speakers to word play.

His wife, Plum Blossom Jones, now standing before an altar to Guanyin and a sepia print of Whitby purchased while visiting his ancestral village in Yorkshire, had a sudden flash of inspiration.

"Ooh," she said, "You get big pocket money this week."

This was a new one.

"Carry on," he said.

"I pay you good price."

"Uh huh…"

"Money back if not satisfy though."

There was no turning back now. A private account for secret liaisons across the border in ShenZhen – he could get the address from his father-in-law – then he would not be just a gweilo, but a Feijai, a playboy, a big man – it beat a wet Sunday afternoon in Peckham. As he wife unzipped his trousers, he could feel Hong Kong tightening its grip on him.

A TOUCH COLD

Ah, he was a quare fellow ol' Micky was. There was the Big Fella on the top bunk bemoanin' a head from the night before an' a shiverin' under his blanket as the wind ripped in through the sky-light. I told him the top one would be nearer the cold but he said the heat from me breath an' the heat from all the udder fellas feet would rise like it was a swedish sauna full of steaming blondes. An' in walked Micky to this, bringin' from the outside a sharp blast of cold. He smiled like a dement on comin' in an' everyone thought he was deranged but when he talked all the boyos listened.

Micky looked at the Big Fella and seed the top bunk there. He said he'd like a place with a view an' gives the Big Fella such an icey stare he shivers like he never shivered no matter how icey that wind.

Now you don't turf the Big Fella out of nowhere. An' remember that the last fella had that top bunk died in his sleep for no reason. No reason udder than the Big Fella wanted it. But Micky gave him the smile an' looked frail an' simple an' the Big Fella just got on down an' stood back dropping to the floor the half brick he'd ready to brain ol' Micky with. I guess he was too surprised to do it.

Micky wheezed like it was his dying breath as he climbed the bunk an' looked round at us all cramped together an' pressed against the crumbling walls. All of us but Micky Boy rattled with a blast of the cold. The sky-light again, at first I thought, but I looks at the old man's clothes an' there they are, icicles, a hangin' off him. His face was an ash blue an' cold was oozin' from him like morning mist from the bogs. I decided to keep me distance 'cause when that cold gets into you, you just can't shake it off.

For a while me an' the udder fellas huddles in the corner by an old plywood tea-chest where stood the primus stove we used to cook what food we could get. But then the oil ran out an' the

Big Fella breaks out his last dregs of whisky. Now dere was one t'ing 'bout the Big Fella, for all the bad feelin', an' anger, an' cursin' in him; when the cold was on you, he'd give you his last drop o' the hard stuff to keep it out.

But the last drop is never enough and I went across the road to the King's Head to watch the people who live in the cozy world. I sat there with me black stout an' watched the decent people, wonderin' where I went wrong an' feelin' the chill creepin' like maggots deep in me, right between the blades. I'd breathed in too much of Micky's air I thought.

I'd once gone for a change of air taking the dust-cart to the countryside tip. Thought I'd get away from all this, escape those I was jealous of an' those I got sozzled with. You know, a better life an' all that; but no sooner was I out in the country then I found meself wanderin' back an lookin' for a bunk.

After chuckin' out time, I finds all the fellas suppin' their soup an' biscuits an' no-one speakin'. So I asked Micky where he's from an' he says the country-side but before I pumps him for more talk, in walks the Big Fella as drunk as a snowflake an' spoilin' for a fight. I stepped back from Micky thinking that the so an' so who took the Big Fella's bunk would be gettin' it this time but the Big Fella is shoutin' an' gettin' at us for not makin' Micky feel at home. Micky smiles that crazy smile an' the Big Fella goes as quiet as a corpse an' Micky brings out a crumpled soggy bag o' fruit he says he found. So there he was, the Big Fella munchin' a mouldy apple as happy as a sweepstake winner sayin' Micky's just like the ol' fella that died.

In the mornin' greyness I'm not feelin' meself an' in the blurr of that damp cold day I seed Micky sat writin' in some faded exercise book an' seed he's fixed up the sky-light with some black sticky tape an' stuck yellowing newspapers all over it. He seed me an' smiled demented like, an' asked me 'bout meself, but there's nothin' much to tell him so I sits and watches a while. I noticed the torn picture of a sunflower he's stuck over the bare bricks of the wall an' I tell him that's the way to live, a soakin' up all the beautiful sunlight an' planted deep in the soil. "Roots man", I said, "Roots!" He just laughs and smiles toothlessly an' so I told him that when the summer comes I'm takin' a job on the motorways an' gettin' set on me feet again. I tells him I'm knockin' drink on the head an' he smiles an' says he wants to go to the pub, his voice thin an' distant.

So we went to the Kings Head an' I pointed out to him all the flash cars an' double flash houses on the way an'pointed out all the greenhouses at the back, all just waiting for the sun. That kind of makes me sad though 'cause I didn't really make much of a go of livin' in the country.

When we got into the pub I looked at Micky Boy an' he somehow didn't fit in. That crazy look in his eyes made everyone stare.

There's me corner an' I went an' took him to it an' over comes whithered black-eyed Rosy, her eyes sinkin' more every time I seed her, an' she brings the grog, but this time she don't stay, she just shivers an' goes. Micky Boy sat with nothin' in front o' him but his cloudy breath. I was blessed if I was goin' to buy him one on the basis of such a short acquaintance, an' so to try take his mind off it I told him of the dead man used to sleep in his bunk. This cheers him up an' he tells me how he used to be a teacher but no-one listened to him which is just as well 'cause they'd have probably all ended up like him. He laughed at that an' his breath hit me round the neck like a draft under a door. A fly could have skated on me pint afterwards.

A few days later Micky was all over the place recitin' poetry an' cookin' us all egg an' bacon in a black fryin' pan bought after he'd recited in the Kings Head an' they'd taken a collection to get shot of him. I seed the Big Fella prickin' up his ears a hearin' the poetry an' he eggs Micky on to say more an' says it takes him back. An' Micky he's a writin' them all over the walls whenever he says he's the inspiration. There was a darlin' one but I've no head rememberin' things but it went somethin' like 'Half a league, half a league, rode the six hundred', or somethin' or other. I've never heard nothin' like it. He could have been a professional could Micky. They just streamed out o' him like a dose of curry after a dog of a night.

Micky cleared out some musty rags, makin' room to set up a scorched table in the corner, for us to play cards. He'd knocked on all the doors a couple of streets away askin' for old tables until he got one that's been burnt by a solderin' iron. The cheek of a flea had the man. But even so the udder fellas they didn't like him, they all thought he was cracked and that freeze he took with him an' that smile, never did nothin' to help his popularity, But they went along with the cards an' food.

One night Micky shows me this crumpled picture of himself in cap an' gown but I couldn't recognise him. I guess it was so old. An' the fella also told me he wrote a play with two tramps who sat about doin' nothin'. An' they were the heroes! Micky had some funny ideas. But the Big Fella hears all this an' he likes the idea an' gets angry that no-one gave Micky his just desserts an' then he comes over in a cold sweat an' shakes an' shivers like a frightened dog. Micky put the Big Fella to bed an' started slapping stinkin' wet-sock-poultices on his head an' makin' him greasy green broths rank as hell.

This was goin' on for days an' the udder fellas they made fun of Micky an' tore his poems from his exercise book an' scribbled in crayon over his writin' on the walls. I noticed then how different Micky's clothes were. They weren't like mine and the others, but more like a schoolteachers only shabbier. An' when I think on it, Micky never drank, not even when the Big Fella offered him one, an' no-one refuses the Big Fella, but then I was no fightin' man those days.

So after the Big Fella got sick an' stayed that way, me an' Micky sat recitin' to the Big Fella an the Big Fella lyin' back weepin' for more poems an' givin' all his whisky to me, lookin' each time at the bottle as if it was exposin' itself to him an' he was a virgin never seein' such a horrible sight before. He said to me, the Big Fella, "I've a terrible feelin' like stainless steel slidin' through me spinal column, an' a numbness in me fair turnin' me brittle, fit to snap at dawn with the frost." An' he calls out then for Micky's cellaphane voice.

On good days we carried the Big Fella to the Kings Head but it's no fun as Micky don't bother with me, only entertainin' the Big Fella. An' Micky, he could be real entertainin' with his singin' an' recitin', but all the regulars hated him, always givin' him a whip round and tellin' him to clear off.

One night we took back the Big Fella an' he was bad, a shakin' an cryin', sayin' the wind is gettin' in on him and his bowels have iced up. I thought it's best gettin' in the Doc to stick him somethin', but when the Doc comes, dressed like Lord Muck, the Big Fella won't have nothin' doin' with him an' calls only for Micky. All the udder fellas they feel the Big Fella should have the Doc but Micky says nothin', just smiles an' so the Big Fella tells the Doc to go an' he checks his watch an' does so, not really wantin' to be among us anyway.

However the Big Fella got through the winter, the worse of it; an' I, with a reference Micky, wrote, got me motorway job. So for the last time we went for a drink at the King's Head, no ice on the road crossin' an' a clear blue sky. Me an the Big Fella got a right skinful on us an' we started singin'and sayin' the poems along with Micky Boy. An' Micky Boy he seemed drunk too, though he never touched a drop. We heard the dustcart rumble up like thunder an' I says let's all go into the country on this fine spring day, although it wasn't spring yet, but it felt like it. So we climbed on the back of the cart when the binmen weren't a looking an' it moved off.

The sun was bright an' the air was fresh even though we were on a gluttonous dustcart, an' even the birds were singin'. The shadows of all the comfy houses were black an' sharp an' we passed a policeman an' waved an' shouted at him. He smiled too, his face swelling up, eyes glazin', gums gleamin', like Micky's. Then we went down the posh rows, like through a foreign land. We hadn't seen nothin' like this all winter, never venturin' so far. "Nothin' in those houses", whispered the Big Fella, "Is as beautiful as a poem of Micky Boy's". An' the Big Fella lies back to listen to Micky talkin' of the time we had an' the snowballs, snowmen, sledgin', an' the Christmas feast, as though it had all happened. An' it had happened, but a long time ago, long before I met Micky and the Big Fella.

Then I noticed the Big Fella, he looked all grey lyin' there amongst the rubbish an' I worries an' feels him. He was cold. An' he was real stiff too. So when the cart stopped, me an' Micky leapt off to tell the driver to take him to hospital but the cart drove on an' left us standin' at the traffic lights wavin' an' shoutin' with the cars tootin' an' bippin' us as though we were kids just havin' the crack. Then the traffic dashes between me an' Micky like old Mo' an' the Red Sea an' I was stuck on the island but when the lights changed to stop an' I could see across the road there's no Micky. He's gone. Then the lights changed an' the traffic went an' everythin' was silent. Nothin' moved but dust as if it were sea mist, leavin' me boots grey.

I walked back hopin' to find Micky but there's no-one about an' everythin's closed an' not even the mad policeman was there to be found. An' then I walked past the nice people's houses an' the Kings Head an' that's closed too, an' I stood by the scaffolded hostel feelin' like a peelin' poster on a demolition site fence, an' wonderin' whether to go in. But somehow I was ready for somethin'. I don't know what, but there was a different kind of coldness in me an' there was no more hurtin' there, only anger an' I was ready for anythin', an' spoilin' for a fight.

ANCHORITE

Last brick in place just a hole for the food to come in waste to go out light for day dark for night pallet on floor kneel during day lie during the night notebook and pencil to record thoughts all I need for the soul of a righteous man is the throne of God concentrate on what is important nothing will distract world of temptations strange that world made that way test of our rectitude.

What is temptation and what is not hard to tell guides written in scriptures handed down by tradition spoken by authority hard to interpret must concentrate consider all possibilities.

We are imperfect will be forgiven though why we were made imperfect why we have to be tested why the world was strewn with traps hard to say would be cruel hateful some times the father must chastise the child but should he torment the child first then chastise it for its being tormented hope to find the answers to these questions.

In the night a dream devil said leave said beg to be let out but I stated in my contract should I beg to leave it will be the devil not me I am glad the struggle has begun so soon.

Asked the Devil why he punishes evil if he is the enemy of God stupid question for how can one get the correct answer from the Devil will tell you anything whereas God will tell you nothing he is not a whisper not a voice nearer than ones own soul made from the very substance of God known without voice if one lets it be known.

Patience is necessary in ones vow for in that one shall keep ones soul.

Many demons only one entity divine indivisible has become flesh as the son not the father saints are not gods have the essence of the holy live forever plead our case.

Fear I know so little might commit great error best not to think simply obey do what betters tell us though they can be false too lead us into error but it is error to question error not to.

Must sacrifice the body if need so martyr ourselves others will follow ask the question whether right or wrong question whether vanity though vanity and sincerity not tests of truth tests of character.

To be correct and vain fate worse than any other revels in adulation truly beyond reproach if one allows others to steal the acclaim all such benefits in this world heaped upon them will be taken in next all the more painful.

Seek a vision to confirm for all that next world is true though confirmation may itself be devil in disguise and believe is the test without confirmation a torture beyond which may also be a desire to establish by contrast the greater glory and glory seeking is vanity.

It is these confusions I fear are errors should eradicate them for God made us loves us keeps and if a wretch like me can be made aware others will be blessed.

Only the devil seems to know I am here I am not safe there is no safety that is safe to be safe is to be lost that is attachment not good for all is impermanent forever lost life everlasting ever after all there is never life before.

Those who say it is wrong are idolatrous with gods as statues where our statues are but saints the Holy Mother Son of God all cycles forever how can we be certain?

I age for certain but no certainty thought it would increase without distraction vanity to wonder how I look it matters not how I look will forget how I looked.

My hands are not clean so much dirt comes in through the holes unless I am dirt I am dust corrupt evil what I see in the dark maybe uncertainty for certain are these my wounds my sufferings my signs growing fingernails that I bite and chew my wounds I do to myself out of vanity to become symbol evoke faith in others it is vain must be hidden away forgotten it is all for me this hellish privilege will save only me not what I intended.

Waking in the night do not know which night mark my days by entries here I fear making entries all errors not the thing my thoughts about the thing lead me to errors have no one to judge do not trust own judgement one word a day all I can trust one true word a day and aeons fall between.

Perhaps it is trust in my judgement I seek do not know hope for enlightenment know poverty lack of attachment to world is path reduce you to nothing but fear and helplessness.

Not poor not unattached am fed should starve to enlightenment what that is do not know allowed this because did not know because asked too much because only one authority could trust would be met here should be release from prison of existence not unlike prisons of world where men become angry bitter know only fear isolation and escape for home live in nightmares hoping to be home knowing no home cannot go back in their eyes what God must see feel for our suffering is his made by him suffers as his creation suffers as his creation is of him but not him.

Euphoria happiness ecstasy in the light of the Lord desire by other means desire not to have desire is desire and lust not far from being desire and desire not far from being lust meaningless here no worse than anything else created for us stolen by us a forbidden fruit in the garden offered in paradise this lust for enlightenment this desire to bask in the glory the light the virgins the music only in Hell lust is denied pleasure is denied.

Pleasure a distraction from power glory truth ask so much answered so little sacrifice so much but should not feel the sacrifice that is attachment vanity a claim on specialness we are nothing special humility saving grace.

All every little thing special looked upon not a soul unaccounted for folly to think one can ever know the truth be at one with the all powerful all seeing all knowing eye the minds eye ego's eye therefore false for there can be no ego.

All feelings that saints and wise men claim to be bliss but lust even lust for pain suffering is but lust am straying into error upon error wonder why so hard for me so easy for unquestioning others who will die for this kill for this care not for thought only what moves their heart their passions they know to be right all seems so wrong.

My plate is empty have I eaten was it ever filled is not clean dry stuck with crust of dried juice licked to see and there it is the faint flavour lust after more not what should be happening should be taken from me cried out in the night one night long time ago perhaps they should not feed me let me fast then return with small tasteless morsels sustain me not enough to satiate me satisfy me be forever hungry help one strive to achieve ultimate goal without need of temporal things of dead animals to sustain us but then these others were there for us look like they feel must be the devils work came as a snake not a temptress normally not condemned as some beasts cloven hoofed beasts evil beasts too were made part of everything the scheme the plan the will the intention beyond my comprehension in error again.

They have changed my carers they do not whisper my name glance by the hole in the wall a brief shadow then go cannot know if they even remember I am here I should not care I required this needed it have it am grateful for my errors will not harm them.

This may be some time since my last entry it is a day in the book time stretches contracts mark it by the entries mark it by the food trays told them to send them at irregular intervals so that I do not count on them so that the fear of absolute poverty of starvation of being totally alone will help me concentrate on what is left the only truth.

They might have accepted that it was the devil that spoke told them not to trust what I said suddenly they trusted they too are controlled by the devil maybe God who created everything his jailor there to punish the evil have said this before or thereabouts have no new thoughts thankfully hungry read the last words those are the devils not mine surely not mine hunger is a taskmaster whipping me on only the one thought whereas his son took away everyone else's sins he only took away my last meal.

No new thoughts the end is obtaining absolute wisdom oneness knowledge time unchanging timeless truth same forever only here do things change in an instant forever the truth the lack of truth consistency ever ongoing process that scientists speak of the reiterations cascades of numbers energies that can do nothing but burst into flame again and again rumble on thunderously forever into the cold flat empty black light of no time no place until mind comprehends then what light snuffs out again awake in the dark again sleep in the light?

A noise pulsing blood in my own veins the drains of the monastery remember where they are should have chosen to be blindfolded taken somewhere unknown maybe I was I am dreaming but kidnapped held hostage forgotten details the pain too great so here with the scriptures only in them longing and struggle and war and plague but a shadow of the true book written in God's mind unquestionable by those who have no authority to question it but it will yield the answer reveal secrets yet it has not.

Prayers silent whispering words become nothing fall asleep am asleep have always been asleep wonder in the darkness if I ever awake did not feel that I could be unless at one with everything.

This was more than for myself was wrong selfish no compassion accuse myself judge myself judge those who bring me my tray those who do not bring me my tray should leave judging to others should but kneel and wish for better things for everyone for that is what all the prayers in the world sound like wishes for better things for health wealth pain free days not to be forsaken left without hope yet it all seems more hopeless relying on prayers cook my own dinner if I did not have others to rely on who are not there any more do not listen to my prayers.

Had to count the entries felt a need so few dreamt I had made many perhaps someone comes in my sleep takes them away removes the errors leaves only the errors for me to correct cannot correct them they take my corrected errors away for they too are errors do they remove the errors or leave the errors do they know which is which why do they not tell me?

I am thankful they are considering me enough to remove the errors of my ways cannot be alone whether they are there or not should not leave me alone here one should find all that one truly needs in the air they would have me breathe despite it not being what I would call air.

Been looking for my pencil for some time do not know how I lost it for when I found it was where I must have put it in the dark again miss the light always seems dark try to stay awake for the light then it comes but the light will go as the dark will my thoughts run away from me.

Noticed confusion wonder if in confusion the thing I seek speaks why it should speak I do not know speak or give visions is not all the world can be not all the all of creation can be must be something beyond in the numbers count my days they are my days.

This is wrong should have no attachments to time or place have been writing Day when it was Night not correct what I seek is truth reality then does it matter if it is light or dark am no longer attached to such things might be good but attachment to non-attachment is attachment the same attachment I must not exist must let what it is be what it is must accept the darkness the last brick in the wall the last sound the end of it all building on the bridge of the world when all else is unknown.

Do not know the words that are words that are but sounds that are no sounds that are merely written privilege given to written words is wrong and to be spoken is wrong and to all sounds all sights but this is wrong and being is incommunicable making progress in the dark in the night in the day without voice without opening of lips directly to the soul.

Pencil worn out finished one word one year one year ten years no word good enough no mark blank black sheet forever no more one more one more truth lie know not good enough never enough never sharper always blunter one sharp stab forever blunter snapping shaving till gone forever no marker to mark with.

ENTROPY MEANT TO BE

I knew young Bob Pynchon when I was a kid. We called him Bob because it was short for Tom. We didn't know any better. It was just after he published his story Entropy. Everybody thought he knew what he was talking about but it was all in the title, the "what" that he knew that others thought he knew was a lot but was nothing. Or something.

Clint on the other hand had been no youngster when he first came across the octopus that glowed in the presence of a missile strike. He thought it was cool. Plenty of time to duck 'n cover. BBQ'd, he thought it gave him the same powers. He played misty on the ukelele after sucking it off the stick. It was his inspiration. Screw all that Rawhide shit, let's get into the movies before it's too late. So when he heard I'd met Bob, he noted it down, filed it in his sock drawer and fifty years later gave me a call growling, "Get that son of a bitch, we gonna make a movie."

He decided to make it in Japanese because hey, nobody would know the difference. There was always something Anime about Bob. Just take a few glimpses. A monster streaks across the sky and the sub-clauses pile on as it reeks its message of curling smoke making those names that sell the toothpaste, cue for a jingle of the tingle tongue taste fresh as mountain stream after a case of never alone with a strand, though woodbine was most likely preferred. Those were the days when "Hello Kitty," meant Sherrif Dillon wanted a blow job. And Bob was a sailor, so one thought, though in reality Bob was a mechanic in a hot rod speedshop, all crewcut and red neck, an oily rag and a college football shirt giving one for the old gipper.

I met him when he was twelve with a superman comic in his pants running around with a cape and making his magic creature call that seemed to sound like the leader of a north Korean communist dynasty. His jokes were always with himself. There was no pushing it out, tongue in the cheek, how's your pussy missus, like a cheep vaudeville clown off the slummy back streets of thirties London. Which is just as well as Clint, like Margaret Dumont with the naked Marx boys, would never have got that. Though apparently they gang banged her in a train. "I've never been so insulted in my life!" "Well, just stick around some more!" What Bob did get was the mystery, the man with no face, riding into town with mad cap bag full of rantings and raving calling down doom gloom and the apocalypse: an Elmer Gantry with Eng. Lit. in his GI Bill knapsack. It was all hysteria. Roofs fell in. Missiles zoomed across the universe, OM! Nothing will change his world but a quick hunt for nothing, no motive, only motivation, robotic, pre-programmed. That was the essence of Bob, or Trebor as his permanent pack of mints to disguise the alcohol stench from his parents would have it. Trebor became Tobor, the first cinematic Robot with a heart of gold. Hence Rob, Bob, not Tom. Tobor was a great Saturday morning picture house favourite among the Batman serials where the guy always jumped out of the car you saw falling over the cliff the previous week. Trebor walking backwards for longevity calibrating the frequency German submarines communicated at, was never fooled. He noted it down and phoned it through to Mr V-V-Vonnegut.

So did Clint and now he had the money, he wanted in. What a wheeze to film the unfilmable, to create the events that slide by with each sentence, a film stunt in itself. He would use a big close up on the pen as it was all written long hand in a cold water apartment on the East Side somewhere because it is always the East Side and it is always some dingy little apartment somewhere where the artist is supposed to discover themselves and then be miraculously found. The truth of course is that he stank of money and paid the unpublishing house to take him off their list and let the New York socialites promote him and bribe all the academics of UCLA to write PhD thesis on the deathwish mechanoids of Manchuria, all made of Bakelite.

Clint loves Bakelite as well. He would use no other telephone but the Bakelite bone if he could, cheroot in mouth, chewing the backy and swallowing instead of spitting. Which of course means there is gonna be one hell of a bit of day making trouble. You don't get no tougher. All an act of course. He watched it backwards in the editing room and saw everything reversed. Mincing around in his frock and his long curly haired Shirley Temple wig, "Call me the love that knows no name." If only the world knew, but they would not want to, because icons are icons and it takes more than an ugly wife to blot the horizon. But that was the appeal of Bob for Clint, the sense that somewhere over the rainbow there was a silo just for you and the walls would come tumbling down, as the song goes: Off comes the roof, down comes the ceiling, out goes the door, in comes the windows, it's all out of control! Good old William Slothrop, centuries forgotten, and out of print!

Holy Cephalopods, the plot is impenetrable, but then that is not necessary for the list, the word horde, the guarantors of immortality for they circulate words forever until of course they do not. That was the trouble, this writing for posterity, it always assumed that it mattered when it never did. It would all come tumbling down, turn to dust, and no-body would be able to find the old programmes that could read the code anymore. Which is why Clint wanted to update it all because no-one reads this stuff anymore, they just watch it, in three minute chunks if possible.

So I called Bob. He was drunk. In fact he was always drunk. He wrote what he knew: the sailors in the dance halls, the life on Mars, the whole seventies modus operandi. Cut Ups, inner worlds, the consciousness unconscious, the drug fuelled Lawrence Ferhlingetti of it all and if you could just do it at such great length you were literature and if Clint could do it at such great length, three part, four part, five hour long versions for the Blu-Ray aficionados, and do it quick, cheap, hand held, no fuss no muss with all the interns who would all be glad of the opportunity, then there would be light. Or at least a Kazoo! "Who dat man!" "Why, dat is Gabriel!" And all God's chillun got bombs! Anyway, that's how I put it to Bob. He was easy to find. Like I said, you just gotta know the right , a-huh, bar.

Open a door at random and yell "Bob", you'll find someone.
"Hi Bob, fancy meeting Clint?"
"Sure. Whatever."

And then you bring the man in, in his hat. He always wears a hat. His head is cold. And you can't see his eye. He has only the one, the one staring eye above the beak. It is a little known fact that Clint has eight arms. It makes him a multi-tasker of enormous capabilities. You can see that for Bob is was love at first sight. He rolled up his sleeve, unzipped the latex and hit the love function. It was a mess. There was Ink everywhere. It was as if Anaiis Nin had met a football team and squirmed like a squid sandwiched between them all. It was a great spectator event, college football at its all American best meets monster truck rally, with the great bar strung out bar after bar of infinite regression, sailors, salesmen, gunslingers and gangsters, tier upon tier, four dimensions, five dimension, a pyramid of cheer leaders without their pants twirling on well greased baseball bats. It has to be seen, to be believed, this land of red-haired, green-eyed baboons, white skin with a few freckles, kissing thin brunette girls in slacks.

"I guess it does," said Bob," listening as Clint explained his beatnik mission.

"A man has to know his limitations though," Clint said giving the "but" to the pitch. "Unless of course you can supply some of the funding."

"And er, if not?"

"It'll look like shit."

"That's the way I like it."

"That's what it'll be then."

"Deal?"

"Done."

And so the real work began because the writing is nothing, just a deal breaker, just a slab of words for the money men to rest their cigars on. The writer disappears and the re-writers re-write and they too disappear and in the end, the houses fall, the exits are blocked, the screams cancel each other out as white terror turns to white noise. Rock n' Roll wrecks the seats. Multi-plexes as tight as refrigerators replace the People's Palace, the walls tumble and here we are with the screen a dim page spread before us, white and silent. The film has broken, or a projector bulb has burned out. Everything, not just the movies, has got smaller. Fin.

THE MANY FACES OF YAM TAT WAH

The first thing to read and the last thing to write is the face. It is the finishing touch, the coup de grâce. You start your tattooing career with the arms, the legs maybe, but never the face. That's the what-the-fuck moment, the end of the sequence, the part where you commit purely to being what you have written under your skin. And the tattooed man wrote what? He wrote the names of Hong Kong movies on his body.

If you are to indelibly ink over your features then one might imagine a great work of art is necessary. But no, in this case, not even the sublime Mickey Mouse sketch, the anchor, the serpent or the highly original dragon, but an injected scrawl of text lifted off the back of pirate DVDs.

The movies may or may not be great cinema but are they a bold statement on the fragility of life, a philosophical utterance that will transform one's outlook, a statement that will change the world? If one were to make oneself a monument, then one would expect it to be a monument of some great significance. Maybe within the titles there is a secret code, a message of great significance. Or maybe it was just the use of Chinese characters that enticed the Tattooed Man. They appear to be more mysterious, more meaningful, and can fool everyone. And these characters tell a story, but for those who do not understand, they tell only what they imagine could be there. Assuming they imagine anything at all. And the imagination is powerful.

So with a smile to begin with, we read that Don Law from the House of The Lute, turned informer on the twins. He lived by night and killed green things, so it was goodbye mammie, get outta Chinatown, Big Brother! Hence the tattoos, the sign of the triad, the sign of the outsider, the sign of those who were once inside, locked up, all at sea, all of one tribe, all of an us against a them, or an it, or just seeking to disguise themselves; all written on the face, saying it all, and much more, or less.

Don, AKA, The caged tiger of Osmanthus Alley, took a lighter out one night and burned Snow, scarring her for life, or scaring if the sub-titles are correct, and though she escaped, she ended up in jail. Don thought her free but no, she was there living hard and stoking the fires of her ambition. It was a lucky star that saved her, a Chinese cop out, framed for her own safety because Don was a wild one, the man with the coconuts making the final run, and he would have burned her more. He juggled four loves. He was a big man with many little affairs. But he would have hunted Snow down, made her bleed, and stuck a bullet in her head to kill the romance.

The face was a pirate-DVD cover printed in Shenzhen and translated by a computer. Stay away from me, says this face. Don't screw with the Don, says the face. Thirty-seven Hong Kong Dollars, says the face, and you will be lucky if the entire film is on the disk.

You turn away and catch sight of the arm. Lurking in the shadows, other stories leap out. Here we discover how Don the gigolo, embraced the Cyprus Tigers with a fatal determination to terminate his return engagement. Life is a cycle, and death follows life and life follows death. It meant nothing to him. One day he held a doctor's heart in his hands. It was all part of the plot where he was a bullet for hire, a great pretender, and a lover of whores.

Literally on the other hand, the black cat made a deadly deal with the sea wolves. He turned over the cards and queen was high, and in the good, the bad and the bandit on a mission of condor, he invited Don and Snow to the banquet where Guns N Roses played and they reprieved their gigolo and whore routine. They brought the good, cash on delivery, and once upon a time a hero in China arrived.

Such was the back-story for the face is the last place but the arms among the first, the first disguise, the first area of embroidery undertaken to impress, to join in with, to frighten, to declare one is bad ass, bored, bitter, in love, and dedicated to Jesus, The Devil or the vicissitudes of fortune one way or the other. Here is the beginning of the disappearance, of the immersion in ink, and the display, for the arms are naked and shown, as is the face. But then comes the stranger but more often illustrated regions, the areas rarely shown but in private.

Kicking off at the feet we discover that Dr Lamb, before his heart was ripped out, was the Friday Gigolo. He rode out in the night naked and killed the powerful four with his full contact holy weapon. It was a killer's love, incorruptible and without a policeman in sight. Pure insanity. You can't stop his crazy love for anyone. It was love among the Triads. The first shot came from the warriors and their black panther. Trained as the future cops to bring down the prince of Portland Street in the final judgment. The feet are but a trailer for what might or might not come to be, depending on the finance available, and rarely on display.

Here is the iceberg depths, the frantic pedaling to stay afloat, the depths, the fear, and on the souls of the feet the secret sign of whatever sect requires it, whatever secret sign, old will, myth of weakness and strength is hidden. Here the tales of the birth reside but none are true. The feet are liars but the more they lie the further away they take us.

They ran, the Dr and Don, and they killed, but they were raped by an angel called Rose who they loved, truly heroically, awaking a tragic fantasy in the Tiger of Wanchai, as Don once was called. Such was the folly of youth. He was a drunken master three times removed, crossing the crystal fortune run. They opened the devil's box and their passion twisted the police confidentially, killing the dragon that snaked up the haunch because of the lies. Darker and darker are the secrets, as only those who pay the price will view what is available in these regions. Here one would expect to find hidden truths awaiting discovery on death, or love.

Snow and the Doctor love guns and glass and rob all, even their dearest, with the ghostly bus. The disconnections are disconcerting, for there must be a reason but it is merely the spare space that had to be filled. Here we begin to suspect that that is the motivation, the filling of empty space, the desire to take something from out there and wrap oneself in it, for fear that one is not enough and that only that which has claimed a space in the cultural consciousness is valid. Here the tattooed man joins with the wanted men who were kings of robbery and on Bloody Friday, they all of a sudden became No. 1. Street Angels. They were young, dangerous and remembered to be scared. For in that, there was power. In the scared and scarred moment was truth. Here was simplicity, never elaborated, always hidden and then revealed, to intimates. It is only a matter of time for the penis, the red head, the snake, to get a spider tattooed on it, or a bolt placed through it.

Here the tattooed man lost heart. He wanted to do something but only thought of hardware insertions, which must have been painful. But there were no names, no titles, just ink to blacken. Here there was no story to swallow. It was what it was and no disguise. Action and not words was all that was hoped for. It was the reader's respite from gang lore and a tale of whores and dollars and brothers in arms, a moment where what lay beneath displayed itself momentarily and perhaps it was the only bit left, the thing that was never intended to be disguised. For sex is part of the tattoo. Sex and virility are supposedly enhanced by taking on the power of the signs, the magic of a blue skin, for even the red fades to a darkish blue.

It is when we read the back that we begin to suspect that there is more to this than the story, but we expect the unexpected and somehow the back is a relief. Here we look for the main feature, here is what everything else is a lead up to, the big work, the big image. This is operation billionaire, where everything is a Casino and a hit man is on the way. That was Don's mission. With legendary speed, at the Trust Me U Die Night club, Juliet fell in love with the model from Hell. This woman from hell was cold and signed up to deathnet.com, where Don belongs. Here is Snow, the woman from hell, the cold woman, the deathnet.com woman. But Juliet? It is wrong, such a wrong name for this world, a transliteration, but then so many things are wrong for this world, this world of Hong Kong movies. When it borrows it borrows blatant and does not digest and Juliet, a name of nobody, has no dimension but then most of the characters are but names of no dimension. So wrong and without a character, a piece of Romanization among the Chinese characters which one hopes are more than they appear, at least for the target audience. But ones suspicions are that even to them, even to the billion, even they feel it is all but skin deep.

She, Juliet, or Snow, a generic female much beloved of generic film makers, wanted a man, a fulltime killer, a final romance, and flew at midnight when her left-eye saw ghosts. Then such a let down as the back fills its space randomly with scenes of domestic mass marketing where Don and Juliet are partners obsessed with Lara Croft Tomb Raider, The Cradle of Life. Instantly the era is labeled on the back, forever. Don looks for Mr Perfect and joins the PTU, where the eternal flame of fatal attraction burns. The news breaks, and the wake of death commences for Mob Sister, another fatal attraction, another cold lady, another void to be filled.

With such a gap in the leadership an election in this outback back was required. And the Dragon Squad finally came into their own, exiling the eye in the sky to the triangle, a simple sign, a three sided figure and sketched out pieces squeezed in, unfinished. A women's prison has gone ballistic, a fatal move for the sparrow, the thief, where an ocean burst into flames and human nature found no way out.

There is now no more space and yet there is more to squeeze in. In gaps randomly discovered, Ip Man, with partners and comrades in arms under cover of night and fog, seek vengeance on the storm warriors. And the bodyguards and assassins pay the black ransom, leaving much bad blood with the blood bond and echoes of rainbows.

It was obvious, the tattooed man never imagined his hero would have such a career, pile in so many roles in so many films, and even though the skin came to an end, so Yam Man, Hong Kong's star, forever working, forever producing character after character, went on. But the skin would be confined to the fires with the body, unread mostly, unheeded, and secret, as all things are. Art is not forever and cash pays the bills, but so often cash is sacrificed for the ephemeral that poses as eternal.

How strange to spend a lifetime accumulating the signs, hoping for a skinning, to be turned into a rug, a lampshade, a suit of cured sign and signifiers, but knowing it would not happen. In the end is cremation or decay. And nobody would ever read it. Except for me, and I am nobody. Nobody would do more than glance and remember you were the blue man, the man covered in characters of a certain dimension, a blue kind, a Chinese mash of many dialects and languages, unappreciated by the rest of the world. And not even appreciated by the world that might have understood, or cared, who shared the dream, the dream of Snow and Don and a dance of guns and brawls and gambling debts and Kung Fu warriors. No longer the sick man! A banal inspiration, but inspiration nonetheless, and life nonetheless, a life, the life, written one character at a time to say one was there, one was touched, and one day it will be finished, complete. But instead, time and space merely ran out.

THE END OF FICTION

What's the story? I've been asking this for years. It's how I deal with the world. What's the story I say and have to conclude most of the time that there is no story. Life sort of happens in a messy mix of accidents and processes beyond one's control, though all your own fault. It happens, whatever you do, and the story is just not there, though you might want it to be. A story is a beginning a middle and an end? But there's something lacking; a moral mostly. A story means intentions and obstacles and triumphs and failures. Where's the story in just being born and dropping off the end of the conveyor belt? Where's the story in getting up and going to work? Where's the story in getting by, having a drink, toasting a sandwich, having a chat on the phone and cashing a cheque? Stuff happens, intentionally some times, in reaction to other stuff mostly, and largely in accordance with a logic not of our own making, unlike in fiction where we can choose everything and make the story work.

The lack of story could be a story I suppose, in a post modern, or is that post-post-modern sense? Make what you will of that. Critical discourse long ago became about counting consonants and kicking the author out of the equation rather than trying to work out why something was better than something else. Coolness perhaps became as good as it got. But we all know that it's the story, stupid!

And that's the case with history and our grasp of the future. If history is reduced to statistics and processes we aren't interested, but find a love story, find a struggle between good and evil, a great warrior who believes in their destiny, or a prophet trying to live life according to some fiction, and our attention is grabbed. And our money taken. The story is a commodity. The reality of history, like wars, is statistics, or perhaps music though it can be pretty ugly music. And you concoct a story to make people willing to play a role in it. Nobody wants to be just a note on the stave, a cog in the wheel, a number in the statistics, and so how can an entire society exist and flourish that has no myth, just a set of numbers? Or is it that it could exist, only nobody would care or notice? Which brings me, in a very round-about way that all the naff books on how to write essays tell you is wrong, to Hong Kong, the point! And that is the point because the point of anything is a fiction and the fiction of Hong Kong has a strange and pointless nature. If the myths of the communist motherland are not to be swallowed, then nothing else can be! And if they are, then whatever that story is, it won't be Hong Kong's.

So what's the no-story of Hong Kong? It was born, it grew and maybe there will be an end. Cities do end; some abruptly. And some evolve into other cities. Climates change, rivers run dry, economies collapse, and fashions start coming from elsewhere rather than ones own creative dynamic. Cool turns to naff. And Hong Kong one day will be either too naff to live there, or under six foot of water and the playground of monsters or midgets as yet not evolved. So when people ask what has changed in Hong Kong after sixteen years under Chinese rule, one searches for a story to tell them, an illustration of change, of moral intent, a point of departure, an end, a beginning, a hero. But one has to manufacture it, falsify, fictionalise and in effect make a primitive judgement just to please an audience. The truth is just statistics, though one can romanticise and start looking for the tune.

So has the tune changed? Have we slipped out of the incessant march music and eight tone scales of the West into something less rhythmic, more pentatonic, more shrill and operatic? I even have difficulty in pin pointing any change in tone. What you get are statistics and processes and complexity and the certain knowledge that come 2045, the assigned date for the death of the Hong Kong SAR, a forgotten component of the agreement between the UK and China, that one is still going to have exactly what one has, though maybe some fantasy history will have emerged that, in this town where nobody gives a damn about history, history will make not the slightest bit of difference. Any discussion about Hong Kong turns into an infinite regression into parenthesis.

Hong Kong used to have a crowd-pleasing story. Hong Kong was founded by drug dealers, so the story goes, though if you want to be pernickety you can look a little more closely and discover it was not quite as cut and dried as that. There was even a Hong Kong before the British came, for a start, and the Hong Kong history museum now likes to present all that and portray the English bit as just a blip.

The Convention of Chuenpeh 1841 ceded the island of Hong Kong to the British and if we think of Hong Kong beginning when the British came, maybe it ended when they left. But then, who has left? The British government left, but they more or less had little to do with the running of the place from the time the Japanese invaded. And it can be argued that much the same people run the place now that Beijing has in theory taken over. And in some respects they are much the same people, some of them direct descendants of the Chinese who threw their lot in with the British when they first started doing business in the region. Though that starts making the story very complicated and the story begins to fall apart and turn into this unheroic, unspiritual, amoral, progression of stuff that just happens when lots of different individuals with certain drives and needs come together in the pursuit of those things.

But let's get back to the story. Was the founding of Hong Kong a noble, outrageous, piece of adventurism? Hardly. It didn't even warrant much of a Boys Own Spin at the time. Everyone involved got sacked, reprimanded, stabbed in the back by someone who either thought it should never have happened or was too pathetic a reward for so much effort. Charles Elliott, who signed the Convention of Chuenpeh, was made chargé d'affaires in Texas, which was very much a punishment appointment, if you consider how he would have to host dinner parties for the dismal bunch of drunks and slave owners who had seized power there. And for that matter the Chinese Mandarin, Lin Tse-Hsu, who set his sights on destroying the opium trade, also lost his job for in effect doing his job! The escalation into war was more to do with Beijing's inertia and inability to support its own administrators. Lin was after all, a man of humble origins who had worked his way up, and the aristocracy were not inclined to communicate with the likes of him. Too clever by half, and suspiciously logical and hard working, he was sent off to the newly annexed Illi basin in Xinjiang, to host dinners for Kazakh opium addicts and slave owners – a little bit of Chinese imperial adventurism conveniently forgotten in all but the name of the province: the New Territories.

It was a mix of misunderstandings, double-dealing, bribery and corruption all in the service of the needs of the then level of technology. To trade with the East you needed a base to fuel your steamers. And to deal with complex commercial regulations you needed laws that recognised the concepts used to organise the economies of the West. Chinese law could not handle it and the Chinese quite sensibly thought steam engines dirty noisy affairs that frightened the cows. There is the story told of Chinese backwardness where the ignorant Mandarins tore up the railway lines to Guangzhou because they disturbed the countryside. In my youth the history books used that as an example of why the British Imperial mission, morally dubious in many aspects, was also justifiable. We modernised the world. Nowadays one can look upon those Mandarins and think them perfectly sensible people. They would weep at the polluted state of China's cities and point out how not just China is destroyed but the whole world. Bad Feng Shui! That's what Global Warming is… And now I've lost the story again. Other stories seem potentially available, if we find it useful to pick them out of the noise. What, we may ask, is politically useful? Which, we may well ask, is the most lucrative commercial story? How can I serve my own purposes? Or should I just be cool and knowing and enigmatic, hinting I know secrets that you do not know and have powers and connections that you do not have? Us Brits can be inscrutable when we want to be.

And so, 1842 and all that! History reduced to the best bits, only, in Hong Kong, well, there is an awful lot of noise in Hong Kong, a lot of selves to be served and not many good bits. So after 1842 and all that, the official founding of the city of Victoria – a name that never quite caught on, though officially still is the Hong Kong Island part of the city – much as the City of Hull is officially called Kingston, though nobody much cared for the King and thus the locals called it Hull, after the river. I digress.

Where am I?

Ah, yes, 1842 and all that!

So we find Hong Kong history a list of squabbles, infighting, bewildered moments where the place sought a role for itself and much about drainage and sanitation. The story then became China and not Hong Kong. Though Hong Kong did produce the Tai Ping, a murderous and free loving Christian sect with socialistic leanings that in the end frightened the Westerners as much as the ruling Qing Dynasty. Could the Falun Gong of 2007, much given to large drum beating processions through Hong Kong mysteriously without any media coverage whatsoever, be a modern descendant of such mysterious forces in the Chinese soul? They ooze a boxerish vibe and Tai Pingish religiosity. To paraphrase Basil Fawlty, "Don't mention the Falun Gong!"

And to paraphrase Jiang Zemin, to rid us of this evil cult, the Tai Ping that is, Chinese Gordon, eventually of Khartoum, led the Qing to victory and the next thing we know is a rather dull little medical student at Hong Kong University started thinking China needed to get rid of its Emperors and institute modern institutions of Government. Sun Yat Sen goes on to be possibly the dullest revolutionary ever recorded in history, but undoubtedly the founder of modern China.

And here is something curious about Chinese history, it so often is a sweep of processes rather than great heroes. The individual is buried in the waves of history. Or at least that is how Chinese history is studied. Its popular variant is a confused mess of stories without much care for chronology or accurate depictions of the era they come from. And the stories are often wild and woolly with gods and demons thrown in for good measure. It is all opera! And as everyone knows, you can never really follow the story in an Opera, you are supposed to know it somehow, but you never do, not all of it and often not the same story. And perhaps since all history is just this mess of stuff, the Chinese are right. Collect lots of boring records and annotate them and let the popular imagination create wild stories and call it history, while the real history is the number of bricks in a great wall and how many man years it took to build it. Somewhere in all that is a lingering idea of the good man, versed in literature, arts and good taste in general, but where the West came in and destroyed the lingering remnants of the Chinese story, came the idea that man is only as good as the system makes him. Power without check inevitably destroys virtue. The game is everything and what makes for a good game? Good rules that everyone understands and can, if they produce boring results or unjust ones, be changed. And so Cricket arrived in Hong Kong but would the Chinese play it? No!

How come the Chinese never cottoned onto the one game that could shame the colonialists and prove themselves more than their equals? One has a sneaky suspicion that most Chinese who emigrated to Hong Kong either did not notice the British were there or were glad they were there instead of the Qing. But essentially they ignored them, as they pretty much do today. The then Chief Executive Donald Tsang announced, if my reading of the *South China Morning Post* in April 2007 was correct, that "the opinions of ex-pats" are of little importance. Maybe they misquoted him. But probably not.

What changed the rules of Hong Kong's game rather abruptly was Hong Kong's falling into the hands of the Japanese. It has its stories, its moments of tragedy and high farce: the Japanese were slaughtering and raping nurses while the Australian forces, idiotically dumped in Stanley in a futile attempt to bolster up a pointless defensive stance, broke into the bars and got drunk. And as the British propaganda machine got into gear portraying the Japanese as sub-human devils, British officers entertained their counterparts in the Japanese army to sit down banquets with plenty of wine, as a prelude to their dismal internment. This is perhaps where the Hong Kong of the British Empire died and what was born afterwards was an afterthought, a misalignment of historical forces. The Americans did not want it. And they, more than the Japanese, were the enemy then. They wanted Hong Kong handed over to Chiang Kai Shek but the Brits in the internment camp of Stanley had other plans and reclaimed the colony. Nobody here argued with them and the British swiftly sent the navy to make sure they got there before the Americans. If the Americans had been quicker, if Chiang Kai Shek had not been mired in organisational chaos, and the Brits in no mood to compromise, Hong Kong would have died then and there, becoming a windswept backwater, pillaged by the communists, and left to rot. What a story the place would have had then! Its pivotal role in the modernisation of China would have been dismissed as a joke, a desperate imperialist conceit confined to a few footnotes referencing obscure academic papers that once bothered to argue the point. Instead it became the refuge of Shanghainese businessmen, retreating Kuomingtang, and Cantonese refugees and the modern Hong Kong of sweatshop labour, and plastics factories. Suzy Wong grew up amidst all this and started writing stories about The Miracle of Hong Kong.

By the time the handover came, it was as though the rest of China had caught up, but was still an unknown quantity. With the Soviets collapsing, China looked set for regime-change of some sort and Hong Kong would thus, so some said, take over China! Perhaps it already had. The blunt use of the military to suppress unarmed student protestors in Tiananmen Square in 1989 put paid to that and conjured up images of the old China, Stalinist policies, and "M"ist excesses. Hong Kong shook and for a moment the story of the Handover began to look interesting, for annihilation does produce a sense that they deserved it and a moral makes a story. Would it be a case of rampaging People's Liberation Army troops blowing up shopping malls and arresting dissidents? Was one a fool for hanging around waiting for the internment camps and mass executions? Would there be daring escapes? Would there be heroic encounters? Would there be a song and a poster image of a banker beating off a retreating tank with his briefcase?

And the press flew in, hoping for a story, desperate for a story, and all they could come up with was the revelation that White Men actually do labouring jobs in Hong Kong. Or at least the couple of white guys they found doing a bit of furniture removal for a Chinese boss were held up as a sign that White Supremacy no longer ruled, forgetting the rather blue collar origins of the sailors and soldiers that propped up the bars of Hong Kong since its inception. One wonders how much money the man who concocted that piece of copy got from the syndication rights? The best image was of a kilted squaddy at the War Memorial caught in a gust of wind revealing that nothing was worn beneath his kilt and all was in perfect condition. This was perhaps the anti-dote to the labouring white men, for it proved that the devils in skirts were still to be feared, if the film "Carry on Up The Khyber", voted best British movie of all time, is anything to go by. Private Widdle would no doubt have approved. (I implore you to see the film as it explains everything there is to know about the English.) And there was something Widdlish about the whole handover ceremony in which both sides managed to out-kitch each other in a display of pomp and circumstance and Gay Soldiery that proved that the plot had long ago been lost and everyone really knew the concept of national sovereignty was draining away in the face of globalisation.

And so, what the press found was rain and a T-shirt featuring the Union Jack being painted Red. The icon was perhaps more prescient than it was intended. The flag was not so much changed, as merely painted over for beneath Hong Kong remained, well jacked, and not unlike Hawaii, with its Union Jack vaguely protesting its annexation by the monster next door. Now that is an odd story that lingers in the footnotes of history, why the Union Jack should represent Hawaii and why Sun Yat Sen conducted much revolutionary activity in Hawaii? Rich ex-patriot Chinese with American passports hover in the shadows of the founding of modern China, and now, American MBAs in hand, newly acquired Putonghua, their grandsons and grand-daughters head for Shanghai and its business opportunities. And curiously, the seemingly conservative emblem of Imperial Power presides over a rather bolshy, stick-it-to-the-man attitude, capable of giving anyone, claiming the mandate of heaven in all its forms, a headache.

To continue the great and glorious history of Hong Kong and its "Miracle"...

In the lead up to the 1997 Handover, the Brits half-heartedly tried to keep rioters from the streets by allowing for greater democracy and boosting up the economy with great works like the Airport. But afterwards, the Chinese returned the government to the old bureaucracy, though kept the airport. It looked nice.

There seemed to be a story brewing: here was the disastrous economic down turn and the even more disastrous new Chief Executive, Mr Tung, hell bent on producing a Singaporean style benevolent dictatorship, which turned into more like a re-enactment of Ferdinand and Imelda Marcos's last days when he managed to get half a million people protesting on the streets against him. But underlying it Hong Kong was much the same. There had been riots before. There had been strikes before. There had been upturns and downturns and indecisive governments before and anyone who had been in Hong Kong long enough would know, the very pulse of the place, the music if you like, assumes what goes up, comes down and sometimes you get lucky and sometimes not.

It was all taken in its stride. The heart of Hong Kong beat much the same as ever. Even when the Plague, a much loved depleter of Hong Kong's 19th century population, returned, in the form of SARS, and the old Hong Kong politics of drains and sanitation resurfaced. There was even a tragic fire, the Garley Buildings, like many other tragic fires from the Happy Valley Racecourse fire of the early part of the century to the Shek Kip Mei Squatter Camps of the middle part of the century. Fires, Plagues, street demonstrations, bureaucratic paralysis and rapacious tycoons sewing up monopolies of property and service industries backed by dodgy money from gun runners, drug dealers, gambling syndicates, corrupt officials, crazy fung shui masters etc. etc. etc. etc. and etc. are the every day fibre of Hong Kong's way of life. Anyone who enters Hong Kong throws themselves upon the rough waters and hopes some wreckage comes along with a handy bit of gold hanging onto it. And in this messy piratical world, enough luck is generated to keep everyone hoping for their turn. Nobody is rewarded for hard work, for brilliance, for exceptional abilities. You either get lucky or you do not and that is all there is and Hong Kong would like to think that this tune is its very own but one finds it hummed throughout the world if one does not live in a fantasy. Though to say that Hong Kong people do not live in a fantasy is perhaps overstating the case. People literarily do get sold magic beans on the street. Little old ladies have their savings prized out of their bank accounts by unscrupulous flim flam artists peddling magic beans that restore good health, good fortune, and full heads of hair. They have been known to tragically blind babies by rubbing magic incense ashes into their eyes.

In a world in which policemen have gun battles with each other and write poetry about the meaninglessness of existence, if the evidence presented in a 2007 court case featuring Officer Tsui who was given to robbing banks and taking his mother on exotic holidays is anything to go by, there is no moral to the events of Hong Kong, thus no story. If the case of one of the richest men in Hong Kong being kidnapped and scolding his wife for paying the ransom without negotiating it down and then being kidnapped again and disappearing, rumour has it, over the side of the boat speeding him to Taiwan when intercepted by the Chinese navy, is anything to go by, nothing happens without an element of absurdity. The now very rich wife took to sporting pigtales, wearing mini-skirts, and queuing up for cake coupons while the money languished in probate. Then there was a lawsuit from the aging father who already was rich enough. Then, on her winning all the money, she quickly dies a premature death and a mysterious fengshui master lays claim to it all. And then hefty doses of media management crank into gear as questions start surfacing suggesting that all of this saga might be the tip of a very iffy set of circumstances. Follow the money, one might say, but it could be very dangerous to actually do so. And so...

Where was I in this absurd soap opera? Nowhere!

The facts of Hong Kong lack moral content, let alone the fictions. Hong Kongers prefer spectacle and absurdity, to coherent story telling. Mo Lei Tau, nonsense, has been perfected and art has never made much headway, perhaps because reality has outstripped it and similarly not made much headway. So what is the story? There is no story, there is Film Director and comic actor Chow Sin Chi turning out live action cartoons with a deft use of the non-linear editing suite. There is process and the process continues, repeating, recycling, reforming and eventually one assumes dying. It is a piece by Philip Glass endlessly cycling through the circle of twelfths, and fading out in a clatter of Chinese gongs.

Has the handover changed anything? It docs not look like it. Have the Brits finally gone and the whole place reverted to the sleepy Chinese fishing village it once was? No. But then the whole of China has changed. Has Hong Kong joined the rest of China? Not quite. It drives on the left hand side of the road for a start. It does not arrest government opponents; it rather invites them to endless lunches and onto endless committees. Has the English Language disappeared? It was never there in the first place. The Chinese slept one side of the bed and the English the other. But the English were never here in large numbers and although there are fewer Europeans here, an awful lot of the Chinese are not exactly Chinese nationals, but rather products of overseas education if not nations. The ABC, BBC, CBC – American Born, British Born, Canadian Born Chinese – are everywhere and some of those are more American, more British, more Canadian than the Europeans who arrive with their dreams of exploring oriental culture.

Globalisation has changed the world but not Hong Kong for Hong Kong was a product of the globalisation process, is the epitome of globalisation. The market made Hong Kong. Trade Routes made it. And although the steamers do not need a fuelling stop any more, the airport is one of the largest in the world and the container terminals, shipping goods in and out of Hong Kong, are still there. Economics drives the place, not personalities, and it remains a first rate place for third-rate people. Talent is scarce and business opportunities are many. Buy cheap, sell high. That's it! That's the story. A city that struggles to be a city instead of a workers' dormitory! That's not a story. A city that was never quite a city, but more a depot! A city that has no soul! A city that lacks culture and taste! A city that is hot and happening and ever changing and never changing! An exciting city! A city of dullards and dimwits and dickheads! The ignorant rule. Nobody rules. No story. Just stuff. A lucky place to be in! Especially if you like dancing and horse-racing.

Mimi Wong, an HSBC banker, paid US$15 million for Tango lessons! And quite rightly got most of it back when her instructor called her a lazy cow. Only in Hong Kong could US$15 million fail to impress upon someone the need to be at least politely diplomatic when confronted with an idiot.

Maybe Hong Kong is learning diplomacy. It's learning about China. It is gathering more information about the new China and finding it not the monolithic evil force in the back yard, but rather a mess of bits and pieces, some with good investment prospects and others as ever rife with warlords and corrupt officials. Beijing has become nicer, in as much as the men are younger, though not young enough to forgo dying their hair an alarming jet black to keep looking vigorous despite their age. But the age is sixty-something rather than eighty-something nowadays and the men are professionals, engineers, economists, political science graduates, experts and general managers who create focus groups and committees and study papers. China has no crusade. It struggles to replace the irrational with the rational and provide the framework for everyone to play the competitive game and not exploit those who have not as yet got the message.

Hong Kong might not be learning to love Beijing, but it is losing its fear and learning that there is a game to play that might have some harsh rules, but all one needs do is accept certain principles, the primacy of the communist party for a start, and then everything else is negotiable. And even what actually constitutes the Communist Party seems to be negotiable. Membership has been thrown open to all the "Advanced" social groupings, meaning technocrats and businessmen can be "Communists" now without having to accept Marx as the last word in Economic Theory. Meaning, if you pay your money, you get into the good seats at the Olympics reserved for important officials.

But that is assuming too much. Hong Kongers are a little gauche, a bit naïve, a little cosseted by the good times, and products of bizarre devilish deals. Mainlanders are hardened to the ways of the Mainland, come in two forms, ignorant peasants out to grab whatever they can, smart well educated graduates out to grab whatever they can. And the notion of the communist is lacking in Hong Kong discourse, unlike the every day of China. There is but government, authoritarian yes, but as was always the case in China, the Emperor is but one man and is a long way away playing with his concubines and communing with the forces of heaven. Everyone else is putting their bets on which horse will win, and sometimes if the recently excavated radio controlled drugs dispensers planted at the starting rail of the Happy Valley Race Course are anything to go by, working on elaborate means of cheating the whole system. And the suspects were mainlanders, as they always are. So the love and trust of China, of Beijing, is but a sycophantic hope for someone to protect them from the rapacious hordes. The Chineseness of Hong Kong is a throwback, called upon from folk memory, half forgotten and barely relevant to modern China but that does not matter! And that is the odd thing. Whether one can conclude that this has changed anything in Hong Kong is a moot point. The story is a mystery, a chaotic soap opera with no end, except when the Aliens land and inform the entire cast that it was all a dream.

What Hong Kong means is that stuff happens and one can turn a story on it if one likes, but the story is a fabrication, a piece of propaganda, and indicates a need to manipulate, to gain control, to establish an order, and in Hong Kong one finds that this is remarkably lacking. And so a coherent Noble Lie for those who vie for power here and do not really want it that much. There are no great leaders. They all follow in the wake of Sun Yat Sen, in being dull professionals who somehow get assigned the role in whatever the system is churning up. We have an eight hundred strong committee to vote for the Chief Executive and since only the man Beijing thinks suitable will win, it seems pointless opposing him. But recently opponents have somehow emerged. A sort of Loyal Opposition has been sanctioned. And, so the argument goes, since it is pointless, maybe someone should run in opposition to expose the pointlessness and it will at least make the chosen winner explain their policies. And this is ideal for people who actually do not want the job very much to at least show that they think policy decisions by the government matter, even if the ones announced and discussed in public are not actually ones that the government really does much about. The point though is to create a fiction that some can believe in, that there is a mandate, and that the elected Chief Executive has addressed the public, whose opinions matter to the eight hundred electors. But as the desire is not really there, there is no story, just a fragmentary drama with a few good scenes, and ultimately nobody suspends their disbelief for long.

Since the handover there have been no riots, and arrogant officials have a habit of ending up in the courts exposing their arrogance to the public who find them all rather embarrassing. Whether it is contempt for the ignorance of the general public, or even the "stupidity of Hong Kong teachers", as discussed in another recent court case concerning government interference in academic freedom, it all smacks of an uniquely Hong Kong muddle brought on by uncertain powers and the ever-levelling effects of back stabbing and envy. There is no prize left unscorned and it is just far better to keep your head down, avoid conspicuous displays of idiocy and wealth, and definitely side step ambitions in public areas, and muddle on in a very British way that sits very well with the natural anarchy of the Cantonese. Render unto Caesar what is Caesar's and get on with your own business, especially if you happen to have some nice off-shore earnings and property in various places around the world.

How can I conclude this overview of the Handover? I feel I should just end in mid sentence, like most conversations in Hong Kong. Nothing is concluded. Everything is talked away in lunches and pointless meetings. Decisions do not get made, but things happen and we all live reasonably well, some a lot more reasonably than others, but they do such stupid stuff with their money as to make one realise that one actually can have too much money. Or at least Hong Kong can. They prefer to horde it for a rainy day, for a future ancestor, for HSBC bank, or buy a bag of magic beans, or a pack of Tom.com shares from Richard Li.

If one wants to look for a great pronouncement, to find something the Western newspapers want to write about, or the historians even, the story must be about democracy and its failure to be implemented. The story though is the non-story, for only when democracy happens, will the British Colonial legacy finally die, except that it died a long time ago with the Japanese invasion, so whatever ran the place, made the place, was the place, had nothing to do with democracy which would be the end, or beginning, but somehow the hunger for democracy does not motivate anything much... well, not much more than a sharp intake of breath.

The dynamic that fuelled Hong Kong was the isolation of China under the revolutionary period and now China embracing the market economy drives Hong Kong. External forces rather than internal take the lead and a democratic Hong Kong will probably find itself in much the same situation with everyone moaning about how useless and indecisive the democratic government is. Democracy is a brave attempt to create a moral and make a story. Freedom, democracy, and the opening up of the Hong Kong society and thus a cultural renascence, a flowering of many blooms, a resurgence of the film industry, a gathering of creative literati and visual artists, are all possible, if enough actually care. History will have progressed. The Story has a happy ending. Or it just goes on. And who says the place wasn't democratic in the first place, because, essentially everyone does exactly as they please and those with the most money get to buy more than those who have less, but so it goes, that's not going to change in this world, in this life-time, anywhere!

Another gasp of polluted air, devoid of oxygen and packed full of toxins...

So Hong Kong the cool, forever! And that is it. Hong Kong does what it does, is what it is, and languishes as a footnote, and does not give a damn. And the non-story of the British is, what a success the handover is! And the non-story of Beijing is, what a success the handover is! And the non-story of the Chinese is, how clever we are, and the non-story of the Ex-pats is, hey, here we still are! So it's a happy ending. So how cool can you get?

ABOUT PROVERSE HONG KONG

Proverse Hong Kong is based in Hong Kong with long-term and expanding regional and international connections.

Proverse has published novels, novellas, fictionalized autobiography, non-fiction (including autobiography, biography, history, memoirs, sport, travel narratives), single-author poetry collections, children's, teens / young adult and academic books. Other interests include diaries, and academic works in the humanities, social sciences, cultural studies, linguistics and education. Some Proverse books have accompanying audio texts. Some are translated into Chinese.

Proverse welcomes authors who have a story to tell, wisdom, perceptions or information to convey, a person they want to memorialize, a neglect they want to remedy, a record they want to correct, a strong interest that they want to share, skills they want to teach, and who consciously seek to make a contribution to society in an informative, interesting and well-written way. Proverse works with texts by non-native-speaker writers of English as well as by native English-speaking writers.

The name, "Proverse", combines the words "prose" and "verse" and is pronounced accordingly.

THE PROVERSE PRIZE

The Proverse Prize, an annual international competition for an unpublished book-length work of fiction, non-fiction, or poetry, was established in January 2008. It is open to all who are at least eighteen on the date they sign the entry form. Unusually for a competition of this nature, there is no restriction based on nationality, residence or citizenship.

The objectives of the Proverse Prize are: to encourage excellence and / or excellence and usefulness in publishable written work in the English Language, which can, in varying degrees, "delight and instruct". Entries are invited from anywhere in the world. Semi-finalists to date include writers born or resident in Andorra, Australia, Canada, Germany, Hong Kong, New Zealand, Nigeria, Singapore, South Africa, Taiwan, The Bahamas, the Peoples' Republic of China, the United Arab Emirates, the United Kingdom, the USA.

Founders: Verner Bickley and Gillian Bickley. To celebrate their lifelong love of words in all their forms as readers, writers, editors, academics, performers, and publishers.
Honorary Legal Advisor: Mr Raymond T. L. Tse.
Honorary Accountant: Mr Neville Chow.
Honorary Judges: Anonymous.
Honorary Advisors: Bahamian poet Marion Bethel; UK translator, Margaret Clarke; UK linguist & lexicographer David Crystal; Canadian poet and academic, Jonathan Hart; Swedish linguist Björn Jernudd; Hong Kong University Librarian, Peter Sidorko; Singapore poet Edwin Thumboo; Czech novelist & poet Olga Walló.
Honorary UK agent and distributor: Christine Penney
Honorary Administrators: Proverse Hong Kong.

Proverse Prize Winners Whose Books Have Already Been Published By Proverse Hong Kong

Laura Solomon, Rebecca Jane Tomasis, Gillian Jones,
David Diskin, Peter Gregoire, Sophronia Liu, Birgit Linder, James McCarthy, Celia Claase, Philip Chatting.

Summary Terms and Conditions
(for indication only & subject to revision)

The information below is for guidance only. Please refer to the year-specific Proverse Prize Entry Form & Terms & Conditions, which are uploaded in April each year onto the Proverse Hong Kong website: <www.proversepublishing.com>.

The free Proverse E-Newsletter includes ongoing information about the Proverse Prize. To be put on the E-Newsletter mailing-list, email: info@proversepublishing.com with your request.

The Prize
1) Publication by Proverse Hong Kong, with
2) Cash prize of HKD10,000 (HKD7.80 = approx. US$1.00)

Supplementary publication grants may be made to selected other entrants for publication by Proverse Hong Kong.

Depending on the quality of the work in any year, the prize may be shared by at most two entrants or withheld, as recommended by the judges.

In 2015, the entry fee was: HKD220.00 OR GBP32.00.

Writers are eligible, who are at least eighteen on the date they sign The Proverse Prize entry documents. There is no nationality or residence restriction.

Each submitted work must be an unpublished publishable single-author work of non-fiction, fiction or poetry, the original work of the entrant, and submitted in the English language. School textbooks and plays are ineligible.

Translated work: If the work entered is a translation from a language other than English, both the original work and the translation should be previously unpublished. The submitted work will not be judged as a translation but as an original work.

Extent of the Manuscript: within the range of what is usual for the genre of the work submitted. However, it is advisable that novellas be in the range 30,000 to 45,000 words); other fiction (e.g. novels, short-story collections) and non-fiction (e.g. autobiographies, biographies, diaries, letters, memoirs, essay collections, etc.) should be in the range, 75,000 to 100,000 words. Poetry collections should be in the range, 5,000 to 25,000 words. Other word-counts and mixed-genre submissions are not ruled out.

Writers may choose, if they wish, to obtain the services of an Editor in presenting their work, and should acknowledge this help and the nature and extent of this help in the Entry Form.

KEY DATES FOR THE PROVERSE PRIZE
IN ANY YEAR
(subject to confirmation and/or change)

Receipt of Entry Fees / Entry Documents	14 April to 31 May of the year of entry
Receipt of entered manuscripts	1 May to 30 June of the year of entry
Announcement of semi-finalists	July-September of the year of entry
Announcement of finalists	October-December of the year of entry
Announcement of winner/ max two winners (sharing the cash prize)	December of the year of entry to April of the year that follows the year of entry
Cash Award made	At the same time as publication of the work(s) adjudged the winner / joint-winners of the Proverse Prize
Publication of winning work(s)	In or after November of the year that follows the year of entry

NOVELS, SHORT STORY COLLECTIONS
AND OTHER FICTION
Published by Proverse Hong Kong

If you have enjoyed *Odds and Sods* by Lawrence Gray, you may also enjoy Lawrence Gray's *Cop Show Heaven* (2015).

**You may also like to read the following
(all titles in English unless otherwise stated)**

A Misted Mirror, by Gillian Jones. 2011.
A Painted Moment, by Jennifer Ching. 2010.
An Imitation of Life, by Laura Solomon. 2013.
Article 109, by Peter Gregoire. 2012.
Bao Bao's Odyssey: from Mao's Shanghai to Capitalist Hong Kong, by Paul Ting. 2012.
Black Tortoise Winter, by Jan Pearson. Scheduled 2015 / 2016.
Bright Lights and White Nights, by Andrew Carter. 2015.
cemetery miss you, by Jason S Polley. 2011.
Cop Show Heaven, by Lawrence Gray. 2015.
Death has a Thousand Doors, by Patricia Grey. 2011.
Hilary and David, by Laura Solomon. 2011.
Instant Messages, by Laura Solomon. 2010.
Man's Last Song, by James Tam. 2013.
Mila the Magician, by Zhang Jian. 2013. (English / Chinese bilingual)
Mishpacha – Family, by Rebecca Tomasis. 2010.
Odds and Sods, by Lawrence Gray. 2013.
Paranoia (the Walk and Talk with Angela), by Caleb Kavon. 2012.
Red Bird Summer, by Jan Pearson. 2014.
Revenge from Beyond, by Dennis Wong. 2011.
The Day They Came, by Gérard Louis Breissan. 2012.
The Devil You know, by Peter Gregoire. 2014.
The Monkey in Me: Confusion, Love and Hope under a Chinese Sky, by Caleb Kavon. 2009.
The Monkey in Me, by Caleb Kavon. Translated by Chapman Chen. 2010. E-book. 2010. (Chinese)
The Perilous Passage of Princess Petunia Peasant, by Victor Edward Apps. 2014.

The Reluctant Terrorist: in Search of the Jizo, by Caleb Kavon. 2011.

The Shingle Bar Sea Monster and Other Stories, by Laura Solomon. 2012.

The Snow Bridge and Other Stories, by Philip Chatting. Scheduled 2015.

Tiger Autumn, by Jan Pearson. 2015.

The Village in the Mountains, by David Diskin. 2012.

Tightrope! A Bohemian Tale, by Olga Walló. Translated from Czech by Johanna Pokorny, Veronika Revická & others. 2010.

Tightrope! A Bohemian Tale, by Olga Walló. Translated by Chapman Chen. 2011. (Chinese)

University Days, by Laura Solomon. 2014.

Vera Magpie, by Laura Solomon. 2013.

OTHER GENRES

We also publish in other genres, including autobiography, biography, children's illustrated books, educational books, Hong Kong educational and legal history, memoirs, poetry, teenage / young adult books, and travel. Other genres may be added.

WRITE TO US!

We are interested to read your response to
Lawrence Gray's *Odds and Sods*
and any other of our publications.
Please write to our email address, proverse@netvigator.com,
giving us a few sentences which you are willing for us to
publish,
giving your comments on this book.
If what you write is chosen to be included
in our E-Newsletter or website,
we will select another title published by Proverse
and send you a complimentary copy.
Please include your name, email address and mailing address
when you write to us, and state whether or not we may cut or
edit your comments for publication.
We will use your initials to attribute your comments.

FIND OUT MORE ABOUT OUR AUTHORS AND BOOKS

Visit our website
http://www.proversepublishing.com

Visit our distributor's website
<www.chineseupress.com>

Follow us on Twitter
Follow news and conversation: <twitter.com/Proversebooks>
OR
Copy and paste the following to your browser window and follow the instructions: https://twitter.com/#!/ProverseBooks

'Like us' on Facebook: www.facebook.com/ProversePress

Request our E-Newsletter
Send your request to info@proversepublishing.com.

Availability
Most titles are available in Hong Kong and world-wide from our Hong Kong based Distributor, The Chinese University Press of Hong Kong, The Chinese University of Hong Kong, Shatin, NT, Hong Kong SAR, China. Email: cup-bus@cuhk.edu.hk

All titles are available from Proverse Hong Kong and the Proverse Hong Kong UK-based Distributor.

We have stock-holding retailers in Hong Kong, Singapore (Select Books), Canada (Elizabeth Campbell Books), Principality of Andorra (Llibreria La Puça, La Llibreria).

Orders can be made from bookshops in the UK and elsewhere.

Ebooks
Most of our titles are available also as Ebooks.

www.ingramcontent.com/pod-product-compliance
Lightning Source LLC
Chambersburg PA
CBHW051340020726
47501CB00007B/2200